Awakening the Ancients

Awakening the Ancients

ARIANA WOLVSHIRE

Black Lyon Publishing, LLC

AWAKENING THE ANCIENTS
Copyright © 2014 by Ariana Wolvshire

Our books may be ordered through your local
bookstore or by visiting the publisher:

BlackLyonPublishing.com

Black Lyon Publishing, LLC
PO Box 567
Baker City, OR 97814

This is a work of fiction. All of the characters, names,
events, organizations and conversations in this
novel are either the products of the author's vivid
imagination or are used in a fictitious way for the
purposes of this story.

ISBN-10:   1-934912-62-x
ISBN-13: 978-1-934912-62-1
Library of Congress Control Number: 2013954502

Published and printed in
the United States of America.

Black Lyon Romantic Adventure

For you.

Chapter One

Roman in Red,
the Last Priestess awaits
when the final winds cry.
Lost in the sands of
Orion's Hourglass.

My name is Ariana. I am heiress to the old religions, collector of history, gatherer of the Ancients. I wish I could say all magic and wisdom were mine again, but I'm human now and have been for a very long time.

Our newfound haven, tucked away inside trees and mist, is far from the places where I saw history made into monuments. Apart from these remnants of long-ago ways, my writing comes easier somehow. It's more comforting here to explain how I have watched and witnessed, seen the mates to my soul walking the road beside me.

Countless times I've questioned how to begin this part of the Record, our tale set to paper. For how can I really summon the proper words when I don't remember for myself exactly when it all began? The Whispering always says to begin with those I know, to begin where my heart always travels, and so I shall. Daen. Winger. Ryuichi. Cibrien. All precious to me now, though I can safely say the path that ended with us fleeing Cairo to this place did not begin here this time—or in this life.

Early on, there were two things I knew to be true. The first was that the divinely whispering voices of creation and fate didn't reach everyone. The other? That the dreams, which carried me through the night, were too intense to write off as childhood imagination. They came to me more as memories, and I always suspected that was exactly what they were. For me, past lives were real enough to believe in.

The Whispering started quietly for me, scattered in bits that reached my ears from time to time. Each message carried was familiar, hinting of a recollection of things I had been born knowing and lost along the way. Above all, I wanted to know everything, to recall the tiniest of details in this grand mystery locked inside my own soul. Of what to do with those details, I had no deep plan or intention other than to satisfy my own curiosity.

Christian Winger, my friend and protector, was the one person in my untried world who also heard the Whispers. If ever I'd been sure they were real, Winger confirmed it. His opinions never came in shades of gray, and he was certain that Daen's presence was a bad omen that risked some noble future purpose related to those Whispers.

Daen? I started to sense him one summer before I'd even heard his name or set eyes on him. I just knew he was out there drawing ever nearer, and I always had the feeling that he was never quite gone from my mind even when I wasn't thinking of him. When he finally arrived and stood close enough for me to touch, the Whispers reached the point of a scream, transformed from a nagging intuition to something nearer a voice that spoke in times of consequence and decision. Daen's presence ignited something in Winger and me, even if Winger would never admit it.

Then, all those years ago, Daen suddenly left.

Afterward, I tucked myself away inside hallowed ivy-covered halls, studying and waiting, before the Whispering came again and pulled me from my home in America to Tokyo. I should have at least had the sense to be a little timid, cautious, afraid … But I wasn't. I took a small job at an English tourism office just outside the city, and dove into the quest Winger had predicted.

I waited, wondered, watched for some sign of purpose in a country about which I had never given thought. I didn't intend to stay for more than a few months anyway. Maybe, just maybe, there were wondrous others like Daen and Winger out there after all. The Whispers hinted of it.

While I waited in limbo, Winger wrote to me of his own smaller adventures, his words painting it into my mind. I could see him with his shoulder-length brown hair streaked with sun-bleached blonde as he walked between trees, light flickering when he pushed each evergreen branch aside. He moved smoothly and silently as if city life had never touched him. I don't think it ever had. I laughed to myself.

That we weren't quite normal never bothered us and I wasn't about to start worrying then. If we had known the extent of Gifts, our afflictions, we might have reacted differently at the onset. For things long buried have ways of climbing to the surface, and destinies are not easily shaken.

My attention turned again to Winger who stood still in the far-away sunlight, knowing through that measureless connection of ours that I watched. He always knew. His teeth flashed brilliant white against his dark stubble, blue eyes stunning against tanned skin. His smile could seem sensually wicked or strongly assuring given the right combination of his mood and eyeteeth, which were slightly sharper, longer than they should have been. Gift of the Wolf, they were. He smiled when he told me that. He said he had earned them.

"I wonder how long it's going to take before we figure out why I've been drawn away to this place," I told him one evening on the phone.

"Well, at least you're not missing anything here," he said. "I haven't booked any guests for my wilderness tours this summer just in case. I'd hate to have to run off in the middle of the night and leave them alone in the woods if you need me."

I laughed. "Winger, my dear, I think the Whispers are leading me into something that would be much simpler to avoid."

"Ah, to open the proverbial Pandora's box guided by the Whispers. Sounds nice. Maybe your purpose in Tokyo isn't to find some thing, maybe—"

"It's to find some*one*," I finished for him. "Crossed my mind."

We were right. I knew we were right the moment I walked into a small music shop across from the train station the next day. For a moment the air around me stopped moving, like I had passed into the center of a storm and if I took another step, the winds might push me past the point of return. There was a wide screen above the shop's checkout counter, and it suddenly loomed silent and black with the end of a video.

The first beats of an entirely unique song filled the store. The screen was solid blue for seconds, then solid red. I watched spellbound as the band members of this group danced on the flat screen. Then, as a mere silhouette, the singer appeared against the red background. His profile moved with each word he sang and the outline of his hand shifted sometimes to his hair, sometimes to his face.

It had to be him. It absolutely had to. An energy that felt more like a slap caught me. This was no Whispering, no connection with a friend, no intuition finely tuned. My head involuntarily turned away from the video as the pictures in my mind attacked. The intensity of the scenes was like nothing I'd ever seen, ever felt. The scenes demanded audience.

Then a man's voice echoed behind the images with the kind of sound deeper than a thought—not quite internal, not something said aloud. *Do not look upon him. Do not look upon him.* I stopped and twined my fingers through a metal mesh shelf for support.

The warning carried with it the vision of a Roman soldier, an older man with silvered hair and a closely clipped grey beard. How stern and commanding his face, how tightly he held his helmet under his left arm even though none would dare take it from him. The cage sat behind him on the ground, all bars and not built tall enough for a man to stand upright while inside. The man enslaved behind its bars crouched down with one knee planted in the sandy earth. He, too, wore the tattered reds and earthen tones of the Roman army. His hands clutched the bars, a jagged section of brown hair showing between them as he watched a woman walk away. The anguish in his eyes …

I saw the woman at first as if watching a movie. The long hair—a color I couldn't place—was captured in a single, loose braid down her back. The sky blue of her dress, the tiny triangle necklace at her throat, the contrast of her dark skin and darker Egyptian eyes—all dreamlike. She turned her back and walked away, beautiful collarbone and shoulders accentuated by tightened neck muscles, the choked breath held inside. The next moment I was this woman, knowing he reached out for me, seeing life through her eyes.

This impression lasted only seconds, but the vision was so consuming, so saturating that I could hear my own blood rushing through my veins, pounding in my ears. I turned toward the screen again, feeling strongly that I shouldn't. The soldier had warned me, hadn't he?

The singer turned his face away and I waited. He reappeared, still in silhouette, then hidden in shadow. Light began to fade into the final frames and when it hit him fully, he covered his face with one hand, glancing only once through his fingers. But, that once was more than enough. Two of his long, artistic fingers brushed against his forehead just between his eyebrows. It struck me that this gesture had meaning, so familiar it seemed.

I waited for the name of the band to flash across the screen. Ashes of Rose. Then I bought all their DVDs.

Do not look upon him.

But how could I not? Drawn, I raced homeward, then sat back on the cool tatami to watch the first disc. A song began and there he was, years younger, thick hair down to the middle of his back, but him nonetheless. The band wore full gothic makeup for this song.

His eyes were painted in elegant kohl as he sang the tale of two people locked together in the cycle of eternity. He was the tormented child, the wandering vampire, the angry one through his songs.

He stood on the stage before a small audience with arms outstretched to his sides. His head nodded down until his chin nearly touched his chest. Gentle, deliberate destruction. The glow of the colored lights behind him shone through the thin silk of his long, white shirt. I could imagine the Egyptian woman on her knees before him, hands reaching up to his chest, sealing the surrender in his crucifixion pose. How indescribably beautiful.

The next song blended into being before my eyes. Ashes of Roses had found its sound. The heavy bass and solid drumbeat mixed with the singer's clear, warm voice and the tortured scream of a violin only sometimes. He looked older now, as though I had watched him bloom into adulthood on that stage. His black hair now fell only to his shoulders. The gothic makeup disappeared, but black outlined his eyes even still. He sang of mystery, love and magic as he sank into ocean waters under a glorious moon.

Again his hair changed, cut short at his neck and around his ears, left longer in front so that the layered bangs would fall into his eyes. No makeup touched him now, only his bare skin, his brown eyes, and always this theme of longing. Always surfaced the search, the hole in the center of him as he begged and beckoned.

"Forgive me. Forgive me," he sang, "so I can love you again in this world."

He was taller than me, though not tall in the least compared to Daen. Body disciplined, muscles lean and taut, he cut a slender figure. He was powerful and compelling, a laughing, dancing rogue with the secrets of life lurking inside his soul. *Potent little imp*, came the thought. The names of the band members ran with the credits. *Ryuichi*.

"Dear Lord above," I said to myself. "He's like Winger and me, isn't he?"

I reached out with my mind and found Winger sleeping. My own thinking didn't even sound rational to me, and I laughed out loud. As my excitement grew, the wind picked up outside and threw bits of dry, used, useless things at my window. But I continued to watch Ryuichi sing. I studied every move he made, every gesture of his hand, every change in his animated face.

At times he was lithe and feline. Then he became masculine, strong and solid. It was simple really, too simple for me to tell which songs stirred him and which were mere words. My finger pushed the rewind button on my remote as I heard him speak in English. The quiet words came quickly, nearly fading into the music.

"I wish you'd try. Find me."

He cried out words describing Ancient Egyptian temple ceremonies as if he knew them. The thing most chilling was that his words so mirrored mine. His lyrics translated to English were nearly line-by-line twins to the poems that filled my own notebooks. He chanted tales of fallen angels. He moaned through times of his greatest loneliness, called upon God, described the suffocation he felt living among skyscrapers.

More English followed, this time only, "Fly to me."

More of the fraught invitation …

Finally, he sang of a countdown, of mankind's final hours on Earth before judgment. He sounded so desperate, as if he were facing one final chance to tip the scales in his favor, a last opportunity to save his soul. By his actions, he would show his inclination toward good or evil, as the temple rituals he sang of dictated.

Whatever Ryuichi's inclination and past, he provoked a curious stab of pain in me that still seemed minimal compared to whatever he must have done to himself to inspire such lushly desperate music. I needed to decide what to do with the information I received in the music store. If only Winger were near.

The evening darkened. I was exhausted and could no longer dwell on this ill-fated musician, this Ryuichi of Ashes of Roses. When morning came around, I hoped I would realize I had been star-struck by a charismatic rock idol and just imagined the rest.

•

As the days passed, I was convinced that my first impressions of Ryuichi were absolutely right. The sensation of him wouldn't fade so easily. In fact, it didn't fade at all. It held on as tightly as Daen had, refusing to be shaken, and using my own desire for it to forge the connection. I wondered then about the small details of this present lifetime of his. Where did he live? Was he married?

I knew that I could track him if I had to, and find his essence more easily in Japan than in my own country. In Tokyo, I had the advantage of my coloring, the novelty of my appearance. If I went to a concert, he might see me in the mix. If I walked by on the street, he would notice. But, I couldn't present myself to him as a fan; that, I was not. What I needed was to stay as far as possible from his fame so he would be sure of me.

Concerts, CD signings, and everything else related

to his career were strictly off limits. I had to meet him unexpectedly in the grocery store, pull up beside him at a red light, cross his path at the airport. I had to see him by chance with his hair unstyled and his jeans worn thin.

On weekends I visited more music shops, restaurants and trendy hangouts. I asked about him when the mood and the company were right, but no one ever knew anything. My wandering at last took me back to the same secluded music store, back to a sign and some photographs thumb tacked to a wall. He had been there. Three days after I had stood there shaken by a silhouette on a screen, he had followed.

The camera captured the expression in his eyes so that it was impossible to miss, yet no one seemed to notice. The pictures showed customers gathered tightly around him, smiling broadly, making peace signs, ecstatic with their good fortune. But Ryuichi's eyes were dead things—hopeless, exhausted things.

I stood in front of the picture, riveted to those desolate eyes, alone without him and without answers.

"Excuse me," a tentative female voice said. "You like Ryu, do you?"

I nodded as she continued.

"I was here." She pointed to her own image in the corner of the photograph. "Ryu say he came to meet someone, but no one here. Nice guy. Not like some famous people."

She had my attention then. "Did he say where he was going?"

"He only say he must leave. I think he have to return to new home in Tokyo."

A breeze swept softly past, moving my hair ever so

slightly. Disturbing, reassuring. I wasn't sure what to say to her, but she smiled and kept talking.

"I don't know where is his home," she said. "Ryu like English. Maybe near *gaikokujin* areas so he can practice." The woman nodded to me, smiling as she walked away out of the store, waving happily as she disappeared into the train station.

For a moment, the gentle sound like a flutter caught my attention and then was gone. No doubt about it, I had to find this Ryuichi of my visions. My quest depended on it.

So my search began anew. I scoured Tokyo, searching blindly through so many of its sections that I lost track of where I'd been and where I hadn't. Along the way, I found I could conjure some intuition to find this unknown singer—something like the heightened sense that came with the bond between Winger and me. Something like the Whispers.

I traveled to places where I thought that Ryuichi had often been near—only not recently. I got lost in another record store for an hour leafing through dozens of magazines with his image inside. But that's all the magazines captured, an image. They had no tales to tell. The feeling, that connection, grew stronger and more confident with each picture I saw and each song I heard.

I moved from train to subway station, from park to shopping center without finding a clue. It was on a walk from Tokyo Tower when I saw the red Ferrari displayed in the glass showroom on a corner. I ventured inside just for a minute of air conditioning. The rear bumper had a tiny smudge and I reached out to wipe it away. The instant my hand touched the silver metal, a shock ripped through my body. The response would not be squeezed from my hand. It fairly burned.

He had been there! The moment I touched the car I saw him—saw him run his hand along the bumper, saw him slide across the leather seat, saw even his reflection for a moment in the mirror with the sides of his hair now clipped evenly above the ear. I didn't know what business brought him to this area, but it wasn't finished. I searched the bars, restaurants, and shops, gathered information, listened to rumors, and finally found where he just might go.

The next evening, I walked into a tiny establishment so dimly lit that I could see nothing at first. My boots scuffed along the dry wood floor. My eyes adjusted, taking in the widely spaced tables to my right, the private booths to the left. I couldn't see Ryuichi. A bar took up the center of the place, its wood marked with tales of years. Rows of corked bottles lined the shelves behind it, the door to the kitchen to the right of it. The rich, sleepy color of the bar's wood further darkened the room and absorbed the faint candlelight. Rain slid down a single window, so high on the wall that nothing but dusky sky showed through.

Moody, surreal, and quiet it was, shutting out the world beyond its door and creating one of its own. The few customers inside looked to be European or American for the most part. This was a place obviously not favored by the locals as part of their usual nightlife ritual, and I suspected that was the exact reason he had come here.

I turned on my heel and walked through the shadows to the restroom. Alone, I braced myself against the sink, trembling with something other than cold. I looked up into my own eyes in the distorted mirror. Makeup flawless. Hair glowing like dark gold down my back in the odd lighting. Green eyes alive. The outside was fine, but inside I was not so together. Inside I tingled and spun with the knowledge that he was near and my search was coming to fruition. I could feel him, more darkly glimmering, more brightly vibrating than I had ever imagined. His presence filled the bar.

With the greatest breath my lungs had ever accepted, I walked back across the room, past the door and the bar with all its sparkling bottles, past safety.

Do not look upon him. Do not. Do not look.

The booths stood empty—except one. On the high dividing wall, the movement of a single person cast its comfortable shadow. I sat down in a booth near the opposite corner. Had he sensed me, too? What if he possessed no sense of me at all? Had I lost my senses? Only one way to find out. I stood.

This time my boots were noiseless on the floor. My legs felt lighter the closer I came to his table. Then I stopped, letting my hands drop to my sides. In the candlelight, his hand stopped moving against the paper on the table. The pen slid to its side, away from the fingers of the poet, my philosopher-priest.

For just the barest of instants, he thought that a fan had found his hiding place. But this run-and-hide instinct fled as quickly as I felt it pass through him. I saw for the first time the eyes that held all the glorious, radiant power of his words, the source of all the pain, hope, and desperation his lyrics cried. I couldn't see the bottom of this well. The energy flowing from him literally and physically wrapped around my heart. Unmistakable temple training. There was no turning away.

Where was Winger when I needed him? He should

have come to this country with me.

This man simply had to remember something, recognize something, but he didn't speak. Instead, he gestured silently for me to sit as he blushed like a startled child. He felt down in his soul who I was even then. I know he did. But he wouldn't simply begin a conversation with a complete stranger that could bring his sanity into question any more than I would have. He would not pour the words from his heart that way.

He brushed his fingers along the side of his face as he took in my hair and eye coloring. "*Nihongo … wakaru*?"

I nodded that I understood and folded my coat a little too carefully beside me on the bench as I sat down across from him. I had hunted for him for so many days, and now only a table separated us.

"You understand English, too?" he asked quietly at length.

Again I nodded. *Do not look upon him.*

"My name is Ryuichi."

"I know."

He reached out and met my hand in a tentative handshake. Oh God, the warmth of his hand. He truly was flesh, no dream at all.

"Who are you? What is your name?" he asked.

I reluctantly took back my hand. "Ariana."

I heard in my head the words of his songs mixing together, all the torture and lament of his stories, all the never finding her. Me. And I felt an anger that must have sprung up from lifetimes ago rise in my chest. What had he done? *Do not look upon him.*

"I am a singer. You know my group? You heard my songs?"

His face was deadly serious, inky black brows slanting dramatically upward, drawn down toward the top of his nose. The Japanese accent caressed his words rather than slurring them, a singer's voice trained in persuasive strength and clarity, born to seduce and soothe with a whisper.

"Yes," I said, unable to force out another sound.

This was not the way I wanted to react to him. But the sensations began to battle in my chest the moment I saw him in person. I had not expected the loving fascination I felt watching him on those videos to mix so suddenly with this cold fury. I wanted to punish him with stubborn, hateful silence. I grabbed my coat and started to leave. The quest was over. So there were others out there like Winger, Daen and me. I knew it now. That was good enough.

"Wait." He stood faster than me, stopping me with his hand gently on my arm. "Who are you?" I couldn't decide if I saw fear or hope in his expression, but the death I had seen in the photo was gone from his eyes. "Who?"

The soul remembers what the mind forgets. I simply looked at him and we sat again. Amazing how the single touch of one man can carry with it more intimacy than an entire lifetime with another.

He spoke again. "I remember you."

"Yes, I know that, too." It was only a whisper.

He leaned forward studying me. Strands of hair fell down across his forehead on either side of his face, that luminous black hair coming together in the hint of a widow's peak. Shadows hung in the hollows of his cheeks, light falling on high cheekbones, warm Asian eyes.

"I looked for you every place. I waited for many years. I always sing for you. Band members think you are—not real."

My throat still threatened to close itself to speech entirely as I thought to myself again that I had been right. Winger and I had been right. But what had it gotten us?

"I see you in my dream for years. Not your face, but you," he said.

I couldn't leave. The Whispering told me this was too important, that I had to cast the shock and fear aside. My journey to find him was crucial somehow.

"We need to remember, Ryuichi." A chill shot down my spine at the sound of his name aloud and from my own lips. Words hold the power.

My reaction didn't go unnoticed. "Forgive me," he whispered. "Forgive me."

"I can't forgive you. I don't even remember what you did. What separated us? Betrayal? Sacrilege?" He looked puzzled as I said the words. "You destroyed something holy in Egypt."

"Holy." He inhaled the sound, slightly flaring his perfect nose. "I know this word. We began holy. Then I did something wrong. I took you with me? I have dreams, but they are never clear enough."

"I don't know exactly what happened either. I only have one tiny bit of a memory, and all I'm doing in it is walking. I do know that whatever happened, you weren't responsible for my part in it. If I even had one."

I thought we shared for that silent moment some vision of a memory from long ago, some clue from the time I had walked away from the cage. And they had killed him, the Roman soldier.

He hung his head. "I will never do the wrong thing again. I promise. But I do not know why I—" He searched a minute for the words. "Why I fell from grace."

His voice was a caress set to sound. He reached across the table and took my hand in his, examining my fingers. He placed my hand back on the table, but didn't break the contact, still touching my hand with his fingertips. This semi-touch was almost unbearable.

It was my turn to take his hand in mine and with the full touch came the past like some great, silent blast with the power to knock us over the edge. The sensation was like standing on the brim of the deepest of ravines and calling out a word into the emptiness where, with each reverberation, the word grows ever more faint until it disappears. This memory was an echo in reverse, flowing back to us instead of away, growing steadily louder until it reached the full intensity of the original word.

Ryuichi and I were allowed by whatever divine influence to recall the story carried on that echo. The things we saw came from many centuries before, and they were no doubt the binding ties that brought this man and me back together in the present. With Daen. With Winger.

After my quest through Tokyo to find Ryuichi, all it took was the most innocent touch of our hands to trigger memories we hadn't really even known were lost.

Chapter Two

No memories before You.
View our second time,
Roman in Red.
Caged Soldier
shadowed by the moon
behind our temple.

Back in time my mind went.

I remember neither the time nor the date. Such manmade numbers weren't of importance to me then. My wisdom had taken me past them.

My facts came from the alignment of the heavens, the universal, geometrical truths around me. I was the woman, the priestess, the goddess. I was Nephthys under the moon, Isis in the Sun. The temple was mine and so was the magic.

The One God, said to have created life at Zep Tepi, the First Time, smiled on me from beyond the stars. He knew I heard His voice when the Pharaohs had long since ceased to listen. They took the statues and called them gods, offering sacrifices, attempting to manipulate them to serve human whims. They never realized that the One God was never swayed this way, that the One God demanded more. Eventually even the language became corrupt, and skewed meanings justified actions. I think now that these were the final elements of their downfall.

I knew that those they called gods had been created as guides and messengers. Some were the giants on Earth—Neteru, Urshu, Elohim, called angels by the Greeks. Some were simply terms given to divine actions, never beings at all. The old tales said that offspring of such beings walked the Earth with mankind while the angels ruled the air.

All these guides carried out individual tasks of the One God, or at least were supposed to. Some triumphed, some fell, but never were they meant to be worshipped as the One God was. Even they cringed at Egypt's blasphemy.

And how I wept. For I knew that the wisdom was soon to be lost and truths once widely known would soon become what man would call mystery. Even the priests had grown stupid and corrupt. My temple, the Temple of the Sun and Moon, stood alone in wisdom next to my dear friend, the High Priest's, Temple of Osiris.

Implications of a great army from the North introduced themselves to Egypt at that time. Curious soldiers filtered into the land. It was a time years before the daughter, last of the Ptolemies, would call herself Queen and reach her destiny at the age of marriage. Royalty recalled only the corrupted language and would marry this daughter to her brother, the son of her own father. In the time of the Neteru, all men and women called one another brother and sister, and so brother married sister in a sense. It had never been meant to be taken so literally. Common sense should have told them so.

It was easy to foretell Egypt's future, for she was knowledgeable in the ways of man and his politics, yet infinitely blind to the wisdom of the spirit.

We had a history already then of assimilating prisoners of battle into our society, and the influence of other armies, other lands, had further altered us. So when the soldiers wandered into our city that day we welcomed them. In fact, most scarcely noticed their presence. These were not the first wanderers to pass our way. Entire armies had come and gone.

I remember when the five dusty soldiers knelt on the banks of the Nile in the midday sun. Light bounced off their helmets, their weapons, all strewn hastily through the reeds and the lotus plants. The bottoms of their sandals were nearly worn through. This was the second thing I saw as I watched them scoop the Nile's water up into their hands. The first was the soldier nearest the edge.

The younger priests from the Temple of Osiris walked toward the soldiers, but I hung back near the buildings only to turn away before the soldiers could rise to their feet. I ran to the Temple of Osiris and called out for the High Priest. He appeared from the shadows inside, nearly an apparition of a man, hunched and shrunken, eyes blue with the hazy veil of age. I counted on him to still possess the inner sight that is not affected by tired, old eyes. None of the other priests could truly see.

"Romans have come."

He drew a ragged breath. "And what makes you pay

such heed to these Romans?"

"There is one among them. He has the Gift."

"My priests will bring him here with the others. They cannot journey so far upriver. I feel they are already lost. They will rest with us."

"I only wish conference with the one."

The High Priest nodded and disappeared back into his sanctuary. He would grant my request, I knew. He had chosen me for the training, seen the Gift that flowed so strongly in a young girl. He had cleared the way for me to rise to the position of High Priestess in a time when women were often excluded from Temple hierarchy. He would entrust the Roman to me this night.

The priests gathered around a fire that evening when the sun had faded and I was Isis no longer. I was again Nephthys, reveling in the moon, the night, protectoress of the dead, witness to the cyclical design of life itself. This was the role in which the Roman must first see me. I waited in my temple, dressed in flowing white trimmed in deepest purple, hair loose down my back. I waited while the soldiers ate the roasted offerings by the fire. I longed to be only the woman now, for the role of goddess had tipped the balance of time too far in its direction that day.

My novices scattered in the temple, fluttering away like silly, frightened butterflies. I knew the High Priest had sent him. I sensed the Roman's uncertainty as he stood in the shadows of the doorway. With a wave of my arm, the novices left the temple free to seize the night, giggling as they passed near the Roman. So without hope, their training.

He walked toward me under the light of the torches, and suddenly was before me. Face to face we stood, each studying the eyes of the other. The years of the Temple could not control the woman in me at this moment. It was shameful almost, had the feeling not been so delicious. He smiled then, realizing I shared his temptation, and the smile carried with it no falsity or malice. Ironically, this was the thing that warmed me, the thing that made me sure.

"You have the Gift, Roman. I have seen none other in this life so strongly in possession of it."

He stood mesmerized by the sound of my voice against the temple walls. He watched the movement of my lips as I spoke. I saw myself as he saw me in the reflection of his eyes.

I laughed. "I know you can speak, Roman."

"You are the High Priestess?"

"You expected another? An old crone with teeth blackened?"

He nodded dumbly and then collected himself. How fortunate that he knew to regain his composure then, for I grew short of time.

"I summoned you here with another invitation, Roman."

"What do you have in mind, Priestess?"

"The High Priest will soon close his eyes for the last time. Surely you must have seen this. The funerary rights will continue, but I am Nephthys alone. The ceremony is only half with me."

"What good could a lost Roman soldier do?"

"Stay with us and become the Priest. I will train you."

The Roman sat down on the stone step before the altar and put his hand over his mouth as he thought. "Abandon my army? There are other priests sitting just outside. Why not one of them?"

I brushed aside his question. "The idea tempts you, Roman. Search your soul. See if the path you're on is your Way."

"Are you a sorceress? Do you see through this chest into my heart? You tell me."

It was I who smiled then. "I see your path, Roman. And you do not yet walk it. Anubis. This is who you are."

The sound of the word ran through him in a shiver. I watched it reach him as he rose to weary feet. "I cannot. There is no excuse to flee the army. I would be killed. I am no traitor."

I watched him struggle with himself. So exhausted he was, so very tired of Rome, so amazingly charming without even a word or movement. I took the decision out of his hands then.

Smoothly I glided past him up to the altar itself. My feet made no sound as I moved, leaving only the gentle stirring of the air to assure him I had passed. I was past vanity for this talent. This was a trick he would soon learn easily enough. I took the dagger from the altar and raised it high above my head, calling on the One God, blessing the blade with a soft kiss. As it is above, so it is below. Somewhere in the heavens the stars created and reflected this moment. I turned and plunged the dagger into the Roman's side.

The soldier crumpled on the stone floor, horror on his face as he watched his thick blood flow down the altar step. I could smell the warm metallic salt of it. More horror as he looked to me. The strength of his body flowed away with the blood, yet the strength of him did not.

"Do not worry. I would not harm you." I knelt, smoothing back the hair from his face. I knew the agony of the physical pain he felt. But he would not die from this wound. "You fell on the knife and cannot make the journey with the other soldiers. You will stay behind to heal."

"And when they return for me? What then?"

"It does not suit you to sound too uncertain, Roman. Weakness is not yours." The gash bled more than I liked. "Place your hand over the wound. I go now to bring the others." The memory became mine alone then, as he shut his eyes and lost all sense of the world.

I remember the face of the High Priest, amusement lighting his feeble eyes. We nodded in mutual understanding of the thing I had done, what had had to be done. Oblivious were the priests, the tired soldiers. So easy it was to turn their minds from the truth, to turn them away from the temple and accept the lie. Some of them helped me carry the Roman to my home, for I did not want to care for him inside the temple this night. Already his blood stained my dress.

The fever found him in the night. I suspected he would have walked away from the small stab of a dagger at another time. But his strong body was worn from miles of walking in the sand, miles with neither food nor water. Moonlight flooded through my window as I laid him out on my bed.

Ah, the sight of him was heartbreaking. The poetry of the universe danced inside him even while he slept. I washed him gently, wiped the beads of sweat from his chest, kissed his still lips. I took away his soiled clothing and covered him against indecency.

He moaned, "Nephthys," and I kissed him again.

The blood ceased to flow from his side long before morning when the soldiers came to my door. I do not believe they recognized me as the Priestess from the night before. My hair and skin grew lighter with the rise of the sun, darker with the moon—and they would never comprehend, never see beyond the illusion. I had heard men refer to the twin sisters of my temple when in truth there existed only me. They looked to the Roman on the bed, grunted, and began their journey anew. I watched from the door as they walked far from sight following the banks of the Nile.

Again I sat beside the Roman. How gentle he seemed with his skin aglow under the sun. Its warm rays would awaken him soon. I bent to kiss him softly one last time, but this time his lips moved against mine. I jumped back and watched a smile shape his mouth.

"Nephthys." He opened his eyes. "How far have they gone?" This was his game, playing this role of the dead until the soldiers would leave him behind. Did he not know it could mean his true death to kiss the High Priestess?

•

I looked from the eyes of the Roman now centuries gone, to the eyes of Ryuichi gloriously alive and sitting across the table from me. Back in the present, the waitress stopped to refill the water in our glasses. Ryuichi recovered his breath and leaned away against the back of the padded booth.

"This explains so much about you."

"What does?" I asked.

He smiled again with lips that naturally curved up at the corners, formed two perfect little arches under his nose. Impossibly cute, that.

"The way you move," he said at length. "Your hands and arms. The way you walk. In silence. Almost liquid.

Like the rain down the glass." He nodded toward the high window with its streaks of water from top to bottom.

"Is that how you see me?"

"It does not matter. I see you."

I could only sit in awe of him then. No one had seen me in a long time, saw through me except Winger, except Daen. I never allowed it. How beguiling that he should cling to that tiny observation when the rest of the memory loomed so large. But then, he had written some of the details into his songs, hadn't he? Some of the memory must already rest comfortably inside him. He grew slightly embarrassed by my scrutiny and ran his right hand through his hair. The gesture served to hide his face for just a moment before he met my eyes again.

"You know, it also explains why you and I were looking for each other before we even knew who we were looking for," I told him.

He smiled. "It does."

"There is something I don't see in you right now," I said.

How delightfully concerned he looked.

I continued, "The smugness. Arrogance almost. I felt it in the Roman you were, in that kiss, but not so much in you right now in this moment."

He paused for a second, going over my words to be certain of the English. There was a touch of sadness in his smile and he rolled his pen back and forth under the palm of his hand on the table top.

"Not so much, but those things you said, they are still in me. A reporter asked me a question one day. I was young then. She asked who my favorite ... favorite *ja nakute*." He searched for the words again. "I am out of practice. She asked who I think has the best mind in the world." He raised his eyebrows. "And so I said that my mother does."

"Why is that wrong?"

"I said it was because she raised the world's greatest artist—me! My interview was in all the magazines. People talked about my bad attitude. They were right. I had no respect for anyone, only love for myself because I knew I was different than them. Better. I meant what I said to that reporter. I was very angry."

"Have you found peace along the way?"

"I just have, I think."

"Peace does not come so easily." I refused to be shaken. "I don't feel the anger so much in you now, but I definitely saw it in your videos."

"Band members still do not understand me. Their alcohol, women, parties—those were never seductive. The power was seductive. The fame. But I do not want to talk about that now. I am clear from those things. It was the anger I had to conquer. The anger and the pride. They clouded my eyes before, but only for a short time in this life."

He smiled that smile again, melting me back into the memory.

•

It had been the anger even then for him. And it had indeed been the pride—the all-consuming, ever-present pride of the Roman that jumped up and kicked aside his training. He was blessed with the gift, but the curse of his own character barred its use.

Calm and charming he was as I turned him over to the High Priest. But, I heard him storm more than once from the temple, though I never gave him the satisfaction of seeming to notice. Neither did the High Priest. He simply continued with his teachings whether the Roman was present or not. How damaging the blow to his soldier pride. The High Priest repeated nothing, and what the Roman missed, the Roman missed. The others simply carried through as though he had never risen to his feet, cursed at some minor frustration, pouted and raged when he was not chosen to demonstrate a lesson. In the beginning he always returned, expecting some kind of distinguished consideration and finding none. Insatiable appetite to be noticed.

The patience of the High Priest proved to be a contagious and powerful thing. It stimulated even the petulance-clouded intellect of the Roman. The same pride that sent him storming from the temple now kept him inside it, for he saw finally that his missed training was detrimental only to himself. Gift or no, he required that instruction. He would not reach my temple again without it.

The High Priest taught him the intricacies of the ceremony. He spoke of the time to perform them, when the stars and planets mapped best the Way, when the hour fell most effective. He gave lessons of truth and fact only. He revealed the words and the methods, but never the secret of how to unleash them. He instructed on color and dress, tools and herbs and incense. But these symbols and settings would remain eternally meaningless without the unlocking of the Gift. That task was one reserved for Nephthys alone. And I awaited.

I am assuming that much time passed before the Roman appeared in my temple. The hair that had been cropped in the style of his army, now hung straight and silky, not yet touching his shoulders. He should have shaved it away as the others did, but I was pleased at least with that small part of his rebellions. He came to me in the style of ceremonial dress appropriate for our meeting—the flowing robes of black, eyes painted with Egyptian perfection. Gone were the grime and edges of the bedraggled soldier. In his place stood someone otherworldly, someone whose skin reflected the moonlight and whose eyes held me.

I met him in my flowing, gossamer white trimmed in purple, and how marvelously we blended. A sensation ran through my body.

"I trust your wound no longer pains you."

"Not since your kiss," he said with a smile.

"I forget how incomplete your training still is. Sit. We begin."

We sat on the hard floor on opposite sides of the small fire. Its flames danced between us as we looked at one another, face to face at last.

"You do realize your training would have been so very different had you been born and raised here?" I asked.

A nod only.

"You must first learn to control your body."

Suppressed laughter in him now.

"I don't mean in that manner, Roman. Stretch out on the floor. On your back."

"I'm ready." More of that infuriating, silent laughter.

"Yes, I can see that." Secret laughter of my own, but he must not sense it. Not yet.

"What will you do with me now, Priestess?" Impetuous, insubordinate man-child.

"Listen to me, Roman. We will speak as man and

woman outside the temple, or outside training at least. In here, in training, we are priest and priestess. You will not desecrate my ground this way. Now lay your arms on the floor at your sides."

Sanguine warmth soaked into the temple walls from the fire. "Like this?" Delightful shadows caressed the room like the curls of gray smoke from the fire and the incense.

"Yes. Now close your eyes. I want you to focus all your energy on the tip of one toe. Feel the flesh, the bone, the blood there. Can you feel any tension there? Relax it. In that tiny bit of flesh, imagine the tension melting away."

"It's lighter."

"Don't speak. Now move to the next toe, and the next. See how simple this is?"

I sat quietly by the fire watching him continue this way, moving his mind up each measure of his body. He seemed an insensate manifestation on the floor for many heartbeats.

"I can't release the energy from my chest."

"Breathe deeply and with each breath, feel some of it flow away. It will be difficult near your neck and head also. I'm pleased you were able to free your stomach and the area between your legs."

"Respect for the priest-in-training, please."

I would have laughed aloud then, but it would have broken the last shred of his concentration. "I'm serious, Priest. Your body possesses several points of most focused energy. These are the most difficult to relax, but also the most necessary."

"I am as water solidified. Not frozen, though. Warm. You understand?"

"Good. Now I want you to tense your muscles one by one. Undo what you have done. You are replacing the negative force you have collected with your own positive strength."

The Roman sat up on the temple floor, his eyes shining too brightly, like a child's after a nap. "There are no words for this."

"You must do this in the twilight before you sleep and in the dawn after you wake. Do it whenever your mind wanders to it, until it becomes natural to you. That is all for now."

"The end of our lesson?"

"For now. I think you do not realize how long you were on the floor, Priest. I want to show you just one thing more. Our greeting. Our parting. You will need to know the gestures."

"More symbols?"

"You cannot show another. Watch."

I raised my arms slowly above my head in the most elegant and eloquent of movements that I knew. My wrists turned and fingers curved, set to music I heard yet didn't. With each movement my arms formed the moon above my head, mimicked her rays sliding to Earth as my hands turned and waved downward. When my fingers reached my chest, my palms faced outward to him, tips of thumbs and edges of forefingers touching, forming a delicate triangle. And then it was done.

The Roman stood transfixed before me and I knew that it was not only the series of movements that captured him. He had felt the magic for the first time, heard some gentle piece of the music carried faintly to his ears.

I had his attention now, and it made his training

all the more effective, easier. The Roman set aside his thoughts of me as a woman and decided to learn from the priestess. So comfortable this made our interaction, the rhythm of teacher and student.

We met in the evenings with that delicate beckoning of the temple greeting. He thrilled each time as the music of movement vibrated through him. He captured the euphony so naturally, took more joy in it even than I did, I think.

I taught him to sit still in one position for hours and hours, falling away into the night with ultimate control. He had a way of pulling the music of movement to him even in stillness. He pulled its energy inside him to keep himself company, and would sit trance-like so long as the song was there for his listening.

The time came next to teach him to truly hear. This, he could not grasp. He clung to the music of our gesture with a tenacity that he could not bear to relinquish.

"But you hear only one tune, my Roman. You miss the rest." I leaned calmly against the wall. "Do you know that when I choose to listen, I can hear more music in fire, on the wind, flowing with the Nile? And there are other sounds. There are the sounds of the thoughts of men. They are general whisperings of mankind as a whole, and separate thoughts of one man. Have you ever heard the Whisperings from the One God? How can you be fully alive without them? Simpler than that even, if I listen, I can hear a conversation across the desert."

"I understand the music, but the Whisperings? Where do these come from?"

"The level of the soul. There exists here a record, the Akashic Record. It holds time, thought and all things in its grasp. Surely the High Priest told you."

The Roman stared at me for a moment. "I still do not know how to get there. How do I find this information? And, I wonder this: Can you hear my thoughts, my Whisperings? Is my privacy gone with you?"

"Use your energy to bar me if you wish. It takes little effort on your part, a single conscious thought, really. Not even the most powerful can shatter your block if you do not wish it. Simply place your wall, but do not battle against an intrusion with anger or fear. Those emotions will transform your protection into an invitation to war." I spread my fingers out against the stones of the wall. "And the Record? It will come. It is like the pyramid. There are many ways upward, but there is only one vertex. You'll find your way. I cannot carry you up mine. It is not my place to even consider it."

"Is this inside your soul? Outside? In the stars somewhere?"

"All those places. It's where the physical and the spiritual come together as one."

We exchanged the gestures of parting then. He had not learned to raise the barrier I had spoken of. His joy reached out and wrapped around my heart. He blessed me with this wealth of glad intensity without any effort on his part or any asking on mine. All the Roman knew was that he at long last had been made full with the pleasure of life. His pleasure carried the essence of him into me with a breath.

I chose not to see him outside the temple. He was young and delicate in his training then, and I wanted him to bloom. He came early in the evenings, chasing away my novices as a routine. I didn't care. Their minds were not made for the temple, their souls too young, too unlearned.

Though I chose not to see him in a setting other than mine, the time for the next level had come. He would begin to see shades of the woman in me no matter how I presented myself as Nephthys. The task was mine to control this unveiling, to use it to further his understanding of mankind. He sat in a state of utter relaxation and control while I prayed. The torrent of silent words swirled around my body and left through my upstretched arms, leaping off the tips of my fingers to the heavens.

"You are truly beautiful to watch, Priestess. I try to hear your prayers, you know."

"Do you catch a word now and again?"

He shook his head. "Nothing." His concentration was broken. He ran his hand through the coolest part of the fire's flames. "But I think I see smoke around you sometimes. A mist of purple or of gray."

"I must admit this surprises me more than a little. You might even catch a phrase or two now, if it were thought loudly for you." I stepped down from the high altar. "If the seeing of colors comes as naturally to you as the music does, the training will be easier. I think we will just talk tonight."

"No practices and tortures? No riddles?"

"We'll have enough of those later. Come, let's walk."

"Aren't you afraid I'll see that you are human?"

"I am hoping that if we talk more, you will learn to hold the stupidities of insolent thought inside your head. Do you think before you speak? Or simply speak to provoke reaction?"

"Consider me humbly chastised." He bowed in exaggerated fashion under the stars.

"You have learned the fundamentals of our religion. You understand many of the truths. You begin to hear the music and see the colors. Mastery of an art is important for you now."

"The High Priest did mention that once. I would choose music, if that pursuit is acceptable as training. I do not think I can draw. I tried it before and my hand won't create what my mind imagines."

"Music would suit you well." I paused now, seeing him clearly in the bright night, letting the glamour slide from me so that he would truly see me in return.

"You remove your shell for me?" He laughed. "Ah, that's the face I remember above the bed when I was wounded. That beautiful face."

I shook aside the memory of his kiss before the blood could rush to my face. "The High Priest and I have spoken. He fears your training will not be complete before Egypt needs you."

"I go already to the side of the dead. I assist the High Priest with the paint and prayer, bring a feeling of beauty to the dead. I have assisted with the procession."

"He is pleased. I am pleased. But, time grows short as I have told you."

"What shortens our time?"

"That, I cannot say. I do not know. We have a sense of it in dreams, in the signs. So, I must hurry your training to the next level and depend upon you to master the music alone."

"I can. Bring me to the next level."

"You have heard of heka. You've even learned to use it in simple ways."

"When I bring control to my body?"

"Yes. Heka is something of a life force. It's the energy

in your body and mine. It's the spirit of the One God. It's the magic and vitality of the fish, the plant, the stone. We are each individual, you see, separate and wonderful. But, we are all bound together in creation by this force. It joins us as one. We are each a finger on the same hand."

"So we are separate, yet not." His dark eyes flashed. The picture of masculinity he was, jaw line and stubble. I looked away.

"Yes."

"Odd that this makes sense."

"We will learn to filter and bend the heka tomorrow. I will show you what you need to know."

He stopped walking. "I need to know what purpose this all serves. My mind grows, but I have done nothing to affect anyone or anything with this knowledge."

"That's because it's still knowledge with you. The knowledge will provide you with interesting stories around the fire. But when the knowledge becomes wisdom in your heart, that will affect everything."

What struck him, I do not know. He stood still, absorbing this for moments, studying me. Then he turned and continued the walk in silence for just a while.

"Do you ever feel loneliness here?" he asked.

"Sometimes."

"Good. Because I feel it most when I'm with you. I know you're beside me now, but I can't find you." He stopped again. "You make me question the training. I'm not sure I want to assume this role if it removes me from all intimacy."

His words stung. "This is my shortcoming, Roman. The training should bring you closer to life not remove you from it."

"Then stop speaking to me in great cryptic riddles for a time. Give me a woman's sympathy. Tell me about your childhood or about your passions."

"I cannot. Not yet."

"Priestess, coward." Yet it was he who turned and walked away across the sand.

I pushed his words aside and buried myself in Isis. Homes were in need of blessing, children in need of healing, lessons in need of speaking. And always the writings required attention if I were to proclaim myself an at all worthy scribe.

He came the next morning as the would-be Anubis again, his male Roman pride cloaked at least for the moment. He watched patiently until I set aside my ink, and then walked over to me.

"I am sorry for my words, Nephthys."

"We will become closer, but you expect far too much too soon. I cannot bend to your wants."

He took my hand in his then. Were it anyone else, he would have been punished. No man touched the priestess-goddess uninvited. But his contact was a comfort. For an instant, the sight of the Roman before me was the vision of another man, him yet not. Still he held my hand. Still I allowed it.

He transformed before my eyes into a being surrounded by light—golden, resplendent. His feet touched the earth. And there were others beside him. I retracted my tingling hand. The vision fled without enough substance to analyze, and now my body responded to his touch.

"Thank you," he said. I recognized the manner of heat in his eyes.

"Can you set aside this physical energy for one day?"

He grinned wickedly, lighting his eyes. "Not with all the training in the universe."

I blushed furiously. "Then we shouldn't meet this day. We tread dangerous ground, my Roman."

Chapter Three

Roman in Red.
Priestess in White.
Blooming in the Nile mist.
Embraced by a thousand stars.
Potent binding.

The little restaurant closed in the wee hours of the morning, though we hadn't been aware of the time passing. Time never stood still for us, if our memories were any indication. Ryuichi still held my hand, solemn yet excited beyond words as the awe of our discovery clung to us. We had been together before and our dreams of past lives were very, very real. We had proven these things beyond the shadow of a doubt in our separate searches and separate memories that had come together as one.

We stepped out onto the sidewalk and walked to the back of the restaurant where his car was hidden away in an alley. We moved like lovers reunited under the soft glow of the streetlights. I saw in his every expression the face of my Roman soldier, but more captivating still, the face of Ryuichi. If it were possible, the centuries had made him a thousand times more breathtaking.

He saw in me the last goddess, and that brought out something almost protective in him. I could see it when I looked into his eyes, looked straight through to the center of him. I wondered then how much more he saw. I wondered what Winger had always seen. And we both recalled more of the memory, but it was not until we would meet with privacy again that we could allow it to continue. The past had already eaten away the first hours of our present as it was.

The cool night air pushed against my face as we drove with the windows open. I hung my arm down the side of the car, feeling the wind between my fingers, never having been so thrilled and so at ease in my life. This thriving, dark combination of opposing emotions filled me. Ryuichi looked at me and then back to the road again. The scent of him drifted to me as we stopped at a light. No noxious cologne, only the warm clean smell of his clothing with just a hint of dryer sheet and the golden essence of his skin.

"What are you thinking, my Egyptian priestess?"

"I'm wondering how a lifetime together was enough. How one farewell was enough to keep us together forever this way. We have a lot to uncover before we'll know."

There must have been a reason, a tiny voice in the back of my mind suggested. Someone else. Something else done.

"I am thinking of all the lives we missed. I thank our One God that I cannot remember them now." He lapsed into silence for a moment. "I want to spend my time with you. But my work takes much time. I would pay you to write songs with me. You would be natural for that." A hint of a question hung in the air.

"That wouldn't feel right. You're amazing on your own. Besides, your songs are basically my poems set to music anyway. I have notebooks full of almost all the same words."

"My songs were prayers designed to find you."

He watched the road but never stopped watching me really, aware of my thoughts most likely. The dashboard lights played across his face. His hair fell down over his eyes and he shook it back. The collar of his coat was half turned up. It was stunning that for the flash of a second, I didn't even care what he had done or what I had done. I reveled in the intricacies of his words, his actions, his soul. And that wiped the slate clean somehow, or so I pretended. Winger wouldn't agree. Neither would Daen.

"We'll find a way to see each other even when you're busy. No rest for the wicked." I wished as soon as the sentence left my lips that I hadn't spoken it. Shiver down my spine.

"I will drive to your apartment. It is too late for the train."

"Why did we choose now to be born together this time?" I asked. "Did we choose? And why did we choose to be away from one another until just now? Why is now so special, Ryuichi?"

"I do not think we were supposed to be together again until now. Can you feel it?"

"Feel it?"

He nodded. "It feels right. My world has been so dead for the past thirty years. This life. This time. I was miserable."

"God, don't let me live in a pastel and stale world." I had heard the words in a poem somewhere, sometime long before.

My words struck him and he said, "That is exactly my meaning. I feel alive only when I am on that stage— and now with you. Nothing around me has made sense. Those are the only times when I have been stronger than the emptiness. I did not have a purpose. It is not right. I have to solve this in myself. And I have to understand all the dreams."

"The dreams," I said. "I used to have these vivid dreams about these wonderful people and places. But over the years I've come to suspect they're memories. Now we know for sure. That's the least pastel thing I've ever heard of." I couldn't lessen my smile. "I can now say I remember the feel of the sand between my toes on a warm Egyptian night. I remember dancing in the grass of the Scottish Highlands, and wading in a pebbly creek in Ireland. A castle rose garden in England. Life was wrapped in grace then. Maybe we've found your lost grace again."

"I do not think so." Ryuichi gazed at me for a moment with the glow of a streetlight flickering across his face as we passed it. "My other secret is that I do not suit this time. I would not have chosen it if I did not have an important reason. I have money, but I do not care about it. I hate these skyscrapers. I hate them," he said. "And the dirty air. And I am angry and hate these people who say they love me, though I know it is wrong. So many of them have no richness now. The magic shows up in little sparks only sometimes."

"I think you needed to find others like you, that's all. That's why I came here looking for you. Winger and I planned out a quest." His contagious disquiet soaked into me.

He shook his head desperately. "What if this is our last lifetime?"

"Do you think that's why we found each other? Why we're here? Winger and I have had more conversations like this than I care to count. He thinks my need to figure out our strange abilities is only the tip of the iceberg. He's sure God has a plan and figured we needed one of our own or we'd never find out what God's was."

"So God is looking down at us and getting ready to use us for something?" he asked.

I nodded. "Makes you wonder where we fit in, doesn't it?"

"This Winger, he is a friend?" Ryuichi asked.

"For years and years now. We have a connection, too. He'll have to tell you about it, but I think you'll like each other."

"Have you met more with the connection?"

"One other. His name is Daen." I heard my voice tighten with the effort of his name.

"And he is a friend also?"

"No. Yes. I'm not sure what he is. Winger and I haven't seen him for quite a while."

My chest constricted as it did every time I spoke of Daen. Whether it was bitterness or wanting I was never sure. It was probably some miserable combination that seized me whenever he passed through my mind.

"Four of us, then. Do you think I would remember them?"

"I really don't know. Winger and Daen knew each other immediately. Winger wouldn't go within ten feet of him, but he never really got into the details. Winger thinks Daen has this evil aura about him."

"Aura?"

"How can I explain it? I could feel him before I saw him. Like with you, but different."

"Why is that evil?"

"It's not. I'm not explaining it well. I knew when he moved into my town before I'd even seen him. He was like some great, dark, electric wave passing over the land. To walk past him was consuming. Winger hated that and he hated seeing me even speak to the man. He still loathes Daen."

"So this aura frightened Winger?"

"Not exactly. Winger has too much of the warrior left in him." No, it wasn't raw fear, but it was something.

"I have not met anyone like that. I only knew there was you."

Ryuichi stopped the car in front of my apartment building, tires crunching the gravel. "I have a new video in the back seat. Would you like it?"

"I thought I had both."

"Ashes of Roses has three now. A present for you. Ariana." What did he feel when he said my name? His energy caressed the sound of it as it left his lips. He touched my hand once more before I stepped away from the car.

"Thank you, Ryuichi." Again the rush of sensation at the sound of his name, as if to speak it were to summon his soul.

"Would you come to a concert if I asked?"

"If you asked."

He smiled so sweetly. "Do you know what I think? I think we are remembering not just because of our acts. I think there is something important about Egypt for us. Now, I mean. Maybe we will have a chance to visit there together someday."

"You hear the Whisperings. Pay attention to them." I walked away from his car, looking back from the stairs as he turned the wheels on the gravel and pulled away. As I stood on the stairs, the trembling of a small earthquake swayed me. I grabbed the wall. Whether I planned to support it or have it support me I didn't know.

When I tried to phone Winger again, he wasn't there.

•

Ryu and I worked apart during the daylight hours and reserved the evenings for our meetings. On these occasions we laughed and talked, coming to know the details of one another, yet underneath it all, the stubborn continuation of our memory that refused to surface. It was the memory we most wanted, most desired to discuss.

We drove one evening along the streets of Harajuku with its dim colored lights clinging to store fronts, glowing against the concrete walkways that crossed high above the pavement. Ryuichi had shown me the store from which Ashes of Roses bought its gothic stage attire. A man stood smoking against the wall here, and another played the guitar there. People sat on flat, mesh benches along the sidewalks. Cameras flashed at the famous soccer player now emerging from a trendy corner restaurant.

We passed the small condom store with the giant electric billboard above and laughed. We passed the train station and kept going as the rain began to fall again. Where the road narrowed and stone walls guarded each side, and where overgrown plants hugged these stones, the rain mixed with the soil and stirred up the deepest of scents. This was the aroma of Japan, this wave of musky flowers and humid lushness with a hint of something shut away too long. It was the inside of the Pirates of the Caribbean ride at Disneyland relived, the inside of the temple reborn, and it unfurled through my car window on a roll of warm air. Ryuichi looked over at me, and we knew again while the words began to come.

"The Sphinx was built in a climate like this," I said, not questioning where the knowledge came from.

"But there was no rain when you taught me. None at all."

"Lie down beside the altar," I had said so long ago, "and relax as you have been taught …"

•

The Roman obeyed, releasing and replenishing the energy in his muscles one by one. He was skilled at this already. Even the clatter of my dagger dropped to the floor could not shake the trance. I knew he was ready. He folded his arms behind his head and yawned.

"You seem pleased with yourself."

"Yes. I do, don't I?"

"Stretch out on the floor with your head to the north. It's simple to find the direction, as the temple sits east to west."

"Why north?"

"The pull of the Earth and the pull of your energies strengthen each other this way. It is easier for the novice, or so I'm told. Some say east is best. I find that it really makes no difference. Arms straight to the sides. Yes. Not another sound until we are finished. No sight. No scents. Now control your breathing. Breathe in to the count of ten, hold to ten, release to ten. Good. Your breath flows evenly now."

I sat down several feet from him, feeling my thin

skirt caress the tops of my feet. "I want you to imagine that all of your energy is stored in your feet. Then pull it slowly up your body until it reaches your head. Now push it back down. Build yourself, expand, propel the energy until your whole being rocks back and forth—until you become unsure if you lie still as stone in this temple or if you move in the air."

I ceased speaking to the Roman, allowing him the silence to benefit the state he sought. I watched him for a time, not long, long enough. At last he bent at the waist, sitting up slowly to look at me, brows drawn together.

"This is no relaxation trick you teach. Tell me what this leads to."

"Tell me first what you experienced."

"I felt as if a great wave of myself caught me, humming and vibrating. And then it passed."

"There will come a time when you can hold the vibrations. At this time, your body may refuse to respond to your command. It may freeze."

"What should I do then?"

"Ignore your body. It will remain healthy and unharmed. Concentrate on your thoughts. You may even hear a sound like insects flying near your ears as you do this, but don't grow frightened if you do."

"Ignore this as well?"

"Hear it. And move past it. It is the way you will leave your body behind."

The Roman sat still, eyes fierce, brows still drawn. "If you were another, I would declare your mind decayed. Do you mean this as reality, or some lesson cloaked in mystic wording?"

"Oh, it's real. The essence of you will escape your flesh at your command. Thoughts are deeds in the spirit realm. If you wish to fly to the moon herself, you will be there in a thought."

"What if I lose my body?"

"You cannot. Your body will reclaim you if you are away too long. If I lay one finger on your body, you will come sailing back before the touch is gone. And any time you will it so, you can return."

"What of other discarnate souls? Can they capture my body?"

"Some may try. But this body is divinely given to you and you alone. A single thought from you can drive away an invader."

"What use will this all be, if I go sailing through the stars?"

"You will see more, collect more wisdom than you ever will otherwise. You can look back on your past lives, or see into the future. Time exists only for the physical realm. It does not exist where you will go."

"Is it not possible that an evil one could see these things and use it to harm?"

"The One God does not allow this. He watches always. You cannot change what must occur. If you attempt to see an event that you are not meant to, you will find yourself back in your body immediately. If you see an event that you should, but attempt to use it to manipulate another, harm another, you will find yourself back in your body. And the memory of what you have learned in that event may be so clouded that you will never again access it."

The Roman leapt up from the floor and strode over to me. His veil-like mantle sparkled black in the torchlight. His hair shone. His hands found the sides of my face so gently then.

"The Book of Life will be opened for my eyes. There is so much I want to learn."

"You forget yourself, Roman." I knew that my eyes did not convey the threat my words should have held.

"I believe I do the opposite."

He pressed his forehead against mine as I stood too stiffly, hands straight at my sides while his own hands twined into my hair. With a breath of restraint he turned away and left my temple.

The Roman spent his days in and out of the trance I had taught him. But when his breathing stilled and his heart slowed, still he remained inside his shell. Unable to make the separation, he practiced to the point of exhaustion, often slipping across the boundary into sleep. I knew that it could take him days or months or years to make the final step away from flesh. Often when I believed he slept, I turned to find him quietly watching me as I labored over untold writings.

I took him to the Great Pyramid on a night no more special than the rest. His frustration was beginning to block both of us—him from his fruitless efforts, me from the mere watching.

He held his tongue, a habit he had nicely begun to form. After a time of silent breathing inside the pyramid, the grandest of temples, his thoughts had gathered enough for the allowance of speech.

"I know I am not to be initiated. I thought the training through and I know I have not mastered all the levels."

"So you wonder now what entitles you to the honor of being here amidst these limestone blocks. It seems right that you should see the inside now, at this time. I do not know why it is so, but I listen always to my intuition."

"So you think I will never see this while wearing the robes of highest initiation?" Soft laughter in his taunt, and something doubtful disguised by jest.

"I only wanted to sit and speak as friends. Not as Priest and Priestess this night. I am tired."

We sat on the hard, cool floor, exposed to the nuances of the pyramid, far away from the security of a wall to lean against. The Roman looked upward and breathed in the warm twilight air, the kind that smells so comfortably of earth that it scarcely seems to be air at all.

"What is this soft pulling I feel?"

"The stones have their own energy."

He ran his hand along the dark layer of stubble growing across his jaw. "And purpose as well, I suppose."

"They were built far before our time. They are the greatest of temples to the One God, for many reasons. To show a center, to mark a border, to measure … But enough of this. Tell me of Rome, Roman."

"You change the subject. I'm sure you already know much of Rome."

"I wish to see it through your eyes."

"Through my eyes? My eyes are blurred. Rome's power makes a man drunk. You would like the build of our cities. So organized and perfect. That's where all of Rome's benevolent energy has gone, I think—into her stone walls and buildings. But, you would not be listened to there, not seen. Her power is almost masculine and political. Women are kept from positions of obvious power. You would be a walking anachronism there."

"In what time and location do your blurred eyes place me?"

"Something inside you moves with the changing of the stars. What is time to someone such as you?" Only vague, distant sadness flowed with his words.

"Oh, my Roman, that is the surest quality of the Gift, which we so recognize in each other."

"But I am so far from the grace in which you live."

"You think I live in grace? No, you are not so far."

The Roman leapt to his feet as if scorched by the ground, soul tearing apart behind his clear, brown eyes. "I know you, Priestess. I know you. Golden light. Robes. What does it mean, this vision I see?"

I, too, stood. "Roman, I will tell you this secret I have come to know. I have lived a life together with you on Earth before this one."

"I need not ask when. I know you are as I believe, what I believe you to be—as old as creation itself."

"Not quite so old as that. But if we recognize one another and have lived once before together, then doesn't it stand to reason that you may be just as ancient as me?"

"Maybe from Zep Tepi, the First Time?"

"I think it more than likely."

•

These last words were quiet ones spoken from calm lips, yet they shattered time, the veil between lives gone and the present, and came screaming across eternity to Ryuichi's ears.

"Do you know what this means?" He slapped his hands down on the seat beside him. "We've been assuming that this memory was our first together. It isn't. It's just not!" He ran his hands through his hair, pulling it a little, touch of the madman in his eyes. "We were together before Egypt. Before. It wasn't just that you recognized the Gift in me then. You recognized me. You remembered me. We are older even than that, Ariana."

My back straightened and I peered as deeply into his eyes as it was possible for a human to do. He was right. I knew he was right.

Try as we might, we could not gather up the threads of the memory again. The remainder of the conversation in the pyramid was lost to us. I could only guess that the wisdom I had spoken so long ago still rang true—that if one attempts to see an event that should not be seen, anything learned will become clouded and fade away. The knowledge held in our memory was surely included in that rule, and would come when it should.

•

The High Priest died in his temple, so quietly that his own priests believed he slumbered. When they realized his state at last, a howl rose from the people and vast mourning overtook the city. His temple virtually dissolved overnight as the young priests floundered about in sheer confusion. So unfitting a tribute to his life and the training he bestowed upon them.

Anubis removed the priests from the temple and sat alone beside the withered body of the old man in his final sanctuary. He looked up as I walked inside. "We should begin the preservation. Everyone assumes we will take care of it."

"It is our role. But, we won't do that with him. No herbs, no drying. No wraps. Nothing of the sort for our High Priest."

He looked away from the corpse for the second time. "What can you mean? This goes against the teaching."

I looked at him for a moment, sensing a change in his demeanor, and knew that he had recently succeeded with the final separation from his body. How ironic that he should gain so much with the release of his soul and lose so much with the release of the High Priest's in so nearly the same instant.

"I will tell you a secret, my precious Anubis. The common people, and in this, I include Pharaohs and peasants alike, have come to require mummification as custom. It's harmless enough, I suppose. It's a tradition that transforms the idea of immortality from a spiritual to a physical matter. No matter the superstition, the ka would not return to claim the body. The belief affects nothing really. I'm certain men of centuries to come will appreciate their leavings—our processes are intelligent and marvelous. But, our beloved High Priest wished a different ritual. An older one."

"I'm intrigued so completely, and I have no idea with what."

"You do not see the tombs of our ancestors littering the dunes. Nor will you."

"Ancestors?"

"Civilizations long, long since past. And there are peoples now, peoples across oceans who do not preserve their corpses."

"There are burials, yes."

"And there are funeral pyres."

"The High Priest wished this?"

"Yes. It eradicates the trace of a body now useless. Burns away and releases even the tiniest essence left in the flesh. He will make his way more quickly and freely through the Duat and on to another level or back for the next lesson here. Without the pyre, some essence of him will remain in his heart, his brain, until it fades away with time. It's not his eternal soul, you understand, but the part of the personality that breaks away in death—that part, which was his mask, his outer image."

"How can we do this without witnesses?"

"We will perform the funerary rites inside the pyramid itself. You will be surprised how its design aids the soul all the way to its destination. The High Priest waits for the Way to be opened for him in this manner."

"He awaits? Of course he awaits. I know this. But he could continue if he wanted."

"He's watching us now. Waiting. He will hear us say our words of parting and will wait for us to let him go."

"What shall we tell the onlookers?"

"Nothing. They will ask no more once Anubis and Nephthys claim the body for preparation. They see no more except for the procession, which will take us to the Pyramid. They simply mourn. And when night falls, we will carry the High Priest out of the Pyramid and far into the desert. The place awaits. The High Priest himself arranged it."

"And what of the stars? The other lights of night? Will someone not see us?"

"I will take care of it. Go now and prepare your mask, Anubis. I hear you have painted it like no other."

A dense cover of clouds enfolded Egypt as soon as night fell and the glow of the torch blew away with the starlight. Such sadness rolled in with the night for the demise of our magic so obvious with the death of the High Priest, with only Nephthys and Anubis to attend him. We final two children of the ancient temple, acting out our confused roles, speaking the holiest of words simply to close an already written chapter of history with honor.

We placed the High Priest's still body on top of the

lid to the great stone box inside the pyramid. His shell possessed almost no weight at all, shrunken with the decades as it was. There would be no rouge for him, no paint, no herbs. The Roman stood on one side of the coffer and I on the other. When I raised my head under the weight of my headdress, I saw nothing but Anubis with his jackal head and secrets. This aspect of the One God eclipsed the arrogant yet unsure Roman behind his mask.

The words began as we spoke to the High Priest, those of Anubis to set the scales, mine to guide the way. "Let him who is summoned come and hear us. And let him be not fettered. Release him. Send him from us with potent blessings to a role reborn in the stars. Send him to the balancing of his soul, the healing of self, the forgiveness of self. The Powerful One smiles in the Duat, travels in the abode of secrets."

The prayers were more, but never enough of a tribute to the intricacies of life. We knew the High Priest heard. We knew he watched us. We called him and sensed him, and then felt his departure.

The ceremony was complete and we stood in silence. I removed my headdress and placed it on the floor beside the Roman's mask. He lifted the corpse and carried it away into the night while I walked silently behind. His footsteps made no noise as they ground into the sand. So, he had learned my trick on his own, and how appropriately it marked his solemn, silent stride.

The funeral pyre flared high into the night sky. We stood basking in the heat of the flames, far away from the slight glow of the city. "This touches you. I can see it."

"I was not ready to speak the words I have spoken,"

he said. "I didn't comprehend what I was taught until I heard the words leave my lips tonight. They were gone from hearing before my mind captured the meaning. Such disservice to the dead. I am furious with myself."

"Cool your fury, child of fire. That's your element, you know." Water extinguishes fire. Where had the thought come from? "You showed your teacher at the last possible moment that he had succeeded in breaking through your stupidity."

"Wit blowing away gloom."

"It's the element of air in me."

He smiled. "Tell me honestly, Priestess. Tell me what happened when his heart stopped." Stripped down to innocence for a moment, with the utterance of a question.

"He left his body, much as I taught you to do, only his connection with the body was severed. He floated above, as you have done. And now that his ties are also severed here, now that he has heard our freeing words, he will move on. He will meet the One God and the spark of Him that thrives inside will be ignited. He will be shown every entry in his Book of Life. This is the balancing. He will know again every action, every word, every thought. He will feel how these things have affected each person they have touched. He will repeat the good and the bad until that spark inside him that is both God and himself can forgive."

"He showered only kindness on so many."

"It would be a warm, golden gift to relive his life."

"When all this is reconciled within himself, what then?"

"He will move to other levels, as many as he has earned. I do not know how many there are in total. We knew once, but the knowledge is lost. Each level opens his mind further to the nature of God, to his own nature. You could say that each level is closer to the One God. When he reaches the level he has earned, he will begin to prepare for his return to Earth and begin again only to climb higher with each passing."

"Will you feel the pain of the dagger thrust you fell me with?"

"Yes. I will."

"And you knew this before you stabbed?"

I nodded. Ashes caught on the wind and flew heavenward with glowing embers. Stars began to peek through the clouds.

The Roman continued dryly, "My past relived. How far from the Creator I shall be."

"But He will be with you always."

"Will you, I wonder?"

"You begin to turn the conversation to some lower level once more."

He stared at the midnight pyre, straight ahead and calm beyond control. "I know you do not think so little of me as that. I wonder only how firmly our souls are strapped together now. We were carried by whim or by fate together to this time, by the recognition of something seductive and familiar."

"I am certain we continue the Way together, Roman. Is this what you wished to hear? It's inescapable, I fear."

"Inescapable, I wish. I want to see in my past relived, no face more than yours."

I looked at him, profile of the Roman serene, sincere then.

"I sense no taint to your words. I thank you." I grew ashamed with myself even as my words left me. I had allowed the moment to stray somehow from the High Priest's final respects, from a lesson much needed. I had allowed this irretrievable piece of precious time to be overtaken by a woman's feelings. It was not even this allowance that troubled me so. I could have willed my emotions to a halt—if I had possessed one measure of desire to. This final lacking is what struck me so.

Like living things, the flames cried their final cries and faded to ashes when at last they were all that remained of the High Priest. Even those ashes would find slumber under a blanket of desert sand. The winds would see to this during the night, and I would see to the winds.

The daylight hours resumed their usual flow as if the death of the High Priest had never happened. Life has a way of going on unaltered no matter the incident. Strange then, how it can be so easily altered by the tiniest one. My Roman and I searched for any element in life that is not a touching of opposites such as this, and found nothing.

"Black to white, love to hate, life to death. Each is the opposite end of a line," I told him.

"But if one takes the line and wraps it around to form a circle, opposites touch," he thought aloud. "They become both the closest and farthest away. And so the One God instilled in the universe a great pattern of circles, cycles."

I was pleased beyond words with the Roman's insight so true. This pattern of discussion carried us from time to time. I saw the wisdom more clearly than before, and yet a singular perplexity in the form of a Roman soldier knocked me ever off-balance.

I sometimes prepared lessons for him when my

hours as Nephthys came. He went with me from time to time throughout the city while I saw to the duties of Isis. He watched and learned, I think, and spent a great deal more time alone with his meditations. He struggled to assimilate the knowledge he had been given. It is one thing to know the wisdom, and quite another to use it daily, to create a new reality with the invocation of it.

Concern gripped me when the Roman withdrew completely. I listened with the hearing of a Priestess and went when I heard his thoughts carry to me. I found him in the temple of the High Priest, empty now except for the Roman and the lost, wandering novices. He rose and met me by the entrance. We walked away from the place together.

"I'm ready to show you something. I don't wish for the others to see. Have your disciples gone for the night?"

"Disciples? You know they are not that. The temple is in solitude now. Have you given thought to the training of your own priests?"

He gave a twisted grin. "My priests? When my own training is far from complete? But I've discovered a new ability." He fairly ran into my temple, then stood gathering himself.

"Look, Priestess. See what this energy inside me can do."

I grew wary of him. "Think hard between can and should before you act."

"You talk as if you know already, beloved Priestess. Feign admiration then, but watch me."

I heard voices in my temple, building in audible clarity as he stood smiling, not knowing the consequence of what he did. He breathed through his nose, reveling in the growing presence, palms raised and arms to his sides bent softly at the elbow. White teeth in the torch-light, cloaked from head to foot in black, hair like shining silk—all parts of the Roman turned Anubis, priest threatening to become warlock within the single beat of his heart.

I spoke not to him, but rather to the voices. He was beyond hearing me. "At the command of Nephthys of the One God, cease!" Instantaneous control, a tempest of invisible cold flame carried with my words, silent thunder with my will. "Depart from my temple!"

The Roman's arms dropped. "What is this you do?"

"Clearing this holy ground. Why does your arrogance push you to these actions?"

"I have the power to speak with those who have passed on."

"No, Roman, you do not."

"Now who is the arrogant one here, Priestess?"

"There are ceremonies—blessed, measured, sanctified ceremonies for that. And we invoke such ritual only when the reason is most holy, which is almost never. Never in such a way as I have just witnessed. It is sorcery."

"Why expend so much energy for the mere decoration of a ceremony when I can raise my palms, call, and find answer?"

"Do you know what answered you? Do you have any idea what manner of being entered into my temple just now? To this holy place?"

"Those from the other side."

"No. When the souls of departed loved ones return, it is only through the special leave of the One God. These souls have passed on. They return to guard their living family, to finish the unended. Only the confused, angry Earth-bound would answer a call such as yours. And there are reasons they remain in their twilight state. They lie. They torment. They do whatever thing they need to make contact with one who hears. Even so, these beings are far from the worst you will invite with a selfish, arrogant, senseless conjuring."

"What harm could it do to speak with them if I already know their deceptions?"

"You are breaching a veil that you are not meant to disturb. You will understand later in your training that nothing good can come from exercising your power merely for the sake of exercising it."

"I believe I understand now. I simply wonder if I care about the consequences enough to cease my adventure." So full of pride, so impudent again. Would these qualities lurk forever below the surface?

I turned from him then. "Oh, my Anubis. There is no fast way to the command of knowledge that you seek. Only the weak and lazy turn to darker means. Mastery requires work and effort. There is no instant gratification in developing your soul in the light. Instant gratification comes with evil."

He took me by the arm and turned me to him, thrill of foundling power now gone. "I know the truth in everything you tell me. My mind knows it to the core. But something in me lashes out."

I looked into his eyes, seeking sincerity amidst their pattern of brown with golden flecks, and finding it. "I have the sense at times, that in your life, vast years ago, your actions were held tightly in check."

"Maybe I try to make up for it now."

"I suspect."

He took my hand in his and raised it to his lips. I showed him the methods for clearing, cleaning the energy of the temple. How effective the purification was, I couldn't be sure for the strength was lost in my words now. I felt only the excited intensity of that place on back of my hand.

I walked away from my own temple that night, unable to bear another second as Priestess, another moment of Anubis gone awry. In my heart somehow a devotion to the Roman had taken root and grown strong. Here inside myself I took my first glimpse into godly love, an insight so complete into the very core of another, that even if he sins or errs, the dedication remains unshakable. The pain of meting out necessary punishment would sting because of that love. How lethal the combination of pride and arrogant impatience stirring inside the Roman. No, I could not condone his actions. I could not force change. What he would choose to become lay entirely in his own hands.

Fear of all my fears realized—the Roman's transgressions had only begun. My heart shuddered. I walked as Isis from the city, so filled with the power of the goddess-aspect that no one without the Gift saw the true form of my body as I walked. They saw Isis, taller, brighter, cloaked in a glamour unlike the mortal I was inside. I fairly floated across the sand, hair hanging like golden sunlight, skin kissed by the sun's own strength. But the day was fading.

And I know that I darkened only steps away from the temple, slipped out of the skin of golden radiance, cloaked myself in Nephthys. Yes, this was my time. The magic was not lost—it was mine still. Yet what emanated from the innermost part of my temple? Who dare draw uninvited upon the source of power there? This was not the magic, not the benevolence to which I tended. It was the unmistakable presence of the Roman inside, a presence not wholly his. And shades of what he was before he fell.

Hair black as midnight, eyes bluer than the sky, I appeared in the doorway, arms folded across my chest. Anubis stood in the center of the room, waiting for me. No trace of the Roman, only Anubis to greet me.

"What spells have you worked in my temple?"

"You feel the energy. Such a change of atmosphere, don't you think?" His voice was ice. Not the Roman I recognized in any sense.

"You summoned again and found worse this time."

"Look what power it brought me." He gave a grand, sweeping gesture.

"What you have conjured flees from my presence even as we speak. It knows I can banish it, destroy its game with a single thought strongly directed."

The beast shrank from its visible place behind his eyes.

"I can hold fire in my bare hands, Priestess, and they do not blister. I can darken and lighten in the way you do. I can hear the blood flowing through your veins ..."

"You are unclean. You have allowed this thing into your body. You will be barred from training until your flesh has shed the last trace of it."

He sunk suddenly to the ground, all Roman again, the corrupt faux Anubis gone for now. The summoned wretch slid fast from my temple.

He wept quietly, then stopped as suddenly as he had begun. "Forgive me." He stood on shaking legs. "Forgive me."

I whispered, "My Roman, if you do not take the high road to these powers, they will corrupt you. You will be forever lost to me."

He put his arms around me, clinging like a child at first, then changing to the man he was as my energy healed him. Mistake of all mistakes, I let him look at me, truly into me.

Oh, how every moment counts. How could I have chosen what I chose and so wounded myself in a single moment? When had the temptation in my mortal heart so crushed the sense from my immortal mind?

I permitted him to lay me down on the steps before the altar. The same steps once covered in his blood would now be stained with mine. I allowed him to spread my thighs and I took him inside myself. Ritual and sacrifice sealed with each movement so deep between my legs. Ecstasy unbearable, the tangle of our bodies satiated at the foot of the temple. I had failed as a Priestess, and yet I wanted the feel of his skin more than I wanted anything else.

He took me again that night and again I throbbed around him. Over and over spilled his seed, and I knew he had lost himself in me. With each empassioned kiss, each tremble, I wanted him more. My own purpose threatened to collapse into this need for him, but in the back of my mind I think I somehow held fast to it: the completion of my writings. Morning would part us too soon and I ached for all the small things that defined him so sharply to my senses even before he had gone.

•

Where were Ryuichi's discerning words at the moment when the memory subsided? His lyrics had not recited what we had done at the foot of the consecrated altar. My poems certainly had not. He concentrated all too heavily on the highway. I counted painted dashes in the centerline. What could we say that would not lend more awkwardness to this already ungraceful moment?

I looked briefly at him and without really wanting to, saw an aura of light around him. The heightened state, which the memory always brought, must have clung longer than usual. I felt a tremble pass through me. The exertion had drained the energy from my body. I wanted nothing more than to rub my bare feet against my cool futon and fall asleep. All that stood between me and my apartment was a plate of rum raisin crepes eaten in silence and the last few kilometers of the drive.

The car wound its way into the driveway and Ryuichi touched my hand and smiled. Ah, the touch of his hand, so like that first touch across the table that evening. It brought back a small part of the intimacy, as if some warm thing had covered me with its soft kiss.

Yet now there was a new look in his eyes—one I wasn't sure I could return.

Chapter Four

Poet-Philosopher.
Night-soaked metal
chilled my soul, your hands.
Search for forgiveness
to the final breath,
my Priest in Black.

I snapped back the lock to my bicycle and fumbled with the mailbox key. Nothing. Winger was long lost to the mountains' lure, but I expected a letter in spite of reality. I looked for it everyday. I considered for a moment, stretching out and grasping him with a thought, but grew hopelessly distracted with each stair I took up to my apartment.

A small, brown envelope showed through the metal grid of the message box on the front of my door. The meter reader was the only person who ever placed anything inside and he had already come. I reminded myself again to locate Winger as I unlocked my door.

The touch of the envelope eradicated all intentions from my mind. The residue of Ryuichi's emotions clung to it like some dizzying perfume. I knew he himself had

delivered this letter, sliding his fingertips down the outside of the box as the envelope slid beyond retrieval. I
felt the impression of his warm, smooth fingers lingering on the metal. Never before had the deluge of recollection begun without the two of us together. But he
had begun to remember something on his own, taken
the previous recollections and surmised the outcome.
Or maybe the memory had given him no choice but
to relive it. And he gave me no choice but to share the
memory with him. It came crashing down on me with
such an impact that my stomach clenched against itself.

•

With timing of the worst sort, the Roman soldiers
returned. Nothing was settled between the Roman and
me. Nothing resolved. Nothing healed. But these soldiers did not, could not know the impact of their coming. I recognized the men who had knelt on either side
of my Roman on the banks of the Nile, the men who had
not recognized me in my home with one of their own
bleeding on my bed.

These once-lost soldiers did not return alone. They
were flanked by dozens, led by a stern one with his
clipped gray beard. They had come for my Roman. I
ducked into the temple before they were near enough
to distinguish the High Priestess from the rest.

He sat inside on the altar steps with his tattered Roman uniform on the stones beside him, so much the
priest now that nothing could hide it. He held his head
high. "I will not go back with them, you know."

"I know."

"I want more here. I want more of you. I will die if
they take me."

"You will die if you don't go with them, once they

know you're here and you're well."

He stood up, punishing the uniform under his foot. "I cannot hide like a coward. I go to meet them now. Stay inside."

"Consider this more. I can say you died from your wound. They will believe it. I beg you. Your blood boils hot now, and your words, your very appearance will bring disaster."

"Stay inside. If you hold any love for me, do not watch."

"Take care what you choose to do now, Roman. It will be the etching on your soul. If you cannot tell me, you must know it wrong, this thing you plan. Think before you speak. There are other ways out of this."

I did not follow him. I did not have to bear witness to know what foolishness he would do. I sat inside for hours while he talked to the soldiers, tried to convince them that with all the power of the Egyptian temples, it would be best to leave him as guard. He tried to convince them how it would benefit the Roman quest for conquest, to harness the power of our magic. But the Roman general would want evidence, which of course he could not give without revealing himself. He was trapped in the corner of his self-created box, for whatever facts he told would become proof of his connection with my temple. And this was forbidden to a mere Roman soldier. This was an offense punishable by death. The Romans would execute him for acts traitorous to them. Now I was bound by sacred oath to end his life for the same reason.

The Roman council met around a campfire in the dark. I sat still as marble in my temple watching his shadow cross the wall under the faint light of a torch.

He cast a changed silhouette from when he first set foot on my ground. "They're deciding my fate now."

"You decided your fate."

He tore off the black gossamer cloak that covered his shoulders and threw it to the floor. "What would you have had me do?" His voice was an angry thing, striking the walls.

"You could have hidden here."

"Hide like some criminal in the dark?"

"Yes. Hide and live! Hide and stay with me."

"And where would be the honor?"

"We could have hidden away the papyri and slipped into the night. As long as we live, we can teach. Where is the honor in betraying temple secrets, Roman? What were you thinking?"

"They would tear apart your temple immediately if they didn't find me. They would demand the body. There would be no time to finish your writings." Strange that he sounded so unlike himself, grasping at convincing explanations that held no truth.

"I would have finished elsewhere. The One God wills it so. They are going to destroy the temple anyway. That is their intent. It has been from the beginning. To take something they cannot have and cannot understand, and destroy it. But they did not have to destroy you, too. You did not have to allow it."

He hung his head now. "I did not reveal the truths. I told them of the evil things I had done, only they would not think them evil, only powerful. Not of the wisdom. I will be Keeper of Secrets all the way to my grave."

"What you said was as wicked as revealing the secrets. I heard you, Roman. You boasted of your power. Don't you see that in addition to considering you a traitor, they now believe you a threat to them? Listen, and you can hear them say this now."

He closed his eyes, breathing in the night, listening. "No matter what I could have done, the temple will fall at their hands."

"So you thought to save yourself? Oh, I believe in your desire to stay here. I believe in your sincerity when you say you will not leave with them. Shhh … Listen, Roman. They speak of the heka. They speak of using it as a weapon. Most of them do not even believe you. But, oh I felt you. The power seduced you beyond return. What did you think? That the army would give you a position of power? That you could stay in the temple this way? I fear what you would have done with it."

He looked hopeless in the shadows. "I should never have stayed here. Never have entered the temple."

I listened to the council. They used more words they could never have known without him. "How could you tell them these things? You cast aside the One God and the sacred training with such casualness? You have soiled the sacred aspect of Anubis with your pride. These Romans will write your role into history. Do you know this? Anubis will become this laughable, dark creature who brags of summoning demons and wrapping the dead. One more piece of the wisdom corrupted. The future will never know the holy vessel that Anubis was, that you were once.

"Oh, but Roman, this will not be the end. I will see to it that the wisdom is preserved somehow. That is the present role of the Neteru, Roman. To save the wisdom for those who will awaken. You, with the Gift so strong, Neter of Zep Tepi. How could you have fallen so far?"

The Roman stood before me, solemn and without

providence in the moment. "I will make this right some-how. My mistakes have ensured my return to the flesh. I will find you and I will make this right again."

"I have sealed my own return as well, Roman. But, if you have learned anything, you must know that I am not the One to turn to with your guilt. The balance of your soul will be weighed. That is yours alone to carry before the One God."

The sound of marching soldiers carried across the ground outside. I heard them with the hearing of the Priestess. It would take only minutes for them to come. Only desperate heartbeats.

"Forgive me, Priestess."

He, too, heard them at last. He pulled me to him and touched his forehead to mine, inhaling and exhaling to-gether the same heavy breaths. He placed a final kiss on my lips as the soldiers seized his arms, chained him, dragged him from me. Sent reeling into eternity, locked together with a kiss and a betrayal.

"Nephthys!"

I looked into his eyes before the soldiers forced his head down, but did not answer. My focus had to be on the writings. They were unfinished still. He was gone from my view, but I sensed his struggle nonetheless. He tried to move the divine energy into his palms to form a weapon of fire, to escape somehow, and then ceased. He acted with honor in that cessation, his refusal to use his blessed, cursed knowledge for such an ignoble purpose.

The soldiers held him, beat him down until his knees struck the ground. They hacked his hair away in chunks and tore apart his Egyptian clothing. They dressed him in his soldier's uniform again, dull red and brown, soiled, and torn from his wanderings through the desert that day he had been lost. But he had never been so lost as now.

I wrote furiously, knowing full well that when the army's attention fell away from the Roman, it would turn to the temple. They would take away all the instruments of ceremony, loot the wealth there before I could plead to Pharaoh for his army. I could not go to the Roman. The One God spoke loudly and I set his words to written record. Finally, I swept aside the papyrus and ink, exhausted.

•

The memory blurred and I was able to sweep it aside. Had this been the sum of what Ryuichi had remembered alone? The words on the papyrus fell away from my mind as I tore open the envelope, still standing with one shoe on inside my entryway.

I inhaled deeply before looking down.

I held in my hand a concert ticket, front row beside the stage, nearest to Ryuichi I was sure. I guessed at what thoughts might go through his mind if he looked down from the stage and saw the empty space where he hoped I would be. I imagined the mingling of patience and disappointment I could create in him. I imagined myself trying to sit calmly on my living room floor watching television while Ashes of Roses performed in Tokyo.

But, a promise was a promise. I called his driver as his note said I should and found the man indeed waiting for the phone to ring. What the neighbors must have thought when the limousine pulled into the driveway that evening.

I dressed in a sleek, black shirt with jeans and let my hair flow golden amber down my back. I was daring in the night. Hell, I *was* the night. I was the moon and the stars and the darkness. Mistress of the Universe I was, sliding expertly through the crowd, watching it part at the sight of me.

And suddenly there I was, standing in front of the stage, the enormous speakers. Now I was but one tiny person in the midst of the throng, one face lost in a teeming crowd. My heart raced as if I'd run the entire way. My palms grew cold as ice out of sheer nervousness. I was the one with the stage fright.

The lights dimmed and the audience roared. What a decadent, opulent atmosphere the band had created. The spotlights flared, revealing each of the band members on stage so near me. No opening acts for them, I noted. Their music pulsed with the beginning of the first song and Ryuichi captured his microphone. My breath literally stopped, but I would never allow him to know that. How could I ever express how heartbreakingly beautiful I found him.

He scanned the front row and his gaze landed on me. He smiled then, and nearly laughed it seemed. How inappropriate, his smile amidst the visual, gothic creature this concert was. But the audience clung to any gesture, any word he would bestow upon them, and they were charmed.

His voice enshrouded me. Every emotion in the world was at the command of that angelic voice. I sang the words with him, my own voice mercifully lost in the thunder of the audience. He looked down at me, singing for me, with me—this time about the moon. He looked harmless enough from the outside, singer with his angel's voice, dancing darkly with eternity in front of thousands. It looked like a show, an image for everyone's benefit. But, it was another piece of Ryuichi that I recognized then. I questioned again what the centuries had done to him inside. Had they cleansed his soul? Or was there still some terrifyingly powerful, indelible taint lurking behind those eyes?

This benediction, this song to the moon persisted while lights streamed like her rays onto the stage. His gaze held mine as he raised his arms above his head. The words gathered strength as he sang. My own arms took on a life of their own, answering the call of Ryuichi's gesture. My hands swayed above me and came down to form the final triangle of the old temple greeting.

He took the energy from the audience and transformed it into his own. He flooded through me, and I through him. The force of us whirled from floor to ceiling, filled the building. We felt it, tasted it in the air. Still he sang. With this heka, a force such as this, we could have constructed the pyramids together, lifted the heaviest blocks without strain. Thoughts are deeds, remember. But it was an impotent force despite all its potency now. We had nowhere to unleash it, no reason, no recollection of exactly how.

The song ended with the audience in a frenzy. The people nearest me had all stepped slightly away, looking from me to Ryuichi and back, wondering. Oh, we were bound together now, more certainly than ever.

Somehow the concert found its end. The band members all held hands and bowed together, waved goodbye to their fans. His eyes never left mine. How obviously he wanted to talk to me, but I began to turn anyway, exiting with the crowd. Such a mistake my movement was, that simple turn of my head that triggered his pain.

We were not in the present any longer. He was not

on that stage anymore. He was the Roman soldier now, unable to stand, his hands gripping bars, the cage his reality. And I was the Egyptian woman in a dress of sky blue, gliding away from him for the last time, turning my head. Turning my back to him. *Do not look upon him.* He had begged me to wait, but I had turned away.

The seconds were agonizingly slow as I turned my head. Our situation had been futile then. I had left him there because I had had to, not out of the desire to. Surely he understood that now. I had to carry the contribution, my rendition of my portion of the Record to its hiding place. His betrayal and senselessness could not be allowed to destroy the writings. The empty, thoughtless Roman soldiers would never, never find this prize. He was forfeit to the greater good, and he had sacrificed himself with his actions. The pyramids stood gloriously in the distance far behind him with the moon high overhead testifying to his sealed fate. I heard the One God weep for the Fallen One not yet risen.

"Forgive me," the Roman had said. "Forgive me." How he had begged me to wait.

"*Matte yo!*" Wait. Ryuichi's voice amplified over the microphone came as a cruel slap back to the present.

I had the freedom of choice now in this replay of history. The entire audience stopped its exit, turning with questioning eyes toward him. He looked so desperate with his arms hanging limp at his sides, breath coming in great gulps. And I was willing to take the chance, willing to bet that time had cleansed his soul. A murmur rose from the crowd as he stood there silent and imploring. I turned toward him. How could I ever turn away again?

There was no recovery from the public awkwardness. Ryuichi thanked the audience again, bowed and turned off the microphone. Security ran to the front of the stage, pushing away the fans who turned back and attacked it. One of the guards discretely took my arm and led me around to Ryuichi's dressing room.

I quietly shut his door and locked it behind me. Ryuichi paced back and forth, soaked to the skin with sweat. He looked up at the click of the lock and rushed over to me. He threw his arms around me and held me there, tears mingling with sweat.

"It's okay." I embraced him tightly, smoothing back his damp hair. I cried with him, for him. "There's nothing to forgive now. It's all over."

He pulled away to look at me. "Forgive me. Say that you forgive me."

"Fine. I forgive you."

"You were making something … holy. Yes, holy. From the One God. And I told them. How could I do that? I don't understand why I did that. They destroyed everything they touched." He walked away across the room with his hands over his eyes. "And I lost you. I just threw you away. The temple. All of the pain, all this searching—all because of me. Me."

His eyes frightened me. The energy we had generated together in the concert had not dimmed, but instead turned to the memory, turned into a concentration of this anguish. He sat down in a chair, drew his knees up under his chin, and rocked back and forth. I walked over and knelt before him.

"But I'm here now." I put my hands against his face and kissed away a tear.

"The search almost killed me. Again." All color fled his face and his breathing came rapidly. "They. Oh, no.

They killed me. Killed me."

He knew. Because of my vision in the music store, I had assumed that Ryuichi had guessed at how his time in Egypt might have ended, suspected the reality of his execution all along. What had he thought in the beginning, or even after the memories started to come? That I had banished him from the temple? Or perhaps his army had simply taken him back without repercussion? We had not died happily together of old age; it could never have been so. I had known the manner of his demise since before we met, since the time I sat on my apartment floor in awe of a stranger in a video, yet that part of his pain had not revealed itself to him until he was ready for it. Until he could handle it.

He seemed to settle inside himself and ran his fingers against the side of my face. With the taste of drying tears and fading torment, he kissed me. It dulled the memory for him, helped him through it somehow. But always with him this life held the theme of longing and our kiss only increased the ache. Only the scream of Egypt-past prevented us from recognizing the turn the longing had taken. We only remembered then.

•

Under the rays of the morning sun, time came to an end for my Roman. I could not bear to watch as the men lifted the entire cage with him still inside and carried it to the quiet banks of the Nile. I remember how the sun became an angry, blinding thing that fell partially black in the sky. The heavens screaming out against the actions on Earth below.

I should have gone to the banks to see him die. To let his eyes fall on me in his final moments may have been some comfort to him. I doubt the soldiers would have allowed me near. To stay away was no comfort to me. I could see it all in my mind as it happened, even from the refuge of my temple. The soldiers, mindless, merciless, heaved the cage out into the water, so heavy that it could not sail far. It landed on the riverbed with the Nile water barely covering the top. Sediment stirred up from the bottom and clouded the water some, but not enough to block the rays of that miraculous, furious sun.

I watched as the Roman looked at the sun streaming through the water, the bits of mud and rock floating in it. Then I watched the sweet breath he held escape his lungs. His hand slid away from the bars when the Nile filled him and his eyes looked sightlessly at the end of the eclipse.

I stood alone under the vast night sky, searching for Anubis in the heavens. I could have stood for an eternity there, guessing the answer to the riddle, hunting for one star in the midst of such a number. But not even my sight reached so far as that. Only endless, sacred tears for the life of my Roman.

Chapter Five

Gone the beauty
You painted on the Still.
Fallen away in Fate,
your chains and charms.
Do not look upon him.
Words etched in the Record.

With Ryuichi's death in Egypt came the confusion of the memory. No longer were there two of us to combine the distant images into one story, one finishing the sentence where the other left off. It was odd that way, how each of us struggled for bits of a vision when separated from the other. Alone, I remember most clearly the words: *Do not look upon him.* Other than these words, the rest of the Roman soldiers had no meaning for me at all afterward. They were cardboard characters in the game, holding their places on the board for a time, brushed away by the hand of Time itself.

It is very clear to me that I never saw his body, never performed the rites. I longed to for his sake, for mine. I don't recall now what the soldiers did with him. Did they carry him away when they left? They left immediately, so that it was almost easy to deny they had ever been there. Almost. Did they leave him to the meaner creatures of the river? Or throw him to the hungry desert? Still I do not know. Maybe I never knew. I do not like to think about this. For all his offenses, he had once been Anubis, god with the right to the same keeping he had bestowed upon others. He had warranted the beauty, deserved to behold the Way opened for him. Now he would have to find it himself without ceremony. Disgrace for an Egyptian man, ruin for the priest he was, the growth of his soul.

I remember running back to my temple under the hot sun on the day after his death. I remember collecting rolls and rolls of my work from behind the altar. My writings must have been complete then—at least I believe they were. The content of them is a blur to me. Symbols sometimes leap from the past into my mind, straight from the papyrus to the present. Their suggestions stun me, but like Daen, I can't describe them until their riddle grows clearer.

I hid inside the Great Pyramid, where the stones' vibrations cool and soothe, and the gate to heaven stands for those who hold the key. I must have held it then, Keepers of Secrets that we had been, for somewhere inside or somewhere under, I placed the rolls for eternity's safekeeping. A statue guarded there, a finely worked rendition of Isis and all her answers. What more did I place in that room? What was there even before me? These questions haunt me. But, Ryuichi had said it, hadn't he, that we were older even than Egypt. That even then we held memories of one another. This answers at least one of the questions. I was there in that room before me.

The thing that disturbs me most is the wondering of the events after that. My final memory in Egypt is the inside of that Pyramid room. Did the Romans find me there and bring death to me? I doubted it. They had no key and no knowledge with which to earn it. It would not have changed anything had they found me. My purpose, my writings were complete. And I had succumbed to my love and lust for the Roman. Soiled as I was, I could not have returned to my role as Priestess. What had become of me? I suppose these things do not matter much now. I live again.

Ryuichi came home with me that night. He said he couldn't bear being in a room with no one else in it, at least until the trauma faded. "I know the Roman was the past, but it clings. Everything of mine is so entangled. Everything of mine is so twisted." He said no more the rest of the evening.

He slept under a blanket on my floor, this rock idol with a glass heart threatening to shatter. I knew the pain would ebb away with his dreams and that the dawn would bring its saving grace.

I sat in front of the television with the volume turned down to nothing, watching him sleep. The Ryuichi of Egypt had been revealed to us, and I hope that in the aftermath of that revelation, he might find some peace at last.

The road that had brought us back together was amazing at the least. One corner not turned and we would have never been here. I watched Ryuichi's face and knew every feature had been created for my eyes to see again. There was nothing I didn't adore about that face. What I wouldn't give for one full life together with this man, muse and mystic wrapped in the soul of an Ancient. But the blessed affliction of knowing Daen held me still. As did the beloved, cursed shreds of his memory.

Ryuichi recovered nicely under the healing cloak of sleep. I suspected that behind that heart there lurked a spine of steel, which even shards of broken glass could not penetrate. He smiled wolfishly over a cup of green tea. Morning sunlight fell across the table as I sat down beside him. Small green salads, plain white rice, bowl of cereal. East meets West over breakfast.

I pulled my bathrobe a little tighter around me, hair wet and hanging down my back. "You cooked. Kind of."

"You grocery shopped. Kind of."

"Smart ass. Do you want to talk about the concert?"

"No." Expectant pause. "Explain 'smart ass'. I think I should know this English."

"Are you always this happy in the morning? It's sick."

"Never. I'm a creature of the night, you know." Imagine how the blend of a feigned Romanian accent with his rolling Japanese one struck my American ears. "But, I feel bright this morning." He laughed outright. Had I ever heard him laugh before? Soothing. Healing embraced us.

"What are your plans for today?"

"I have to leave for rehearsal in an hour." He put down his cup. "What did we learn from Egypt?"

I answered, "Mostly our weaknesses, I think."

"I spent centuries learning and learning and learning. Regaining, purifying the wisdom I once threw away. Lust is bad. Loyalty is good. Thinking is good. Vanity is bad."

"Lust. I must have been trying to work on that one, too."

"And then you remember one night on the altar ..."

I could see all of himself spring into his eyes again. I wish he would have hidden something of himself from me. He most likely couldn't have even if he had tried. I remembered the night in the altar, not only the details of it, but in the remnants of suffering it left behind to scar the centuries. A brief moment in history had tilted the balance of our souls. Cruel, cruel twist this was in my fate, to recognize the purest mates of my soul and not be allowed them.

I thought of Daen. I looked at Ryuichi. And how fully then I felt the impact of what Ryuichi's music screamed, the torment of its creator. He returned the look from across the table, the knowing of my thoughts etched across his every feature. I wanted to put my hands over my ears and laugh and cry and shriek my protest into the heavens. But instead I could only sit, letting my thoughts float like clouds across my eyes for Ryuichi to intuit. Despite the howl inside me, I knew somehow even then that something more was written in the plan for us and that while we wallowed in our longing and anger, we would never give into it if the sacrifice was the path marked for us ahead. We both knew this in every fiber of our beings, inexplicable though it was, that we must not touch again.

He rose from the table without a word. He held his mouth just a little too rigid, corners just a little too tight. He started to touch my hand, caught himself, and pulled his hand back. He stopped in the doorway.

"What is it that we are supposed to do now? I found you. Why can't I have you? Why can't I just carry you away and forget the world?"

"I don't know. But it would be completely wrong."

"I was sure when I found you, everything would be perfect."

"Well, it's not."

"I hear this Whispering you talk about and it says that I cannot touch you. That the energy of the Neteru is to be given in a holy way. Holy? Neteru? I just want to breathe freely and love you. I want to run through fields like a child holding your hand. But these words do not fade. These responsibilities do not fade."

Nor do the colors of us ever pale. Stray, nonsensical thoughts as Ryuichi turned to leave.

I sat in the morning sunlight with the click of the turned lock echoing in my head. I pushed aside the breakfast dishes and poured every detail of every moment with Ryuichi onto paper and addressed the envelope to Winger. My mind was so muddled that I couldn't reach out and find Winger. Not even a thing so simple as that. He could have been in America or on my doorstep for that matter; I wouldn't have sensed it.

But I could see Ryuichi shifting gears on his drive into Tokyo. I watched him pound the seat beside him with his fist, denting the leather. Watched him try to catch peace with one deep breath. Thank God I had never been sick with emotion of this kind for Winger. Winger was my sanctuary, safe and strong when I was not.

I went over Egypt again and again in my head, not the memories of that life, but of a flash of recollection that had presented itself to both of us in the midst of it. A light, golden Ryuichi, neither the singer nor the soldier but someone or something earlier. Hadn't there been others beside him? Hadn't I been? And then there were Ryuichi's own words to haunt me. *We were togeth-*

er before Egypt. We are older even than that, Ariana.
Here, hidden in the mists of the past, was the key to our
future.

I worked all day writing descriptions of the city's
pictures for my job, changing their order for best effect
while my mind spun in another place. The dreams came
in tumbles that night. In one dream I had never met
Ryuichi, never found him. I discovered him in the music store, but my search led nowhere. I was trapped in
a room watching another video, watching him sing on
stage when I wanted only to find the door. I beheld his
eyes while he sang and as the lyrics faded away, so did
the energy inside him.

In my dreams, he simply gave up, ended the search,
withered away. He died again with me watching and by
his own volition. Notebooks of my own poetry withered
in my hand while the words that had begun to flow so
freely since I met him blew away like unwanted dust. I
held a magazine in my hand, and up at my face glared
the intolerable pictures of woman after woman beside
him. And from somewhere in the void the balance fell,
Libra falling from the sky, angels falling. I prayed against
omens.

It was impossible to remain long in an existence of
mundane tasks and dreams. But I fought the remains of
them that next day, so angry without cause at Ryuichi
for a notion born in my own mind. Another quake
swayed my apartment while the U.S. Armed Forces ra-
dio station murmured in English news of another ter-
rorist bombing. Something was building inside and
around me, something sparked by event upon event, a
series related and not. Everything came back to me and
Ryuichi and whatever it was that the great, wise uni-

verse was grooming us to complete.

Yet this everything was certainly not limited to the two of us. We were not the only two pieces in this scattered puzzle. Winger fit. Daen fit. And even the prospect of four together still could not silence the burgeoning Whispers inside my head. Even we four did not complete the puzzle. What was I to do? The Whispers called. Ryuichi called. And I was the leaf whirled upward between two winds.

•

My vision of Daen came early the next evening just as I began to drift away into sleep. It came as clearly as if I watched him with eyes wide open rather than with a sight from behind closed lids.

I saw him walking down steps in a large outdoor square. It was a place of learning, I sensed, a university or a library even, and not far from the ocean. The landscape looked familiar to me.

Daen raised his head as his foot touched the last step and though I would have thought it impossible, his eyes met mine. He knew that I saw him, saw me in return. The possibility had always existed only in those dark eyes of his, for something to be so uncommonly bright and black at the same time.

He had completed some goal, I knew, and was walking away from this place for the final time. At this milestone, had he been reminiscing about times that included me? Had our thoughts turned to one another at the same second and touched for just that instant? Oh, I remembered now how strong our connection had been. So strong that after all these years, I could catch the smell of him, see the details of his clothing from oceans away, and have the wanting of more nearly bring me to tears.

I felt somehow that I had betrayed Ryuichi with my moment of longing for Daen. I certainly felt no guilt for my time with Ryuichi. How could I when it had been Daen who had gone without so much as a goodbye? Yet for all these many years I held the ideal of Daen up as the stick by which to measure all others. I still did. Winger remained my friend because he hadn't run from me when Daen wished it. And Ryuichi kept me in thrall partially I thought, because I could imagine him standing before Daen without a hint of intimidation even though by all rights he should be scared to death.

The weight of these old feelings mingled with the realization that my work in Japan was essentially finished. I had completed my draft of the copywriting and outlined all the photos for the city's tourism book. The project would soon be out of my hands. I knew that the local editors and translators would take it, and then I would be done. The end of my short-lived job wasn't what held my concern. I only cared that I would soon have no purpose for remaining.

Ryuichi returned with a knock on my door and a smile, as if nothing had ever been amiss. "I've thought about something," he began, closing the door softly behind him. He walked past me to the living room, nearly raising his hand to touch my shoulder, stopping himself once again.

"I'm glad to see you so soon," I whispered.

He sat down on the tatami floor. "You thought my Roman pride would stop me?"

I said flatly, "I don't know what to do."

He looked through me. "*Uso*! I do not know what troubles you. But, I know how your mind makes plans.

By now you have thought of every action you could take. You know by heart every …"

"Every what?" I couldn't help but smile at him, though it made him angry.

"Everything! And it is very annoying that things will always happen exactly the way you plan—if you have any priestess in you still. Now tell me, what is it?"

I closed my eyes. "I'll have to leave soon." The words hung so heavily that I wasn't sure they had yet moved to reach his ears.

Ryuichi nodded. "And what will happen when you leave? What happens to us?"

"I don't know."

"I do not believe that. What is happening inside your head, Ariana?"

What was I to say? That I was waiting for some mystical sign from Daen? "I know that we're supposed to be together now, in this moment. We were supposed to find each other. You wanted to hear it. I can assure you of that much. There. It's said."

"That is not what I want to hear. It is not enough. If we cannot touch—" he began.

"Can't you hear the Whispering? It's grown so loud that my mind screams with it. I'm going to take all the right paths this time. We strayed so badly in Egypt. Would you make the same mistake now?" I questioned. I would be strong enough for the both of us.

"I am not sure we strayed at all. I said I had been thinking. I think maybe we fell into the plan of the One God. If we had not—well, if we had not done what we did on the altar steps, then maybe we would never have found each other again. Maybe we would not be here together now. We would have nothing to correct."

"You mean we sealed our fate?" I asked. "You're saying we needed to be together at this time, in this place—and that was the way we ensured it? That would be no accident."

"The Whisperings, remember. You would not hear them if this were untrue. You know there was no other choice."

"I agree that yes, we must be here now. It was a divine choice. But did you ever think that we would have wound up here anyway? That if we were together in the First Time we were bound together from the start? What we did in front of that altar probably just kept us apart all of these centuries when we should have been together."

And I might have mercifully been kept from Daen.

"It does not matter now. We have this chance. And I am in love with you, Ariana."

How all of my anger drained from me at once. No one possessed such a talent for flipping a moment over on its back as he did. I must have sat down beside him then but I don't remember doing so.

He whispered, "I fought this long for you. I will not give up."

"I can't love you back. Not in the way you want. Something is going to happen soon. I can hear it coming. It's not an end for us, but it will take me away."

"If you are wrong, if this 'something' has not happened by the time your work here is done, will you stay with me?"

"I'll stay." Even as I said it, the image of Daen sprang back at me. The Whisperings grew. Holiness. Destiny. Neteru. I heard these words like a calling. I could see in Ryuichi's eyes that he heard them as loudly as I did.

Hope springs eternal, I suppose. Hope struggles against chance like a waking dream.

Winger's letter came by fax to my office not many days later. My hand shook in fear of the one thing that could prompt Winger to cast aside smoke signals for electronics. Daen was back.

Ryu arranged to have my things shipped ahead to America while I packed my essentials into a solitary bag. How kind he had been, and how sad. My mind cleared only as I looked from the airplane window to the pavement below. With an embrace too calm for the current running beneath it, Ryuichi and I had parted. The stillness of our final hours together in Japan was maddening now as I sat trapped on the plane. Even before the plane took off, I felt the impact of his absence on me as a strange emptiness mingled with nervous anticipation.

I leaned my head back against the stiff seat and felt Ryuichi both cursing and blessing the wings that would carry me an ocean away from him. But I had to leave him behind to wait for a while.

I was headed straight for Daen, same as ever.

Chapter Six

His memories insist,
scrawled upon the soul.
Sanctuary and sunlight,
which the darkness
surely holds.

I knew he wasn't there as soon as I stepped off the plane. The air didn't hum with him. My mind couldn't trace every step, every breath he took. Daen had come—and he was gone again.

Winger knew it, too. He was as I remembered him, all flashing teeth and effortless grace. If I were wind and Ryu fire, then most certainly was Winger earth. The only element left for Daen was water—he certainly evaporated like it. I wore a smile only half counterfeit as I looked into Winger's ice blue eyes. We were brother and sister out of place in time.

Winger ran a hand across his stubble-covered chin. "Ariana, I looked up and saw him across the street. There he was, just standing on the sidewalk watching me. Then the bastard laughed, picked up a leaf, and tossed it into the wind. I knew that he wanted me to tell you, but I thought he would have the guts to see your reaction for himself."

I turned vampire-white. *I was the leaf whirled upward between two winds.* I had flown around the world for him, and he mocked? How could I have gone from my beautiful Ryuichi, gone back to face this demon? I should have ignored the Whispering, forgotten the purpose and the puzzle, and stayed to love.

Winger judged my expression and shook his head. "We both know it isn't as easy as that."

I waited until the airport met the rearview mirror. "I'm wiser now than I was ten years ago," I began. "I can look back and see Daen's flaws for what they were. This is real life now, real fate. I don't care how surreal or superstitious it all sounds—we're players in some cosmic chess match and sin after sin, we forget the moves to make."

A muscle twitched in Winger's jaw. "I think he has some of those answers and you must agree or you wouldn't be here." His wicked teeth captivated me as he spoke.

"How could he do it? Why did he want me here if he just planned to leave?"

"The bastard's jealous, I'd say. Selfish, cruel, jealous, and completely opposed to letting you remember anything that might make him a little less special in your heart."

Odd that something inside me coiled and prepared to spring viciously to Daen's defense even then. He was still too beloved to endure during those times when his memory overwhelmed me. He was what I would have become were my decisions different somewhere along the way—one darker choice leading to a different set of choices, leading to more … This was the manner in which our oneness had divided, but lurking at the core was a man whose soul was created nearly identical to my own—sometime even before Egypt and we had always known it on some level.

Winger's knuckles tightened around the steering wheel. "Don't even start that again. I know your silences too well. The past doesn't matter with him. He's rotten through and through. You see shades of a man who doesn't exist anymore."

"You don't remember him the way I do."

"Oh, you're right there. I remember an evil son-of-a-bitch who wouldn't allow anyone near you." His blue eyes narrowed.

"You managed."

"I matched him power for power."

"He was protecting me."

"From what? Me? He was owning you. Ariana, the man reeks of evil. Everyone else had the good sense to stay away from him."

"I was with him because I wanted to be. No one else was like us. They didn't hear the Whispering. They didn't have the dreams, the memories."

"You, Ryuichi, Daen, and I are all glued together by history, but if that was the pinnacle we wouldn't even need the present."

"I'll remind you of that the next time you go traipsing off through the forest for weeks on end trying to dig up the past. But you're right," I said. "Thank you for waking me up when I need it."

"Don't you get it? We're all awakening."

•

For the next day I visited my family and did all the

things a normal woman would do. I tried to call Ryuichi, but with his tour in full swing, heard only the sound of his recorded voice. I imagined him up on a stage, remembered him there as I had watched him serenade the moon and me, the taste of salty tears on his lips soon after.

That afternoon, in the midst of fallen pinecones and scattered sunlight, I followed Winger into his sanctuary. We fell too quickly into step with the old times, our feet noiseless on top of the dry things that covered the ground, senses alert to the world.

We followed the thin, worn deer trails to the creek and sat on the ground nearby. The remains of Winger's last campfire colored the earth black. He stacked brush and wood over the char and lighted the pile. I laughed as he put the book of matches away. So modernity had touched him after all—my warm, protective Winger.

He crouched down and looked across at me, eyes level with mine. "Do you think you can still do it?"

I nodded. "Let's try."

I stretched out on the cool, rough ground, sweet air filling my lungs and the first strokes of sunset reflecting in my eyes. Winger set the first pungent bundle of sagebrush onto the blaze, and the heavy smoke blew over me. He sat nearby, ritual sentry watching with eyes of sharpest blue.

One by one my senses closed. The face of my Roman flashed before me, an image of him millenniums before, learning the same act I would myself attempt now. I heard nothing, smelled nothing, saw nothing—not even the darkness behind my own eyelids. I sunk deeper into myself under the guide of a single thought containing nothing. More than once the panic and fear jarred me back to semi-consciousness.

The images of Anubis subsided and my body began to vibrate. I pulled this energy up and down myself in great waves. The buzzing whirred with a pitch inaudible to me in any state but this. Now it deafened. Too thrilling that the resounding force of my own being was physical, perceptible and gone utterly unnoticed by Winger as he stood guard.

He measured my breaths, ready to shake me back into myself at the slightest hint of danger. He was more male than any creature I had ever seen, crouched with muscles taught in his thighs. As I rose above him, I saw the shadow of my own lashes resting on still-closed eyes.

This was me, full in glory, flesh cast aside and wandering in the realm of thought. I paused my ascent. Where was I to go? My confused reason rolled about in clouded denseness, and then the single word surfaced: Daen.

Thoughts are deeds. Words are deeds. The mantra flowed back into me from across the ages and my soul laughed. Time had either halted or more likely, had ceased to exist altogether in this dimension, because with the entrance of Daen's name into my mind, I shot across the world to him, stopping as instantly as I had begun.

No, I was neither a ghost earthbound nor a spirit visiting, but rather something in between. The shape of my body was so familiar to me that my essence took its form. The feet that I imagined myself still in possession of touched the very real soil. I sensed Daen, felt him as surely as I felt myself. My complicated, otherworldly senses reigned supreme in this place but I couldn't do a thing so frustratingly simple as smell the damp earth on which I stood. What had been the trick to that? The fact that I remembered mortal vision at all surprised me some. Too much to recall at once, I simply stood surveying the land before me.

Why had Daen chosen this place? The peace of the cemetery, the ironic sanctity of it? He thought I would feel safe here and he liked the drama I supposed. I breathed in deeply of his emotions. A part of him leaned toward desecration and sacrilege. Yes, the connection was as strong as it had been before Daen faded away into the mist. And now it seemed he would rise from it.

On this night the cemetery simply looked like a vast field, the flat headstones completely hidden under a layer of fog born from wet grass. At the end farthest from me, a fountain stood with orange and yellow lights shining an eternal sunset into the spraying water. Just behind the fountain the upright headstones began and the statues stood.

I had been frightened once of these statues, these guardians. Archangels or not, their unfurled wings and swords were no less menacing for all their marble-imposed stillness. There was something of life in them and for the first time, I was grateful for their presence. I wanted them to witness this meeting and to recognize me somehow. I knew that Daen was watching me, a resurrected ghost from my past now grown too real.

"I know you're here." I spoke without intonation. What more could I do when I had no idea what I should be feeling? Felt nothing. Felt everything. If I screamed aloud against the Whispering I would affect nothing. Daen would still lean against the back of the statue, waiting for me to come just one step closer. And I would remain the priestess, refusing to move simply because he commanded it.

I heard the slight sound of his foot turning on the grass. The pulse of my own blood rushed inside my ears. A loose metal sign flapped against the gates far behind me. He stepped out from behind the statue.

And there he was. After ten years of my life spent clinging to fading memories, there he was. Daen stood between the statues with his chin raised and arms crossed, looking for all the world like a statue made flesh himself, except neither of us were truly flesh at that moment. And there was that face, those hands, that smile—everything I fought to recall and fought harder to forget about Daen.

"You have betrayed me."

So surreal his voice, nearly too deep and quiet to hear from across the distance. I walked to him, not knowing how I could move as if this situation had sub-stance. "Betrayed you? You have the nerve to say that? You left without a word."

"You knew I'd return for you." That same soft accent still clung to his voice. I'd forgotten the music of it.

"I lost the faith after the first decade. All we had was nuance and shadow. What would you have had me do? We never had real, physical conversations that meant a thing. You could have been a dream for all the proof I had—for all I have still."

"You above anyone should know the stupidity of your argument, Priestess. We never needed speech for our words to be heard."

Priestess? Oh Lord, what had he heard through that connection of ours? What could he know?

He continued, "And yet you throw away that bond?"

He leaned uncomfortably close to me. "I would tear you apart for your betrayal, if I didn't love you so," he whispered. "We are bound."

I could have sworn for a moment that Gabriel and Michael stood straighter behind me. I could have sworn that Daen's gaze moved toward them if only briefly.

"We are bound, but don't you ever use it to threaten. Manipulation never worked with me, Daen." Surprising almost that the clouds didn't roll in from across the heavens at the sound of his name. I expected thunderbolts and the wrath of God.

His fingers brushed along my cheekbone and his expression softened. "I found our castle, Ariana. The one in England with the roses and the gate of iron. I saw it, and I bought it. Can you tell me that your little rock star erases that from your heart?"

This was the Daen I knew, so divinely beautiful with such an alluring tint of darkness. The full impact of him stung.

"I've learned. I've remembered. I know the nature of our connection now, and I know that something greater is building. If it weren't, I wouldn't be here with you now," I said.

"I've come here to ask that you forget whatever it is you think you know, whatever it is you think is 'building'. Forget the singer. You've never lived a day without me. Never. Not in all your lives."

Then he turned and faded away. I waited until he grew invisible in the distance before I did the same.

•

Winger paced back and forth beside the creek, arms crossed in front of his chest, chin raised. He listened silently as I described my encounter with Daen. I finished, yet still he paced.

"What are you thinking?" I asked, breaking the silence.

He sat down on the sandy ground. "I think we should bring your Ryuichi here. I want the three of us to gather with Daen and sort through this puzzle." My pulse skipped in a moment of panic and loyalty divided. "Come on, Ariana. I know what you feel for them both. I also know Daen. Darkness can be very seductive, but it fades to nothing when struck with great light."

"I'm afraid our light will only illuminate what's hiding behind the darkness."

"Then we face it. We face him. Ariana, if he has been with you in every life, then where was he in Egypt?"

I shook my head. "I have no memory of him at all. There was only my Roman."

"Well, he sure as hell wasn't the High Priest." Winger's teeth began to show.

"No, the High Priest was too ..."

"Good? I know. Could Daen have been the Roman general?"

"I don't think so. His aura wasn't strong enough to be Daen. If he had been anywhere near me, I would have noticed."

"Maybe Ryuichi remembers something?" Winger offered.

"Maybe he does. But what about our last life together, dear, brave warrior brother? Anyone come to mind as being Daen-ish then?"

Winger's teeth flashed in a smile, and his blue eyes flashed to match in the sunlight. "Not a living soul."

Chapter Seven

Forgetting in the flesh.
A tempting, tortured thing.
Soiled angels' wings protect.
Lush misunderstanding.
Granite, rose, and iron dreams.

We didn't invite Ryuichi to join us in America after all. It had taken only a few days without him for me to realize we needed to be together no matter the tension, no matter his desires. I do not say this for the purpose of romance. It had grown obvious to me that inviting Ryu would have been an exercise in futility. Daen would have us on some sort of defensive here, either awaiting him or following one step behind. The advantage was ours in Japan somehow. Not even a suggestion of that country rang familiar in Daen's background. I wondered before how I could have chosen to be born so far from Ryuichi and I questioned the need behind his persistent search for resolution, but now I knew. He unknowingly secured our theatre of war while I gathered the players. Another fragment fallen into place.

And so I stepped back onto the plane with Winger at my side. Solemn or joyous—which emotion should I feel? I carried Daen with me like a splinter in my heart, sharp and bleeding with each breath. A division and a decision both loomed in front of me, but when? And to what end? I left Daen and his answers behind in temporary peace. I could already imagine Ryuichi's fingers wrapped around the steering wheel, his smile, his voice ...

Winger settled into the seat beside me. "It's a flying sardine can."

I turned to look at him—the tanned skin, controlled movement, and glinting smile all so ill-suited to the inside of an airplane. "I've been meaning to run some things by you." I continued as he nodded, "I've been turning some things over in my mind for quite a while now. Did a lot of research." I pulled my notebook out from my backpack. "I want to go over some ancient myths."

"From?"

"A combination really. Egyptian, Hopi, Aztec, Mayan, Kabalistic and Biblical stories all rolled into one. Thing is, they all agree on most major points about creation and destruction."

"Why go over this? I think we both already know all the legends from firsthand experience."

I sat back to stare out the tiny window, and sighed. "The information comes so fast to me now sometimes that I'm not even sure I heard it. The funny part is that I'm starting to think my thoughts back in the same way. Quick. Without words, only feeling and mind—and more complete somehow."

Winger set his hand down on top of mine. "It's like when we used to wonder how someone who was born blind and deaf would put thoughts together. How someone communicated to God without ever seeing or hearing the words."

"Turns out they might have been closer to the angels all the while." I felt the hot sting of building tears. "Winger, who are we? The more we continue, the more changed I become. I don't know if I'm becoming less human or more fully human."

"Both."

"You're a big help." I closed my eyes. What else was there to do if I refused to cry? I thought back to my childhood when I would spin around and around in the cool air crying for the wind to blow until it listened and blew.

I remembered looking forward to reading the book of my life after I passed on. My mother had been horrified that her three-year-old was thinking about death, but I went on to tell her how wonderful it was to review every thought, feeling, every action. I tried to reassure her that nothing was forgotten this way. How frightening I must have been. What I'd begun to write off as childhood imagination was now coming back full swing to slap me awake. Born knowing, fallen asleep along the way.

Winger closed his eyes beside me, and I didn't question for a moment that I knew this with my own eyes shut tightly. There was only the vague realization that these abilities were becoming so ingrained that I didn't question anymore.

My thoughts threatened to stray into that part of me that grieved for Daen and still hoped. The loss was staggering, this elimination of one of only three people with the potential to understood who I was, what I was, when the rest of the world couldn't see me.

As we soared ahead through sixteen time zones, the globe continued to spin beneath us. History continued to build. So did the Whispering. Below us, the weather patterns shifted and the earth quaked more constantly than many centuries had seen. Our plane hit an air pocket just as the great island of Honshu came into view. Winger looked at me in mock meaning as bags flew out of the overhead compartments around us. Portents and warnings.

•

Winger hated Tokyo. No surprise in that. The skyscrapers and crowds were filthy compared to the places he was accustomed to, and that filth skewed his sense of direction. He constantly fought the urge to run to the highest tree and climb it just to look down and find exactly where we really stood. Trees lacking as they were in the city, he rode the elevator to the roof of the hotel instead. He looked out over the madness with his arms crossed over his chest, jeans tight, and boots worn while the city's air blew against him. I left him standing there near the edge, silhouetted by the hues of a setting sun.

I noticed only the grit on the sidewalk and the beat of my heart as I walked. The entrance to a train station appeared on my left, but I passed it by. The condition of my nerves prevented me from stopping. Instead I marched from sidewalk to sidewalk until the tallest buildings stood behind me, until vegetable stands and ramen shops were scattered along my path.

Dusk settled around a home with tall locked gates and lush plants to hide it. I punched a number into an electronic box and the gate swung open, then clicked as I shut it behind me. Now I faced the front door. I exhaled and took the key from my pocket. Was he there? I tried to open my mind to him, to feel him as surely as I sensed Daen, but the shaking key in my hand kept reminding me of my thudding heart and the grit under my feet. Maybe it was the feel of the wind or the way it moved the leaves, but the delicate balance of the moment somehow required that he be there, and I trusted in that.

Kicking aside my shoes, I walked down the sun-starved hall. The unmistakable glow of candlelight caressed the walls ahead and a pen and paper rested on the table. Writing his lyrics by candlelight—I might have guessed that he would. Sitting on a chair in the corner of the room, Ryuichi looked out at me from the darkness.

His hair hung silky and black as ever, eyes silvered with reflections from the candles. His tunic was long and black, looking rather priest-like from the design of its collar. I could have sworn for a fraction of a second that I saw the dark outline of wings embracing him from behind the shadows, like those of the archangel statues in the cemetery. With skin flawless and pale and all expression stilled, he continued to absorb the sight of me much as I absorbed him. He shook his head almost imperceptibly.

"Ryu ..."

He rose suddenly. "I didn't know if you would come back." Then with only a footstep or two he had me in his arms. "I thought he held you too tightly."

"How could I not come back?" I breathed in the warm scent of him, so familiar and longed for.

He kissed my eyelids and my forehead, covered my hair with his quick little kisses. "Now tell me what we must do."

"We have to bring back more of the memory. I see no other way. Winger came with me to meet you. Maybe that will trigger something."

Ryuichi took me by the hand and led me to a chair. "Where is Daen?"

"Mexico now, I think. Yucatan and temples. He wants to be alone with me, but we can't let that happen. He also wants to meet with his rules, on his ground."

"I want to find him," Ryuichi said. "I want to look into his eyes and know him. I can feel in my blood that one thing is true—if we four meet, we will remember more."

"And if we remember everything past, we'll know our purpose now, know who we are. Daen is the means."

"I cannot believe it. We still cannot be together. Not one sin allowed. And the devil himself holds the key." His gaze grew frighteningly intense. "What did we do to deserve this? Have we not suffered enough years?"

"It's not a matter of suffering."

Ryuichi leaned so close to me that I could taste his breath when he spoke. "He is coming for you, Ariana. All we have to do is wait. You are the magnet and he is drawn."

"I'm counting on it."

Ryu's gaze fell to my mouth. "Maybe Winger will bring back some memories for me." He looked up into my eyes. "With enough answers for me to be able to kiss you. And to not stop there."

I pulled back from him and said, "Send a car to Shinjuku. Bring Winger here so we can start." My reaction to his gaze felt diminished somehow, as if something momentarily scorching had now evaporated. I tried not to think of it.

Ryu obeyed me instantly. All it took was a single call and a limo was carrying Winger from the hotel along the narrowing streets to us. We waited and talked, finishing sentences as if the other's thoughts had been aloud. Then the car pulled up outside the front gate, and I went to open it for Winger before he decided to climb over on his own.

Winger grinned at me with comfortable familiarity, showing his Gift of the Wolf to great advantage, and followed me into the house. He tugged off his boots and frowned at the row of guest slippers in the entry until I told him that just his socks would be fine. I don't know what I expected then. Maybe for two such conflicting cultures to clash beyond help. Maybe for two soulmates to embrace like elated brothers. I got neither reaction.

Ryuichi approached Winger with all seriousness and confidence, and Winger matched him mood for mood. They shook hands, exchanged pleasantries, and walked to the living room. The contrast of the two men together struck me fiercely, one with all the beauty of moonlight, the other spectacular as the sunshine itself.

They sat facing each other, watching and waiting. I saw a look of wonderment flicker over Ryuichi's face, but it was gone all too soon. Winger's blue eyes narrowed as he shook his head. "Nothing."

Ryuichi let out a breath. "Not nothing. Just not enough."

"What did you see?" I asked.

Winger turned to me. "I saw the three of us shrouded in golden light. That's all."

"I saw the same vision." Defeat aged Ryuichi visibly even as he spoke. "It is the same thing we saw in Egypt,

Ariana. But why?"

"I don't know. Maybe we only knew each other in a soul-state before we were ever born that first time. That could explain the golden glow," I answered.

"It also seems," Winger said, "that you and I have been reincarnated together often enough, and you and Ryuichi have, but Ryuichi and I haven't seen each other in thousands of years."

Ryuichi lifted his gaze to the ceiling before looking down. "Winger, what do you know about Daen?"

I tried to prevent that cold thing inside me from uncoiling again as Winger answered. "He's an evil bastard. He told Ariana that he had been in every lifetime with her. He's been following her or something. Stalking."

Didn't they know it had been love once?

Ryuichi nodded in agreement. "This means that both of us must know him."

"I don't remember him in Egypt, do you?" I asked.

"No," Ryu answered, "there was no one."

Winger sat up straighter. "Maybe he lied when he told you how often he'd been with you."

I shook my head. "No, I would have known a lie coming from him."

"Well, one thing's certain," Winger said. "The Whispering is getting louder, which means that Daen can't stay away from you. When we don't go after him, he'll come here and he'll try to pull you over to his side."

I watched as Ryuichi and Winger bonded silently in absolute agreement. "When did we form sides?" I asked.

Ryuichi's eyes softened. "The minute we met in that restaurant. Centuries before that. He wants you for himself. He does not care if you have a higher purpose. He would take you and keep you from it. He wants you because of your connection with him, and because he is evil. If he can keep you from something godly, he will do it." I knew he wanted to hold me again. "I can defend you emotionally, and Winger can guard you physically."

"There's so much at stake here, Ariana," Winger added. "We've only begun to guess how much. We're not saying you're some child who needs protection, but you're not strong enough alone to face him. None of us are." He turned to Ryuichi. "I've seen him face to face. His abilities—psychically I mean, are equal to any single one of us. If he and Ariana battled, it would be too close to call."

"There will be no need for a battle. He would never, never hurt me." Battle? I could only guess at all the elements of a spiritual battle. Why were we even talking about battles?

"Because you gave him everything just short of your soul. Have you ever really disagreed with him?"

Yes, I had, once …

I was sure that Winger didn't notice how Ryuichi's face grew cold. Desperately I wanted to soften the blow of his words.

"It was seven hundred years ago," I whispered, "when I loved him. I loved you, Winger, as powerfully as anyone just one hundred years ago as my brother. And Ryuichi, you held my heart in your hands before. Have some faith in me. You saw me in the temple, saw me drive evil away once. You see me."

Winger stood and waved his hand in a great gesture of dismissal. He was the warrior brave again for a moment, with hair hanging to his waist and bare skin bronzed by the elements.

"Enough emotions. I think we should tell Ryuichi

the story of our memories. We know they were real now—our last lifetime together."

I allowed Nephthys to rise to the surface and witness this warrior build a bridge across time with his words, to watch her fallen philosopher-priest cross over history to join us. Stone by stone Winger laid out the tale just as vividly as I recalled it.

"Ariana was just a child then," Winger began, "a child with wild brown hair down to her knees—all eyes and pointy elbows. She was my baby sister. I remember her as clearly as yesterday, but I can't remember the faces of our parents. I wonder if they were alive as we grew up.

"And me? Well, I was the consummate warrior brave, as Ariana claims, except that I don't recall warring with anything—except whichever animal I was hunting at the time. I looked marvelous in the part anyway." He teased and made a face.

"Oh please," I added, "get a grip on the ego."

He showed more of those infernal fang-teeth. "I spent most of my days hunting, like I said, or fishing. And when the sun burnt too strongly, I would take Ariana down to the river for a swim. There was a place in the river's bend where the water was deep and slow, and the willow trees hung over to shade it."

I smiled. "I remember that place. My hands were too small to hold onto yours, so I would wrap all my fingers around your thumb while we walked to the river."

"Hey, who's telling the story here?" Winger had always been good at feigned exasperation. "We'd follow the deer trails out to the clearing. Your little legs weren't great for hiking, but you swam like a fish. You would crawl onto the bank, soaking wet, and then jump up and spin around and around until the wind started to blow for you. The wind really did hear you. The others laughed at the coincidence, when the tree limbs began to sway, but we knew better.

"It was on one of those days that I first saw the two wolves. I thought they were thirsty, but the time of day was wrong, or the place was wrong—something was wrong. These weren't the usual harsh, mangy-looking animals that we would sometimes see. These were two, great gray beasts. They were almost silver in the sunlight and their coats were so shiny that I swore they glowed. The wolf had always been my totem, and I knew that something was about to happen. Ariana knew it, too. She said that the wolves wanted to talk to me, that the Great Spirit had told her so.

"I started across the grass to the path leading back through the trees, but the wolves stopped in front of me, refusing to let me go any farther. I had no inclination to draw the knife from my belt, but I didn't want to walk closer to them and farther from my sister either. They seemed to be watching Ariana behind me and I thought that if they bolted around me toward her, I wouldn't be able to stop them in time.

"And that's when it happened, when the entire world came crashing down in a second. Ariana screamed out, the wind stopped, and the sounds of the river died away from my ears. I turned and saw a third wolf, blacker than anything natural could be. Black, lethal, and bounding toward my sister.

"The silver wolves leapt over me, around me, seeming to fly—and in that moment they looked more human than animal. They reached her just before the third wolf did and crouched down low between her and him.

"No animal's mind could have planned that quickly,

but his did. He turned in mid-air, like he was avoiding Ariana's two protectors, and came straight for me."

Ryuichi moved uncomfortably in his chair. "And so the black wolf killed you?"

Winger was steel. "Yes. Murdered me on the riverbank while Ariana watched, and there wasn't a damn thing I could do to stop it."

Something unfinished snapped in the air around Winger. He had told me this story before, but now the ending hung awkwardly.

"I was killed on that day, too," I added. "I don't remember where the wolves went. When they disappeared, I think I did, too. I remember hearing something about a fever, something about a broken heart. Either way I didn't live out the week."

Ryuichi's face contorted strangely. "You hunted? You said that. Many kinds of animals? So how could one wolf do this?" Ryuichi's mind lingered on the idea now, one that I had never considered asking though it was obvious.

Winger nodded. "Because it wasn't a wolf. Oh, in form for that moment, he was. But I saw his eyes as the jaws crunched down on my throat. Daen's eyes. There was no mistaking those eyes."

"Why? Why didn't you tell me this before? I *asked* you. Oh my God, I knew you hated him. I just never knew ..." I looked intently at Winger, the shock of his words sending a ripple down the back of my neck.

" ... the exact reason? Well, that's one of them. I guess so far what the bastard says is true. He was with you in that life, too."

"Do you think he would have killed me first, if my two guardians hadn't been there?"

"No. Maybe. I don't know. I really don't. He was running to you like a lost puppy more than something dangerous. Physically dangerous, I mean."

Ryuichi stood with his hands flat against his thighs. "So you had a short life together because of Daen. He ended the learning of that time."

Winger fluctuated between rage and calm as he thought of Daen. "Yes, he ended it. But, before he did, we managed to learn a few things—like you two did in the temple. We re-learned things about the elements and the animals, about the force of life and the spirit. Maybe we'd learned enough by then, but it was God's call to say if we had, not Daen's. He just couldn't stand to see Ariana so close to me everyday. Can you imagine what he's thinking of you right now? The soldier-turned-singer who's stealing everything from him?"

Ryuichi smiled gently. "I can more than imagine. I know. I feel him sometimes in the room around Ariana. Just for a second and then he is gone. He would like to tear my throat out in this life."

I thought to myself then that Daen hadn't given Ryuichi enough consideration yet to plan his demise in detail. He underestimated Ryu still, overestimated his own hold on me, loathed Winger in general.

And so our first meeting as a trinity ended. Ryu's driver brought me back to the hotel. Winger stayed at his house, both of them agreeing that it would be inappropriate for me to stay alone with the other. Temptations had a way of resurfacing when serious conversations ended, and so I found myself watching road signs slide by from the window of a limousine. I could hear Ryuichi humming sweetly for me as he walked out into his yard with the lush plants hiding him from the world.

My hotel room was too quiet after the evening we'd had. I turned the knob on the bathtub and let the hot water begin to fill it. I wished I could have seen Winger's face when he saw Ryuichi's Japanese-style bathing room, but I'd missed it with all my preoccupation. The sound of running water, the dimly lit room, and the tiny traffic on the street so far below all screamed with surrealism. I could have been back in the music shop first seeing Ryuichi on that screen, for the nuance and ambiance felt identical. The concrete and tangible wiped themselves away while the Whispering spoke volumes. I wasn't alone.

"Daen?"

I thought I saw a shadow shift oddly in the darkness. Evil lurks, lives, cloaks itself in the night. In the light my visitor would blend in much less, wouldn't he? Revealed by the light. Angels must hide in the light. One single flip of a switch evaporated all the shadows and he fled. Flown away but not quite gone.

I turned off the water and the lights, and stretched out on the bed with only the inside of my eyelids to view. Should I do this again without Winger? The humming consumed my body too immediately, as if someone pulled me from the outside with great hands wrapped around my spirit.

"Ariana, my love."

I willed myself to see. "Daen?"

He stood before me, appearing from nowhere and everywhere at once. Oh, he was spectacular with his black hair and dark eyes flecked with gold.

"Thank you for coming to me."

"Why are you watching over me, Daen?" I pushed the thought over to him. Quick. An angel thought.

"Why do you run from me?" His lips formed the words as if he were in flesh. I think he enjoyed the artistic effort it took to make himself seem solid that way.

"I don't run, Daen. I don't want to hate you."

He cupped my chin in his hand and I could actually feel the warmth of it. "Why would you hate me, Ariana?" The words sounded as if they had traveled a very long way through mist.

"You killed Winger for starters."

"He told you this? You know, he always has had something against me." He laughed low in his throat.

"I told him I would know a lie coming from you. Don't try one with me now."

"I missed you. I needed to see you."

"Then meet me," I said, "here in Tokyo. Come, sit, and talk with all of us."

"You know I won't do that, my love."

"Why? What do you have to fear? You of all people …"

Daen crossed his arms in front of his chest, looking bold and great. Nothing pastel entered *his* world. "Just take this time and talk with me. Let's sit together and remember our time again. Please." He unfolded his arms. "Wouldn't it be nice to just go back one more time? I have so much to tell you."

We sat against a tree on a grassy hillside with the sun setting around us. I marveled at what a convincing scene a thought could build, and he put his arms around me. Oh, I was the traitor now, trading in Ryuichi's trust for one last moment with Daen before the axe fell.

"You remember our castle?" he asked. "I found it— remember I told you?" He held me tighter. His body had always been enormous compared to mine, so very familiar and comfortable as I rested my head against his chest.

"Where?"

"There wasn't much left of it. A few stones here and there, and an old iron gate held up by a single piece of rotten wood. But it still has a small place on this earth." Crushed velvet and bleeding rose petals mingled in that accent, that voice.

"The gate," I whispered, "that gate I loved. It lead to the rose garden, didn't it?"

In the distance, framed by the sunset, our thoughts formed the castle that had been nestled so long in our souls, engraved seven hundred years ago in the ether.

Tears and more tears for our lost joy. Anguish for the old stones now turned to dust. The image faded away, aged as my thoughts turned sad.

He turned my head and pressed his mouth very carefully against mine. Our lips remembered their old movements. Our hands knew each touch by heart. I was forgetting, forgetting everything in a kiss. Horrible. Unbearable. I longed to take him inside myself again, to reunite what had been torn apart. I was sinking into the past with him, and if I went, how would I ever fight the intense desire I had to stay there?

With one final thought containing all the strength I had, I willed myself away into the void, whirling, fading, gone from his touch. *Goodbye, Daen. Goodbye.*

I lay very still in my bed, unable to move much, settling back inside myself. I heard his voice calling quietly to me, suddenly silenced as my body took hold and jolted me back to matter and time.

I waited and waited—still hours before the sun would come up again. Winger wouldn't know what had happened during the night, but Ryuichi did. He already knew, knew as it happened and sensed when I left my body behind on the bed. Only someone with the temple training could have slipped past Winger, and Ryuichi had done just that. I hoped he knew the certain, decided calm I now felt.

Time was slow and drunken when Ryuichi stepped through the hotel door and locked it behind him. I could say nothing, not form a single word to express even a bit of what reality now meant to me. We communicated with fast thoughts and eyes lit with our essence. And without a sound, he wrapped his arms around me in forgiveness and sleep. For the first time, I knew the seduction and the power he had been drawn to in Egypt when the dark thing he summoned, had summoned him in return.

But I knew something more for the first time. I would have known a lie coming from Daen. I was right to think that. Daen had been with me, each time and always. I had never guessed how closely my Roman's fall in Egypt tied in with my near-fall here. And that dark thing that stained my temple? It now had a face.

Chapter Eight

Cry a little.
The other side of desire.
When unsatisfied,
everything was broken.

The war was on, the battle-lines drawn. I half expected my life to take on some sort of tragic texture, but instead it clarified. I took great care to close my mind to Daen. One stray flash of emotion and thought could reveal what little of us remained unknown to him. His willing conduit now closed and refused to wallow in the stream of his memory.

Daen brought new meaning to necessary evil. We needed his presence to unveil the hidden, recall the forgotten. He would be the last puzzle piece slamming into place with a force to shake the earth. We needed him in order to know why we fought.

Winger's unrest settled to calm as Ryu and I told him all that had happened in the night with Daen. He had finally found an assurance in me that he could accept, though he still couldn't fathom how a "citified rock star" had slipped past him as he slept.

Ryuichi left Ashes of Roses that same week. Though he'd never mentioned his intention to do so, the change registered no shock with me. That gentle, deliberate destruction I saw in his videos was a stranger to him now. Gone was the desperate call for love. The thick, tortured thread that held him to that music had been severed with a touch of my hand on his. I watched his face as he announced his departure on television. He was the glowing child, bathed clean in the Nile, baptized pure and resurfacing to the golden sun once again.

I knew his band members didn't understand. They said all the right things to the press, wishing Ryuichi the best of luck, saying the music would go on somehow … of course they would remain the closest of friends. But it was over. I knew it was. Fans cried openly as the news was broadcast over Tokyo's enormous outdoor screens. Girls screamed and sank to the pavement in the middle of crosswalks. I wondered what they thought they mourned.

In the midst of Ryu's decision, Winger took the train back and forth wherever it would take him. He traveled north to the mountains and west to the ocean, becoming enamored with Japan as he never thought he could, never realizing before that there was still a great deal of land the big cities had not yet consumed. He wasn't gone more than a day or two at a time, and I knew he waited for Daen the best way possible. He pretended that he didn't care if Ashes of Roses was splashed across all the newspapers, but he checked in to see the stories anyway.

And I walked wherever my feet took me. I wandered into every interesting store I came upon, read constantly, ate anything new when I saw its plastic model displayed in a restaurant window. It was a healing time, a calm before the storm. Winger, Ryuichi, and I met in the evenings to laugh and talk together, to sip coffee and throw darts at those newspapers.

During one of these evenings, Ryuichi mentioned that he would soon release his first solo single, but refused to sing it to me. He also asked that we set aside talk of Daen for a month. His own Whisperings told him we must wait, and though Winger and I felt no such inclination, we waited.

Winger took Ryuichi up on the offer of a job. He became manager of the English phone line for Ryu's new solo fan club. I questioned how long Winger would last in a job that didn't involve fur and dirt. I took a part-time job teaching English mornings at a private school in Ikebukuro and wrote in the afternoons.

Ryuichi's single, *Hope*, hit the air the following week. All of Japan had heard it before me it seemed. I walked from the hectic train station out into the square, twisting my way through the crowd to the crosswalk. The music carried above the noise, humming along with the sounds of the crowd. Humming ...

I looked up to the giant screen high above on the side of a building, the same screen that had seen fans collapse on the street below at the news of the disband. Ryu's promo video had just begun and with it came the same softly loving tune he had hummed to me from the garden not so many weeks earlier. And this was the beauty it had grown into.

A current of optimism flowed with his words, and he poured it out from his heart with each breath. He was bright and passionate, soothing and simplified— and the women on the street loved him, personalized the song he had written for me. The awed whispers I heard came from the people around me this time. *Ii na ... Kakko ii ...* This sound was what the public longed for, this romance.

I caught a taxi regardless of the price, because I couldn't run fast enough to Ryuichi's house. My body wasn't large enough to hold in all the excitement. Ryu knew I was coming and met me in front of the gate with an enormous embrace. We stepped away from each other before the feeling could sink in too deep.

"Do you know what you've done?" I asked. "You've started idol worship all over again."

Ryuichi drew back from me in horror until he truly looked at my face. He put his hand over his heart. "Not funny."

Winger stepped out of the house and joined us in the garden. "Well ... what'd ya think?"

"It's nothing like Ashes of Roses, but it's really beautiful."

Winger shot his infamous grin in my direction. "You didn't stand still long enough to actually watch the video did you?"

"No. I just listened as I went." The hair began to rise on the back of my neck. "What am I missing here?"

Thrill, tension, and nervousness whirled around Ryuichi and Winger almost visibly. "Winger plays the guitar in the video."

The news didn't lift the veil of confusion. "This was the surprise? And since when can Winger play anything?"

Ryuichi smiled as he did so much more often now. "He was just faking it. Also, the song was for you."

"We're hoping it's obvious." Winger crossed his arms

over his chest. "Do you remember how Daen carried that backpack with him to the post office and how he read newspapers in I don't know how many languages?"

The veil disintegrated. "He said he was monitoring the world and you're hoping this will lure him here."

Winger snarled. "You betcha. He won't be able to stand the jealousy."

Ryuichi squeezed my hand. "At first it was all just for you. I didn't think about Daen. But after it was too late, we realized."

This turn of events was divinely given, I thought. Ryuichi and Winger had set this plan in motion in all innocence and I had been the study of oblivion.

"Makes sense," I finally said, "to use him against himself like this. Greed. Vanity. Envy—most of all, the envy. He could tolerate Ryuichi inside his newspaper, but Winger? He'll be furious. Oh, and if he actually hears the song? Do you think it will be enough?"

I don't think it would have been enough, looking back. But we were never to find that out. The tabloids took the relevancy out of the question for us. The three of us had decided to stay at Ryuichi's house that night, hidden away by gates and plants. But we didn't hide well enough. The telephone rang until Ryuichi unplugged it. A river of paper flowed from the fax machine until at last he unplugged that, too. And in the morning, there it was in spite of us: the catalyst we dreaded and needed. Ryuichi and I were on TV.

Winger glowered at the picture of us on the screen. The TV showed Ryuichi and I locked in that embrace in front of his gate while my taxi was still visible in the distance. We hadn't even heard the click of a camera.

Ryuichi's face was pale even in the golden morning

sunlight, mouth held too tightly as he translated for Winger. "They call her the mystery woman. They say we might be secretly married." He looked at me with eyes hard and luminous. I recognized him most when he reverted to that emotion. Joy was ephemeral and I recalled the video for "Hope." The line between image and reality blurred with him sometimes, and though I shoved the knowing of it aside, his pain hadn't lessened enough. He had simply created an expert image. Irony laughed.

"Ryu—" I began and then the urge to comfort passed. He would be fine. The mood would go by.

"I do not think our plan could be worse. Now I have to pretend I am what I would kill to be. Pretend I have what I do not. We will hold hands together so the camera will be happy, but I will be dying inside."

Winger stepped between us and placed his hand on Ryuichi's arm. "Be careful with your words. You can't take them back. Or your actions." He looked at me for a moment, then left the house to give us some measure of privacy.

Ryuichi and I stood looking at one another while a silken breeze and that morning sunlight washed over us. "Why can I not heal?" he whispered. "I try. And I know we get closer and closer to bringing Daen here. Even that is no guarantee for us. Everything is unknown." He touched the side of my face just barely, but it burned. "Do you feel this?"

"Of course I feel it. I do." My skin was alive where he had touched it, as if we began to melt together as something other than human with the contact. "But remember the energy we are building together. Think of that power and how we can turn it toward Daen and our search for reason. Think how completely we could be lost if we fall into each other again."

"Ariana, you have to train us now. It is the only way to put our energies in the right direction. You have to become the priestess again."

"Look how it ended with us last time."

"We have to prepare. We have to train. If we do not, we will not be ready for Daen. If we do not, I cannot ..."

He couldn't touch me without wanting to repeat the scene on the temple altar. I heard the words he didn't say. He moved closer to me and touched his forehead to mine. My entire body screamed for me to just lay down, to feel my Roman poet-priest as he had once been, uncaged and mine.

With eyes still closed he said, "Do you understand?" His lips brushed against mine.

I instinctively reached out and found Winger walking back and forth on the concrete outside. He sensed my call and started back toward the house.

Ryuichi smiled through sadness. "Ahh ...   Winger the Protector."

•

And so we began our plan and the temple training while awaiting Daen. Ryuichi and I appeared in public together for the first time, hand in hand, speaking in that silent way of ours while showing only smiles. We went to a small Italian restaurant in Shibuya and transformed into actors before the eyes of the world. The role should have been simple, for the desire was there even if the relationship was not. But it was loathsome to mimic such lightness when the depth of our situation was so devastating. We could only hope that the evening provided enough fuel for the media attention to burn straight to Daen, wherever he was. The Whispers told us nothing.

The daylight belonged to our careers or rather, to Ryu's. My employers had politely asked that I not return to work as soon as my face appeared on the T.V. Half of the parents' association thought I would be a negative influence on their children while the other half wanted to organize an autograph session. So, I stayed home and prepared during the day, tried to remember Nephthys and Isis inside myself.

Ryu and Winger returned in the evening and we would become a mock family for those hours. I breathed the wind and listened on a level I'd too long ignored—a purification ritual of sorts. How many day or weeks we would have for this preparation was unclear.

I rid myself of all jewelry and clothing that might bind. Ryuichi grew tired of seeing me in oversized T-shirts, and brought home clothing reminiscent of that which I'd worn in Egypt. I had short and long dresses of the finest woven flax or creamy flowing silk. They hung loosely yet appeared fitted somehow with their gentle pleating. Their bodices revealed nothing in these modern versions, and from the look on Ryuichi's face it was just as well. Ryuichi returned to the fluid black tunic I imagined him in so often, a look that Winger rejected in favor of no shirt at all, loose jeans, and moccasins. We were finding our selves again.

My days filled with clarification and realization. The old patterns that connected words and elements and colors made sense again. The tiny ties that bound the world grew visible. From the lines in my hand to the stars in the sky, I understood.

We began the training without the masks and the

costumes of old. They, along with their ceremony, were largely out of place in this time, though their meaning remained. We might have fallen back to these things if we hadn't effectively stirred the feeling in ourselves.

In the beginning we simply prayed together, sometimes silently, sometimes with hands held and words spoken aloud. The golden light and energy around our bodies revealed itself to one another when we chose to look for it, and we all said the light was the very same we had seen in that brief, shared vision from a time we couldn't pinpoint.

I heard the rustle of a presence in the room with us at times, but my intuition wasn't tuned sharply enough for me to trust such impressions. We became much more adept at reaching out and finding one another with a thought, though this talent didn't come so easily for Winger when I was the object of concern. He simply knew when I watched him. Ryu's house became the temple, but how much could we bring to it in mere days even with our stored abilities slowly unfolding?

Warm Tokyo rain fell hard in the garden one night while we gathered there. Winger paced barefoot on the cement, hair waving in the dampness and rainwater coating his chest. He was restless in the torrent, and Ryuichi had grown watchful, peering through the dense, wild plants. Winger crouched just above the ground and waited, eyes otherworldly in the intensity of their color. I looked at Ryuichi and his eyes held the same concentrated glint.

Something was wrong, and something beyond the garden demanded all of our attention. These two men I loved and trusted were the lions at the gate this night, with such a marked change in demeanor that a rush of adrenaline tightened around my heart. I felt an old, familiar heat wrap around me, that mix of danger and comfort lost to me for a decade.

"Am I invited, Ariana?" The voice was a caress from the darkness.

Winger rose to his feet. "Show yourself."

"Am I invited? Ariana?"

I lifted my chin high and stood straight. If ever there was a time to play the priestess, it was now. "You have been summoned. Surely you must know the difference."

"Ever the strong one, my Ariana." From beyond the lush wall, beyond the shadows, Daen emerged with the subtle lights of the city striking his face in eerie beauty. Ryuichi moved noiselessly to my left—the old temple trick revisited, and Winger came to guard my right.

"I debated whether to come here really," he continued. "You think I didn't smell your game?" He tilted his head and smiled at Winger and Ryuichi before turning his gaze to me again. "I knew, Ariana. And I thought to myself that there's really no reason I couldn't join your little gathering here. Why not? Could be good for a few laughs. Why not?"

Rain ran in rivers down his face, hung in droplets from the ends of his black hair.

"I know who you are now, Daen. I drove you from the temple once. Try anything and I'll do it again."

"It would be much harder now that I'm in the flesh, don't you think?" He gestured broadly. "But I suppose that's why you have these two mighty warriors with you."

Ryuichi shook his head slowly. "You glow silver. I have never seen something so dark look so bright."

"He's never been human," Winger growled.

"Oh, I'm human enough. My pulse throbs just as yours does. I should know. I felt it between my teeth, your pulse that is." Daen laughed. "And I breathe the same air into my lungs as you do, Roman. When they're not filled to the brim with Nile water—your lungs I mean."

Ryuichi stilled himself. "You are a pitiful creature."

"Really? You were fire in Egypt, holding flames in your hands. And mine was the current that smothered you. How pitiful is that?"

"To summon you was a mistake," Winger said. "You have nothing to offer us."

I placed my hand on Winger's arm. "No, he wouldn't have come if he didn't have something for us."

"Wrong," Winger hissed, "he wouldn't have come if he didn't think he could *take* something from us."

Ryuichi added, "You cannot have Ariana. You cannot touch her. You cannot even speak to her without us. *Wakatta*?" He looked as if he could snap Daen in half with a gaze.

"You never did learn." The muscle at Daen's jaw tightened. "I've already touched her. Nations rose and fell while she rose and fell under me. And you think she's yours?"

Furious, perilous silence reigned over the garden while the deluge turned cold and began to mist around the plants. "Why did you answer our call?" I asked.

Daen softened. "A trade of memory. None of you remembers all of your lives with all the others. Oh, I remember all of mine, love, because you were there. But I want to know the rest of the mix. What were the rest of them doing while you and I were busy doing each other? I would sit with you, Ariana, you and them," he spat. "Then we'll all remember the details. After we re-call, I'll leave. We'll all have our knowledge, and you'll be no closer to what you need."

"So simple as that?" Ryuichi asked.

"It's never so simple. You can never be paranoid enough, Roman. I would drown you again in a heart-beat. No, because now you have the advantage of a vivid recollection in Egypt. I wouldn't be so foolish as to kill you while that recollection is still so precious to Ariana. I'll not make that sort of imitation martyrdom yours." Daen turned to me. "I've lost the other half of my soul in you, and I won't stop fighting to get it back."

Winger placed himself between me and Daen. "The consummate liar. I'm always amazed how a few thou-sand years can perfect a skill that way." Winger pushed past Daen and walked into the house.

Daen stepped closer to me, staring down at my body as the rain soaked my dress through to a filmy blue transparency. "You forgave the rock star his sins. For-give me mine and let me come back to you." His eyes were black pools of ink, writing out meanings, revealing lust, amusement, and something of lingering respect.

"Look up the word repentance, Daen. Forgiveness without your true atonement would be utter stupidity on my part."

I walked with Ryuichi into the house to join Wing-er, and Daen followed. My memory had never served significant justice to the majesty he commanded. He was the chiseled statue of a warring angel brought to life, physically and psychically stronger than any of us alone—made of some entirely different spiritual sub-stance. So hard not to be awestruck, loving, or hating of him.

The flashes came for me spontaneously, triggered by our combined energy in the dusky room. They were shreds of memory that chose neither order nor sense. "Sit closely and face one another," I commanded.

The sounds came before anything else. Random beats and shattering glass, high-pitched fury and shrieks like fingertips on a window. I wanted to shut my ears against the cacophony that rang out from a dimension opened by the mixing of our four selves. And the heat, the heat flowed like molten wax around us, through us, and somehow melted the noise into a visible vibration of silver and gold.

Our combination was the key to the doorway of re-membrance. "Zep Tepi," Ryuichi breathed.

I nodded, "So we see our vision of the First Time brought to life."

"This is who we are," said Winger, "who we first were."

Daen laughed low in his throat. "It was our first birth. God had angels enough and men enough—so he made us something in between. Something with no place from the very beginning."

"How can you say this? I hear the truth now. We are the Watchers. The legends. The Sages. Us," I said. "At last I know that I'm human, only begun with a differ-ent purpose. What more of a place could you possibly want?" Colors collided around the room like the aurora borealis.

Daen's entire being glimmered dangerously. "Yes, we walked among men and talked with heaven. We taught men and recorded what must be unforgotten. And where in the hell did it get us?"

"Separated and scattered around the world," Winger

answered.

"Yes—and why was that? Because of the flood. Remember that? It broke spiritual civilization into parts. Yucatan, Tibet, Egypt, America … And we followed to repair while we were still newly born and recalled everything purely."

"I don't understand your view, Daen. I don't follow it at all," I said.

"Still don't get it? Still the good and fearless Ariana. I love you so for that." He breathed deeply. "Well that little deluge would have never happened if God's precious men and angels hadn't acted as they did. And we paid for their rebellion. We had angels using the power of creation for their own. We had angels crawling up the skirts of mortal women. They all fell, and fell hard until that beautiful, glorious civilization we watched crumbled beyond repair and had to be washed away. So there we were, sent out to help ones that were left. But they forgot anyway and some never knew in the first place— they started calling us gods. Remember that? What a laugh."

"Free will, Daen. Don't you see the beauty of it? If men weren't allowed to be unwise and destructive as they choose, how would the good ever be differentiated from the bad?"

"All your struggles with good and evil never got you any answers, Ariana. It never got God any answers either—it just keeps him amused."

"You're wrong, Daen. My answers pour in. You're the one who got lost along the way."

"Lost." Daen breathed in deeply, flaring his perfect nose in a way I hadn't seen for years. "I'm here again with you. Is that lost? I just refuse to be the Watcher again. How's that for exercising your precious free will?" He studied my face. "Or didn't you realize? Your One God is bored and getting ready to clean house again. Why else would he awaken the Urshu? To observe and write the history so that the future will find snippets of it and drive itself insane debating it again. Well, I refuse to be part of the insanity. You think me evil for this?"

Ryuichi rose to his feet with our colors dancing like fireflies around him. "You amaze me. You give your opinions and wrap them up in the truth of our situation. But it is all a trick, is it not? You hope we will not think to question. I see things differently. You laugh at God and throw away our purpose so easily. But if this is all so ridiculous to you, you would not be here now. We must be very important or something as dark as you would not bother."

Winger nodded at Ryuichi in agreement before turning to Daen. "The same thought occurs to me. I look at you and see a traitor. I see someone who turned against our One God and has been following Ariana for centuries. Trying to destroy her writings? Is that what? I can't quite figure out why."

I raised my hand to stop the mounting tension, more keenly aware of the shifts in Daen's demeanor than ever. "Why did you come, Daen? You're obviously more aware than we are of the situation. What do you think we know?"

Silence crackled sharply before Daen spoke. "There is nothing vital that you know, which I would need. I simply came to be with you. You and your friends are the ones who need to remember. And Winger here is delusional. If I'd wanted those writings destroyed, it would have happened long ago."

I finally stood. "No more then. No more attempts to remember this night. We're finished here. It's time for Daen to leave."

"You misunderstand me and my intentions," Daen said through clenched teeth. "What's worse, you misunderstand the Roman trash."

Winger and Ryuichi didn't exchange so much as a glance as Daen rose and walked to the door. A case of strength and anger enveloped him while the windows shook under a new onslaught of rain. Here was our force to be reckoned with caught in one magnificent body. And that force looked at me through a pair of eyes I knew too well until he disappeared out of the garden.

"I can't believe we just let him leave. What were you thinking?" Winger asked, his jaw taught.

"I'm thinking that whenever there's a pattern, we'd better pay attention to it. You asked why, so think back. In every lifetime he has managed to separate us, to keep us apart. He made sure he was with me and you weren't. Don't you see? And I don't know why now is different, but he made a mistake somewhere along the line—or was stopped. I don't know which. But as long as we were kept apart, God wasn't 'cleaning house' as he so simply put it. He's been trying to stop the beginning of something preordained. I think he knows he's going to lose out in the end."

"He's afraid he's going to lose you," Winger corrected.

"If and when we need Ariana's writings to know what to do," Ryuichi added, "we won't know where to find them unless we are together."

Winger sighed. "This just highlights that Daen is what I thought all along. If he opposes our calling and

God Himself, then there's only one other side for him to be on."

Winger seemed tired to me all of the sudden, something in his voice or his eyes. Or maybe it was extreme sadness I sensed. I ran my hands up and down both arms, but the chill there refused to leave. I wondered what I had once held so dear, what we had allowed to stand briefly beside us again, and how we had escaped unscathed. What angels shielded us so that demons slid past?

A weariness lingered in the room, complicated further by that sense of unrest that always preceded a thought unfinished by Winger. I watched my protector and friend pull on his boots, his jacket, his knife. A quick half-smile crossed his face. "Well, who else could track him?"

Ryuichi's eyes narrowed. "This does no good. Why would you leave? You are not thinking. We do not need to find him." He stepped between Winger and the door to the garden. "If you are alone, he may try to kill you."

"I know I'm not making sense to you right now. Take care of Ariana while I'm gone. Touch her and I'll find you." He raised his hand to prevent Ryuichi from speaking again, and Ryuichi moved aside. "Daen and I have a few things of our own to sort out. I'm following the Whispering."

Winger looked at me briefly before stepping out into the rain. He faded away exactly as Daen had, without pause or protest, gone from me. "He's been training for this his entire life," I said. "I just never realized it until now."

Chapter Nine

Such is wisdom.
Catching the rhythm
of your time.

We were the Urshu reborn, the same beings I knew so well in Egypt, spoke of so often. That much was clear at last. But the legends crawled again and again through my mind, telling me that the puzzle pieces did not add up. Some stories recorded five Watchers, seven Sages, even as much as nine or sometimes twelve. We numbered only four. Perhaps the millenniums had skewed the number in their countless telling of the tale. Or perhaps we had wrongly assumed the extent of our progress and some of us had fallen along the way. Guessing brought only madness, but one thing was for certain— Winger was nowhere to be found.

I reached out for him in my mind over the following hours and saw nothing. I called for Daen and saw only mist sometimes, emptiness sometimes. I called on God for a sign, a suggestion, but none came. For the first time in my life, silence overcame the Whispering.

Near the end of the next day, just as the sun began to

slide, Ryuichi and I sat alone together in his house. One gaze held too long told me how effectively Winger had worked to keep us apart. I thought of Winger's warm laugh and strong hands, his disapproving warnings, but it wasn't enough. Across the room from me, Ryuichi's even stare, his skin bathed in orange and gold erased all other images. He sat on the floor beneath an open window, his back against the wall, shirt open. The touch of the sun carried its own melody, shining with gentle, hypnotic notes into the room. The music, the color, Ryuichi's eyes illuminated to dark amber as he continued to look at me.

I sat down on the floor in front of him, down in the golden light. My skin glowed smooth, subtle, and my hair danced with copper highlights as if the setting sun were repainting us for God in that moment.

A breeze waved the filmy white curtains, and Ryuichi rested his head back against the wall and closed his eyes. I reached out and touched his chest, felt his skin warm beneath my fingertips while he shuddered ever so slightly. I prayed that his eyes would stay shut as I pulled my hand back from the caress. As I rose and walked away to my room, I heard his soft, ragged sigh.

Do not look upon him. The words rammed their way into my head again. *Do not look upon him.* Such dread swept over me with the warning. It was a warning after all, and not simply some arrogant command from the lips of a long-dead Roman general. But we were all separated again and I needed him. I knew Ryuichi had followed me into the room.

"What do we do now?" he asked. "Wait for Daen and Winger?"

I turned and looked at him. Again. As always. "No.

I've been thinking my way through this nightmare. I look far back into that golden time and I see the outline of others standing beside us. I think we should try to find them, don't you?"

"I do not know," he whispered. "I do not even think I care. I look ahead and I see only you at the end of this world."

"It's like you've changed, and yet you haven't. It's the same thing from you over and over again." A definitive edge caught my voice. "The thing I cherish most about you is the thing I most despise sometimes. You wax so damn poetic, but you take it too far to heart. And when you do that, you just become narcissistic and destructive."

"I am just trying to find the end of sorrow for us. Maybe you do not give enough time to your emotions in this crusade for the One God, by whatever name He is going by these days." His eyes flashed violently. "I personally do not want to die loveless again."

"You didn't die loveless before. What are you saying? I loved you enough in Egypt to nearly destroy myself over you. What more would you take from me?"

"Take? I thought you gave it freely."

I stopped myself from responding quickly before the moment could lose more control. I wanted to remind him how his actions had caused his death, his weakness, his responsibility, but I only breathed and looked at him.

"The point is that Winger is gone. Wherever he is, he's distracting Daen. We need to search for the others now. It's the only time. Only the two of us are left together now and we need to stay that way."

Ryuichi hung his head, and when he raised it his

eyes held the same look of internal death that I'd seen in the music store photo months before.

"Can we talk about us first? Please?"

"Yes." I sat down on the bed, all strength leaving my tired body. "Let's talk."

The simmering anger left the room. "Do we have a chance?" Do not look upon him. "Do we?"

I looked up into his eyes and recognized myself there. "We might. I don't know if all your expectations can ever be met. The Whisperings come first. Understand. Please understand. We owe each other this much. Because if we don't do things correctly this time, I'm afraid we'll never get another chance to do what we're meant to."

He sighed and held his head high. "You're right. I know you are. I told you I wouldn't fall again. And I won't." He leaned down slowly to kiss me then, and though I had warning, my body registered shock as the very energy in my soul shifted to melt with his. "Love me," he said. Then, I heard him leave and lock the front door behind him.

Maybe we had needed this reconciliation. Maybe I needed only the strength of his soul touching mine again. Regardless of the catalyst, the winds outside screamed and the visions hit against me with a force I had never felt in this lifetime. I saw Winger in a flash, and in another flash came the image of Daen, still separate from each other, still caught in their own private battle, fighting something personal I wasn't sure I had even imagined correctly. The leaves tore through the garden. I was no longer the leaf caught between two winds. I was the wind, calling for the images, beckoning the visions to come as they would in this heightened state triggered by his kiss. I fell flat on the bed and lost touch with my present senses.

•

I looked down at my arms and lifted one in a wave. A golden glow followed wherever I moved. Had I ever been this elegant? I walked several feet and stopped, realizing that while I had no control of this body I watched, I felt its feelings. This was me, had been me at least. The smoothness of these graceful limbs was so familiar to me, the tilt of the head, the posture.

I saw great white buildings with majestic pillars looming across the landscape on the hill above me and far past that. The blue sea in front of me crashed and churned, nearly translucent in its purity. I walked with bare feet along a terrace of brilliant white marble, a large white fountain its only decoration. Not even a thin rail stood between one false step from the terrace and the angry waters below.

I turned to the steps leading up the hill and saw the recipients of my earlier wave. *You made it here, too.* I wanted to say the words, but the lips that were mine once only said what I had said then, leaving no room for change.

Three from the group of figures crossed the marble to me. I would have cried had I been part of this time. And when the tears choked inside me, I realized I was only locked inside the Record, in a memory. This scene was no longer reality. It was unalterable and gone. All I could do was remember.

The men stood with me now, and I had no doubt about their identities—Daen, Ryuichi, and Winger, un-diluted and newly born. Their bodies glowed with an intensity that throbbed against my chest.

"Is the writing carved and hidden?" Daen asked.

He looked from the crashing waves and back to me. Nothing of the sinister Daen, nothing of arrogance or malice full-blown. Yet some hint of the potential, of independence carried to extreme flashed around him. And none of us were enough aware of the dangerous possibilities in him to cry out in warning. We had never seen that before among our kind, I had to remind myself. He was so grand and radiant.

I simply nodded my head, shaking the wayward spirals that fell from the mass of hair pinned on top of my head. So my hair had been soft and chocolate-brown then ...

Winger put his arm playfully around Daen's shoulders. "His feelings twist around on himself." Had they truly loved one another in the beginning? I had come to associate challenge and antagonism with their relationship, enemies to the core.

"Well they should," Ryuichi added. "I'm feeling my own discord for the first time." His voice lulled and caressed even then. Still he captured the music.

"Have you all told me everything you've seen?" I asked and found affirmation. "Then I've written it all as you told me. I can't say that it will ever be known again after this night. I don't see so far ahead as that."

We held hands together at the end of the ocean, four divisions of the same person in one sense, completely unique in another. This was torturous, this see-through wall between times. I could only watch myself and absorb the feelings long since altered.

"Some of the angels have broken out against the commands." Daen's face showed more gravity than I had ever beheld. "We have to record it no matter how painful." Tears slid down his face as if it were natural for him to lament for the world.

"And what of man?" Winger added. "I never thought they would defile Zep Tepi so soon. Our first time, gone."

"I know your emotions, Daen. The water was yours to note, and that same water will now erase it all. Of us all, this time was most yours." I stood on tiptoes and kissed him lightly on the forehead.

Ryuichi squeezed my hand. "This day brings the oddest mingling of sadness and joy. I'm not certain for which reason to weep most. We've never witnessed an end before." He had once been a great teacher, wise and generous. I had forgotten when that role became mine as well, when the wisdom fled from him.

I looked deeply into Ryuichi's eyes, then Winger's, and finally Daen's where my gaze lingered and began to waver. The world around me shook and faded, moving from one genesis of mind and matter to the next, moving out of my memory's reach.

"No," I said aloud. "Let me stay a little longer." Daen's eyes, I was a slave to that last look. "It's up to you, God. Give me more than those moments," I prayed. "Let me look upon them all again that way before you send me back to a time when they're lost to me."

I grew slightly aware of a pain building in my head. Flashes of a great stone wall engraved with my symbols. More flashes of water encircling the stones, swallowing them. Somewhere in a muffled distance of the present I heard the calling of my name, "Ariana." Consciousness attempted a return to me and then turned away, deflected by visions.

Colors and shadows flickered stiffly past me, as if the

universe were caught in a mechanical dance between realities. I fought to seize hold of a sight, fought to slow the pictures of thoughts.

Images of another destruction as complete as the first came to me. Water devouring the world twice, decimating nearly everything on it. A second existence slain, crushed before my eyes. I heard in the Whispers a promise from the One God that the flood would not come a third time.

An answer whispered back, "Why did it come a second time with my hands bound?" I struggled to place the voice. "How am I to bear this?" Daen?

A voiceless, encompassing Whisper assured that the will was its own and the child of water would never again suffer so. Patience. Faith.

"But you send us apart on the waters I so love? Hear my cry and do not will it so. Twice you have cast us into the flesh, each time knowing we become more human. I feel more than godly love for them now. I feel stirrings of lust. I question my humility at times. You make us more human, and then have us watch as mankind corrupts itself and you begin anew. This is too much iniquity to bear. Hear me. Do not separate us. Even your wayward, cast-down angels have one another for comfort. Do not separate us."

Daen's heart screamed out in mute conversation, sounding more like Ryuichi than himself. But I couldn't hold tightly enough to these Whispers. Those words and that time are dead, I told myself as I sailed on through the Record.

I saw Daen alone on a ship floating away from a broken civilization. He was tall and noble with hair gone starkest white and eyes haunting and haunted blue. My ship took a different current, as did Ryuichi's and Winger's. I saw myself standing in an Egypt that was leafy and tropical in places where sands would blow in centuries to come. So this was the life that first formed my calling to return there. I watched Daen continue around the world, his wishes heard but not granted.

I grasped at a passing thread of reminiscence and found Daen again. I yearned to fill my sight with all of us together and knew it was not to be. The rules were precisely as I had once told my Roman in the temple, and I was not allowed to view what I should not. The purpose of my journey became clear: a reunion with my history with Daen, and no more than that. Words are deeds. Thoughts are deeds.

Let me land in the memory of my fullest life with him.
And I was there.

I saw myself sitting cross-legged on a grand bed with corner posts reaching up toward the ceiling. Daen caressed my hair lazily. We knew what a blessing this time was, recognized the extent of the gift. I could feel as I had felt then. But savoring each moment didn't make the moments endure except for somewhere in the Record. The rich wood, the intricately woven tapestries—they were gone.

I peered deeply into Daen's eyes, watching him watch me. I recognized that unquenched element of unrest in him. I was foolish to believe that this aspect hadn't continued from the time the wind caught the sails of his ship through all the times since. We stole this scene from reality and pretended we didn't see what Daen's rebellion had caused him to become. As I stared into him, I felt the center of the hurricane. Borrowed calm surrounded by whirling intensity. He created an oasis in time with his love for me, and I allowed him to do it. But I knew all the while that his faith was crushed and I was all that kept him from being swept away into the winds.

Even more, I didn't care. The skies could burn and the heavens fall, and my eyes wouldn't leave Daen. He was my once upon a time, once upon an eternity. He was the one who heard my every thought and caught my tears in the palm of his hand. He was the Priestess' equal, effortless knowledge, unnecessary explanation. Nicholaus. That was his name then, wasn't it? Nicholaus.

"Are you happy now? Are you happy?" I screamed to myself and the universe. Then my voice lowered to a whisper, "Please let me forget this, God. Please don't let me awaken remembering him. It will take away my only strength against him just when I've found it."

I tried to open my eyes, tried to awaken. Not even desperate thoughts of Winger and Ryuichi could turn me away. No. I screamed in that silent voice. No, no, no. I rocked back and forth like a sobbing child huddled in the corner of reality as I watched. I could see the bright, inky depths of him with heightened clarity. So like me, he was. So like I'd always seen, his face. I was bound to this plane until the memory played out.

Nicholaus rose from the bed and crouched down in front of the fireplace. "I know what you say is right, but it's too late for me to care."

"How can you say this? It took me time to realize that even if the church is corrupt and the churchgoers are corrupt, the religion remains intact. Do you not see? They do damage to the name of God and that religion, but they no more practice it than the stone outside does. The religion is separate from what most men claim to practice, from what they try to mold it into. It has always been so."

"What amazes me most," he said, "is that you can say all that in one breath."

I ignored his remark. "It's all inside you. Why won't you let your faith out again, you, who've heard His words directly?"

"Oh, I tried that once, remember? I walked across lands and more lands. I taught. I lectured. I built. And it did me no good. I still had to watch those billowing, white sails moving you away from me until I couldn't see anything beyond the horizon. Wasn't it punishment enough for you? Wasn't it enough to watch the Fallen Ones flourishing, while we suffered in isolation?"

Dark poetry tainted the stillness he once commanded. I was fascinated by his anger, horrified and in awe of it. I sat there, all moonlight and mastery, while he drowned in masculine conflict and emotion. He was the scent of cinnamon and fresh snow, the tortured knight battling with the saint. I knew something of what he felt.

"Never was it punishment," I said. "Never. I understood why the responsibility fell to us. And we always found each other, didn't we? In the end …"

Nicholaus interrupted. "In the end? There will be no more ends." He rose to his feet and pulled his tunic on over his head, his black hair shining in the firelight. "Fill your leather-bound pages with writing, my love. Fill them with everything you see. But do not try to explain to me why you write. I know you cannot remember why." He sighed softly. "Your calling must be stronger than mine ever was for you to continue the writing with half the Record lost to your recollection." He continued to dress as if he hadn't said a word.

I recalled more than he thought, only I pretended in order to spare his feelings. I remembered the face of my Roman so naturally in that life. I even remembered the temple teachings.

"At least I remember who I am," was all I could say aloud.

Nicholaus nearly crushed me in his embrace. "I remember. Only I've chosen to use that damnable free will you so love to debate. I choose not to be who I once was."

What could I have said to him then? There were no arguments to make against him, I told myself. But I, in my watching place, yelled out a thousand silent words. From the same watching place, I screamed with the sublime agony of rapture as I felt him, this imperfect other half of my soul, come into me throughout the night. I could die a thousand times and always desire this small moment in all of history.

We left the inn in the morning light, riding across fields and hills. The miles revealed themselves in sequence, all at once, immediate and complete. I wondered if time had ever been a real concept or if I had imagined it.

My temperament was consistent with the self I knew from the present. Something of the human in me diluted the obvious intensity of the priestess. Her thoughts—my thoughts—still filled my head. And Daen—Nicholaus—was he truly so broken as he proclaimed?

So we rode on in autumn chill from the inn to a place I was only beginning to remember. I reveled in and absorbed all the tiny sensations of our journey. I would have been reborn for the scratch of my wool cloak and the clean smell of frosty air alone. I held tightly to my writings, knowing from the Whispering what I must do with them.

I watched elation and disappointment cross Nicholaus' face as our destination showed itself. The rolling hills gave way to a plain, in the center of which stood the megaliths like jagged, graying teeth sticking up from the ground.

This place was magic with its silent stone giants keeping vigil over the centuries. How they must taunt those who did not know. I walked around the tall tufts of grass—dry, yellow blades mingling with those alive and green. Scrubby purplish-red plants grew closer to the ground near small mounds of bare dirt dug up by the earthen creatures.

"Were these yours?" I asked.

Nicholaus shook his head. "Mine are across the world in places map-makers have forgotten. Swallowed by a lush tangle, I would imagine."

"Mine are in Egypt. Most likely buried in sand. Entire civilizations are lost in such simple ways." I ran the back of my hand along the stone to feel the vibration, calling the calling, in a sense. "Would that I could see his face, the one who set these. He must have been dear to us."

"No one, save you, has been dear to me for ages on top of ages."

"Awaken, Nicholaus. Open your eyes and find yourself again," I begged.

"I'm more awake than you can know. Why do you presume that because I disagree with you, that I am sleepwalking through time?"

"Does this place not move the old feeling inside you?"

Nicholaus looked at me with an emotional aspect I hadn't been prepared for—laughing and crying in his eyes. From the alternate view of my hiding place, I drew back and saw the full image of him. Tall, imposing, a black mantel flowing down to his boots—I had thought myself his equal at that time. No, nothing walking the Earth could equal him, beautiful and cutting as he was.

"Let me explain something to you, my love. My soul has fallen outside the cycle of the Ancients. I could not place it back in the rhythm if I tried. There are no more human awakenings for me. I am not human. Neither am I Urshu. No more favor with the One God. No more collecting memories as the moment permits. No more nostalgic discoveries."

I stepped away from him and felt an enormous stone come up against my back. I pulled my cloak tighter around me. "Then how do you come to walk beside me, to lay with me?"

"The Fallen Ones taught me the trick of creation. I form myself as I choose." He stretched his hand out to me. "Do not be frightened."

I pulled myself up to full height away from the stone and the wind caught around me. "Frightened? When have you once seen me cringe? Some of the power is mine still. And anger is mine now, too, Nicholaus. Anger that you did not reveal yourself to me before it was too late."

"I exist as I am for you. Time cannot touch us."

Please don't say it. Those wordless angel thoughts flew through my head. "Don't let it be the truth," I begged of my former self. But, the lady by the stones spoke in spite of me.

"I carry your child." My voice held a calm betrayed by the swirling leaves tossed by the wind around me. It was Nicholaus' turn to stumble backward. "Will this child be purely human," I continued, "or will he have the soul of an Ancient? If you are as you say, what manner of being comes into me with your seed?"

Rain cratered the smooth, dry dirt. In a breath, he was beside me, holding me. With my anger-dulled senses, I hadn't seen him move with that familiar temple trick. "Nothing born from us can be other than blessed," he whispered. "Your goodness is enough for the both of us. Enough to shield my corruption from the child in your womb."

I listened to my silent thoughts of old. *This, we will never know.* At least he recognized his corruption. All anger fled and the winds calmed.

"Be still, Nicholaus, before your rain floods the ground."

The answers were upon me, the outcome revealed with such stark clarity that I trembled. I prayed that he would mistake my seriousness for control or lust or duty. The life I carried was an effort made futile by a greater plan. What was to be gave way to what had to be.

"Come inside the circle with me. I will bury my writings."

His brows drew together. "They are not complete now that we have spoken of all this."

"Come." I nodded. "This book is filled." I sat on the ground between two of the great pillars, a third stone bridging them, sheltering us. The vibrations of the circle acted as a spell, casting consequence and everything frantic aside.

I saw in my mind scenes of our fullest time together, what I had asked to see, what was coming too soon to fruition. We kissed in the garden, swung on the iron gate, and watched the sun set from the castle. My husband, once and finally. Oh, to live that again. But I wasn't allowed even to view it all in splendid detail. Only this scene could I watch. Only this end.

"Is this the priestess I'm seeing?" Nicholaus asked.

"Yes. And I see shades of the Ancient One standing before me."

"These damnable stones. They hum with secrets."

"They're fertile with the cycle of birth and death."

Something of the irony and wickedness enticed him, this stepping inside a cycle from which he proclaimed himself utterly separate. He covered my body with his on the wet ground and we laughed at the water and mud in our hair.

Our lips met in a sweet mingling of souls, each sacrificing one breath to take the other's inside. My tears flowed with the water on the ground. I writhed under him, insane with his spirit and his flesh forged into me, insane with the pleasure and the torment. I wept with each movement, loving him so that my sight couldn't leave his face, and his eternal, binding beauty. In this final act of our sacred, unholy covenant, I lifted the leather-bound book from the ground and rested it on his back. With the rumble of the great stone losing its hold high above us, his eyes opened and he saw my tears at last.

•

A force like I had never experienced threw me from my watching place, whirling me into the void.

"Wake up, Ariana, awaken," I wailed silently to myself. Madness threatened to take me. In one last desperate call, I commanded, "Words are deeds. I bid it so. Awaken."

Ryuichi held my hand too tightly, with silver relief tears on black eyes. "Did—did my kiss … ?"

I sat up on my bed, feeling as if my body moved of its own accord while the energy of me floated just inches away. I didn't know whether the touch of Ryuichi's hand or my will had pushed me back into myself. It could have been either.

"I don't know what sparked this," I said. My head hurt. "How was your—whatever you went to?" I asked him after a while.

He looked at me quietly. "What happened here? I felt you leave when I locked the door. You were not here, but only for a minute. Less maybe. Where did you go, Ariana?"

So years had passed while no time passed at all. Legerdemain of the Record, that. My thoughts were drugged. The deep breaths I took and exhaled worked to clear them.

"Do you know how I met him this time? Did I ever tell you? I felt him coming across an ocean to me. I knew he was coming before he even got there. Can you imagine? Anticipation at its best," I said.

I laughed softly despite the ache it caused behind my eyes.

"Did you hit your head?"

"Not physically. Do you remember England? Feel a calling to Britain of Old?"

"No." Ryuichi shook his head. "No, I think somehow that would have been Winger. Do you want a doctor?"

He knew I didn't.

"Winger and his stone giants—"

"Giants?"

"Still sitting there in Britannia from legends," I said with a laugh. "He sure knew how to put his mark on the world."

"Can I get something to drink for you?"

I squeezed his hand and crawled under the covers. "I just want to sleep the day away. Go to work, Roman in Red. My body and spirit will be well settled when you return."

As I slept the day away, Daen's words flowed into me once again.

Chapter Ten

Hateful silence.
White feathers drifting on blue,
to the next secret.
If only it could stay.
That day …

Ariana's Documentation of Daen's Words

Forgive me if I sound angry. My voice will not come through clearly as I write. It's tinted with the color of Daen's feelings, Daen's thoughts. As I write, I'm honestly unsure whether his thoughts come directly to me, or if I have formed them from the Record.

It's as if I heard him say to the universe with all quiet fury, "Do you really think I care about the Egypt of ages past, or about hearing my bones crunch under stones? Of course I do. Those were my lives after all. I also care very much about Ariana, what she writes, what she feels. Call me evil for my wanting. Call me obsessive and see if I give a damn.

"Ariana doesn't remember enough to keep the Record straight. She's been sliding toward human far too long, and without me to bring it all flooding back, as it were, she'll fall from memory to memory to memory. Best to just sum up the memories all at once and move on. Instead she chases a worthless musician—and her pet pest chases me around the globe. Oh, how I'm fighting the urge to squash those two. But I did that before and see where it got me with Ariana. What's an Ancient to do?"

He pointed out to me that my writings have changed in this life—that I used to write only of fact and of what was to be history. Now I write of us—my feelings for them—and he knows I have fully awakened. I can feel it with this potential newly unwrapped.

"No creature was ever so spectacular as my Ariana," he whispered. "Her eternal memory will return and she'll know again all the fears she ever felt, the tears she ever shed, the loves … She'll say her body and soul are well settled—words from long, long ago.

"I remember everything. I have never slept. Never, never allowed it to be so. Zep Tepi rests on the ledge of my memory, encased in pillars of marble and crisp seas. My creation? My birth? They escape me. I opened my eyes in the body of a fully developed male and immediately called out for the others. This was my beginning.

"I was so painfully perfect, so naturally near to God Himself that I couldn't contain my depth of thought and feeling. It was as if I overflowed from my mortal body. And when I looked at Ariana, we each recognized ourselves in the other—fashioned from the same bit of ether." Would Ryuichi understand if he were to read this?

"We weren't alone," Daen continued, "Winger and Ryuichi existed beside us, along with the one who calls himself Grey, the one named Cibrien, and all the lesser others now faded beyond the call of the Whispers. We gathered instinctively to Ariana, a group of newly born men around the lone female. She was the Magnet and the Scribe—and we loved her.

"I could tell you about broken promises. I could tell you the irony of perfect inventions sliding from grace while the imperfect grow ever closer to it. I might describe guardians with wings unfurled or the waters I caused to rise in the flood on command. The ship carrying my soul away from me crosses my mind from time to time. Quetzalcoatl and Britannia, fire and stones. Yes, I could describe all of this, but the recording of all things past is Ariana's. I am very much a creature of the here and now and the hereafter—except when the past puts its chokehold on the present like Egypt and that Roman filth have done. Then I must tell the tale. And it must start with Egypt because there it will end."

I paused for a moment, fearing the tears that wouldn't come. Daen's words streamed into my mind: "As I remember it, Ariana returned to her precious pyramids as Nephthys and Isis, born almost two years to the day after the Roman again came into the flesh. I watched them both, watched them all, and toyed with the idea of claiming a body for myself in which to be born. As the days passed, I found that I didn't need to. Even as a child, she sensed me in the room and stretched out her hand. She spoke to me aloud sometimes, other times in thought. She floated from her body to join me, so there was no need for me to go through the pain of birth. Mistake of mistakes, I didn't—then.

"Time really had no meaning where I existed, and being as unsettled as I was it was probably a blessing. Of course, I use the term lightly.

"The Old Priest, who would become Cibrien, watched over the priestess-child. I cloaked myself from him, or allowed myself to be hidden in the folded wings of the Fallen. Still, I think he knew I was there and could have recognized me from the onset had he been so inclined.

"Years transformed my Ariana fully into Nephthys, beautiful and refined, but there was loneliness in her passion. When the transformation was nearly complete, I realized all too late that I had become a mere spirit to her. She could no longer summon me, as her training now dictated and her newly spoken covenant with the One God enforced. No matter the depth of her priestess role, the human part of her longed for the rest of us to be with her in the flesh. I cursed my own stupidity.

"My communication with her was reduced to dreams. Oh, I missed her. I could have been born as a child even then, but I desired her in a way that this age difference would not allow. I was a miserable, bodiless mass of the emotions I expressed to her in dreams at night, which she forgot by morning's light.

"The High Priest called in the troops, though why he felt the need to protect her from me, I don't know. How could he so misread his old friend? Cut past my frustration and see the Watcher I was. See the knowledge we shared. Yet I was greeted with the telltale sensation of the One God's warriors, greater than any graveyard statue had ever portrayed them. Sounds of a presence too great for me to battle."

I forgot to breathe. I think his words stole my breath.

"Then the Roman soldiers came to kneel in the dust by the Nile's edge. Nephthys watched the one and saw the Gift, and embraced his very existence because of that Gift alone. The same Gift was hers and mine no less, yet there I was trapped in the watching—with her in the amnesia of the flesh. The desert monuments stood testament to this game of judging shades of sin for the prize of a priestess' affection.

"The energy grew around her when the Roman entered her temple. He had been born simply to meet her again—who could fault him for that? Why was he allowed this blessing when I had dealt with the responsibility of the floodwaters? Why, when I was the one forced across the seas and isolated? But she intensified, strengthened, became more beautiful with him near. Her reaction tore through me. His own desire to remain overwhelmed him, and I think he didn't even feel the slice of the knife as she brought his desire to fruition. Warm blood on cold stones. Baptism of the temple itself.

"I raged against the void inside of which I felt trapped, pummeled invisible walls and remained unheard. How dare he feign unconsciousness in her bed? How dare he touch the lips even I had not? The blackness consumes me even now as I recall her first kiss in all of eternity coming from such an unworthy, undeserving bastard as the Roman. No. If you think justice reigns supreme in the universe, you are mistaken. Punished and punished and punished for doing as He bid me. Torture in place of reprieve. That kiss threatened to drive my spirit to insanity … but I gathered myself tightly and calmed somewhat.

"Vengeance, retribution, and bitterness quietly taunted me. Why could she not look inside him and see the weakness there? So undeserving of her, he was, so very hungry to step from his shadows into the sunlight

I had once been to her.

"But I overestimated my own significance. Twisted as His tests always were, one began to unfold on Earth below me. Choose to be human, will you? I laughed. Forgotten the deadly sins, forgotten the covenants that come with the flesh, have you? Roman soldier, how will you manage these temptations without your memory? And so the Watcher in me watched.

"This life, I'm sure, progressed much as Ariana will tell it, but there were things she could not have known. When the Roman called upon the dark spirits, I first held them back. I can't decide if I felt some twinge of nobility, or if I only wanted to see him beg for the power. The Old Priest was too frail and Nephthys too in love to be of use. Intercede or let fate take its course? I stepped aside.

"The monster came into the temple, rushed passed me, and the Roman held it as fire in the palms of his hands. I felt nothing as I pressed my face against the window to Egypt and looked in. I felt nothing until Nephthys sensed me, saw me, connected me with the beast in the temple—incorrect as her assumption was. She sent the fiend screaming into oblivion, but her bag of tricks held no way to dispense of me. Then I swear that for the first moment in all of time she forgot me. I watched for a moment while he prepared to take her on the stone of the altar steps. I fled as far as I could, as fast as I could. Would that I had been in the flesh with the ability to run myself into exhaustion. Instead this prickling, hard agony rolled across my being, crushing me into numbness that refused to subside. They shredded a chunk of my soul with each spasm on the temple floor that day.

"To add insult to injury, she thought me the beast. How she could decide to see my face in the monster, I will never comprehend. I had not seduced her precious soldier. The flaws were his all along, all alone. I suppose the numbness made my next actions all the simpler. I caused the Roman army to return, sent Whispers into the ears of the general and caused his voice to form words he should not have known … Worst and best, I slipped inside the flesh of the soldiers as they carried the Roman to the water's edge in that blessed cage. The pleasure for me was almost sexual, the sight of the river swallowing him, the bursting pain I sensed in his lungs.

"He paused as his spirit passed beside me, memory full of the Record once more. *Traitor*, he accused with a thought. *Demon you've become. Friend no longer.* I blew him a kiss as he slipped away in a layer to which I couldn't climb.

"Finally I found cause for joy. Nephthys turned to the writings of which I was so much a part. So the Roman hadn't taken all of her. He hadn't disturbed the very core of her—I still held it.

"I could see the moonlight sliding across the pyramids after the eclipse fell aside and night took its place. Nephthys wrote with the Roman blocked from her mind and her ink avoided forming his name. His tale was finished for this part of the Record and my jealous soul warmed at the thought. 'I have no choice, you must realize,' she said without looking up. 'We have doomed ourselves to the Return.' She raised her eyes and looked straight through me. 'Show yourself. I know you exist.'

"With the invitation, my will found direction and she saw me. 'My love …' I began.

"She stopped my words with one confident gesture

of a delicate hand. 'I wish no conversation with you, Spirit. I sense the implications of your presence, but the flesh dulls my memory. I will join you soon enough.'

"I followed her like a starving animal as she wrapped the writings in her arms and marched the long walk toward the pyramids. Dried mummies and musty limestone rooms—those were not reality then. The cool sand gave off the scent of earth and rain long since fallen. The air itself grew alert and surreal. Clarity had never been such a heady mix of grief and joy. But Nephthys walked on while the Roman Army rallied in the distance."

•

Daen's words stopped. How long I sat after my pen fell to the table, I couldn't tell you. I was numb. I found innocence in places I thought Daen evil, and evil where I had thought him innocent. And what of the weakness inside Ryuichi? Did it remain?

My body and spirit were not well settled in spite of everything. Memory and present blended well, but my soul didn't feel still. I reached out for Winger with a thought while Ryuichi read my words.

At first there was nothing, no reply to my call. But then, just for a fraction of a moment, I thought I saw something like a beast moving under the sunlight and sliding fast across a desert floor. But there was no trusting my intuition in that moment.

I called out again for Winger and found nothing.

Chapter Eleven

Don't you love me?
The velvet-voiced call.
Forgive me for
when the sun sinks,
I'll meet you anyway.

Ryuichi read everything. His reactions were all you would imagine, but he found courage and returned to my side after some time apart. We knew enough now and I desired no more words, no more knowledge for the moment. These things would only exhaust me when my energy could only be focused here in the present. So hard to cease the desiring when my memories were rich and alive …

"Stop playing with us," I whispered. The lines between God and Satan and Daen blurred for me. To whom did I speak?

We had more than this problem at hand. I couldn't find Winger, and Ryu and I remained too close together with the longing building again. I felt my heart filled to capacity with the frustration of the situation. We needed to go forth without Winger and we needed to find

Daen. Without them, we were stranded between Destiny's steps. But the days dragged on and a silence fell over the Whispering.

And then the noise began.

It began first as a quiet ticking in the distance, scarcely audible at all. By the time it had grown to a hum, it could be none other. Winger was alive and he called out for us.

Ryuichi laughed with eyes luminous in the night as we sang like drunken children tossing clothes into suitcases and dancing around the bed. That he also heard Winger was the miracle of it—that we could tell the new tales of our old past when we found him.

Ryuichi's driver took us to the airport. With hands clasped and baseball caps pulled low over our sunglasses, we ran to a privately chartered plane and escaped Japan without the media attention we feared. We simply followed the Whispering and glided away silently into the night.

When the plane landed we were back in the States. We were in Arizona to be exact. From the mountains to the desert—this transition didn't seem such a stretch knowing Winger's past-life heritage. I rented a car while Ryuichi walked back and forth through the airport trying to comprehend how he could remove all disguise and no one would so much as blink in his direction.

And so we drove with no course in mind, no map in hand. As dusk settled over us in colors and the air began to cool, we came upon a small church near the road and the rocks of red. With one look at each other, we knew we had found Winger. Winger had found another.

I think I ran from the car before Ryu even knew we'd stopped driving. That bright, dark sense of presence that preceded Daen was nowhere, but I was excited to the point of nearly forgetting his absence. The entire church overflowed with a warm, wild sensation of purest elation.

Winger sat in the twilight near the altar, with stained glass windows glowing softly behind him. "Ariana, my dear. This would be Cibrien. This time."

Ryu froze in the open doorway several feet behind me. Dusty light fell down around me and streamed down the aisle in great gold columns.

Cibrien smiled back at me. "It was a lovely funeral pyre."

He was naughty and lovely all at once. And all at once his arms were around me, lifting me off the floor in his embrace. We laughed and cried, and the smoke from the burning pyre crept into the heavens somewhere in our memories.

He took my hand and I was mesmerized by hazel eyes that couldn't decide between green and brown. The old High Priest was somewhere inside that light little mixture of smallest behaviors I saw there, but this man, Cibrien, was something altogether new.

He held me at arms length as if inspecting some precious painting. He winked and laughed, grabbed my hands and swung me around so that I had to sit quickly in the pew to avoid landing on the floor. Winger's bemused expression told me that Pandora's box had indeed opened. Here was the wisdom of the old in the body of the young.

Cibrien looked up and saw Ryuichi leaning against the doorframe. He calmed immediately and walked down the aisle to Ryu, who stood up straight but stayed where he was.

"Warrior of Rome. Still in search of saving and Savior."

Ryu bowed low before his former teacher. "I am not as I was."

Cibrien tilted his head to the side and whispered with no hint of a smile, "Not looking for recognition and a warm place to tuck away your lonely soul? That'll be the day." He laughed aloud, interrupting the church silence with merry echoes.

I thought for a moment that Ryuichi would turn and walk out the door the way he had so often in Egypt, but in this century he would stand his ground. With the dusty light striking his hair, he looked like silken statuary. And though I knew the words had found their mark, he smiled.

"You did not mention my impatience or my anger or lust ..." His accented words rolled softly through the aisles.

"It is something interesting yet other than lovely to see you again, my friend," Cibrien responded.

I moved in that way reminiscent of rain sliding down glass, startling them both and myself. "Cibrien. That was unkind. You do not behave as the High Priest I recall. Where has the Master gone?" I felt the commanding priestess in me threaten to surface.

"The austere priest has gone and another character has taken his place. I can call on the wizened countenance, the patience at will. I am permeated by it. Saturated with it. Believe me when I tell you that all this vitality and zest are much harder for me to come by, and I plan on enjoying them fully in this flesh before I no longer can."

I felt the warm comfort slipping fast away. "What do

you believe to be happening here?"

"It's very simple, Ariana," Cibrien answered. "We Ancients have been awakened together at last, and we are finally gathering. It's time to take sides and lay boundaries. And as He Who Never Sleeps has said, 'God is getting ready to clean house.' Can't you just smell it in the air?" He wiggled his eyebrows up and down.

I turned to Winger. "Does he take anything seriously anymore?"

Winger shook his head.

Cibrien wore his knowledge lightly. "You, my beautiful friends, have all been born again and again and again. I've missed you so. I've missed all this." Ryu looked utterly confused as the man laughed again, but Cibrien shrugged and continued. "Roman in Red, I haven't experienced this corporeal classroom in quite some time. You all really ought to learn to enjoy it more when I give you a bad time." He jumped up and perched on the top of the pew. "I hadn't the physical strength to do even this when you knew me last."

"We are gathering to do something, Cibrien," I said. "We have the chance again to affect what happens here."

"Do you really think so? We are Watchers, Keepers of the Record, Ancients. We teach and remember. And that is all. It is not for us to question God's motives or to step in front of his actions. Urshu and Urshu only. Sages."

Ryu whispered, "I cannot believe we are only to watch." His voice rose. "We have a chance here to change the world. We can do and act this time. We can make a difference somehow, and then we can be free to live."

Cibrien raised his eyebrows in seriousness this time.

"Then you and Daen are not such different creatures after all. You make his argument well."

Winger stepped forward and uncrossed his arms. "That's unfair, Cib. Hell, not one of us is completely certain what we're supposed to do."

"Oh, I'm certain," he shot back. Our words were coaxing him back into the High Priest role every second. "You, Winger. You wish to avenge a physical life cut short by ending Daen's this time around. And, Ryuichi. You want nothing more than to have Ariana all to yourself this time, and to have Daen aware of it. Lust and anger aren't the purest of motivations, you know. Ariana, the quest to remember and find peace with your past might have been noble if it weren't so tainted with desire. You're absolutely torn in half between two men. What will you do when we find the others? The skeletons in the closet should be something amazing to see then.

"Let go of your wants. We're in a privileged position here. If your wants cause you to give up your purpose, then much is lost." Cibrien's words carried through the church and we were all silent for moments.

"Cibrien is right," I began. "He always has been. We are here to watch and record, but as humans this time. We can record the larger details of history and we can affect our own souls. Of course we don't control the One God and we couldn't step in front of His actions successfully if we wanted to. The challenge is in our intent and how we act. Always has been."

I turned and walked outside, leaving them all standing quietly in the church together. The weakening sunshine struck my face and I breathed in the dry air. Just breathed ...

"It's a fine line drawn between us, my love."

I didn't even turn my head. My eyes may have even closed as I whispered in return, "We've begun to take ourselves entirely too seriously."

His fingers touched my side as he stepped from around the corner of the building to stand behind me. *Daen, Daen, Daen.* My mind screamed out the warning call of the wolf in the flock. And yet I cherished his presence, every second of it.

At last I turned to look at him. How many years had it been since we had locked eyes this way? Crimson on snow, iron gate to the rose garden—visions triggered by the mere scent of his body carried in the desert air. He took my hand and led me to the bottom of the steps, where we stood as the doors to the church flew open.

"Don't do it, Ariana!" Winger's eyes were fierce. He trembled visibly while Cibrien reached out to hold him back.

Ryuichi fell to his knees. Faint greens and whites like the aurora borealis flashed in the air above the church. Sand whipped up around us and settled while tears slid from luminous eyes all the way down his face. I broke Daen's hold and ran to him, dropping to my own knees.

"I have to speak with him, Ryu."

He shook his head slowly. "No."

"Have faith," I said. "I have to talk with him, just for a while."

Winger snarled at Daen, "You can't take her."

Daen smiled coolly. "You know the way of the Whispering, comparatively weak as it may be in you. There is no option more right than Ariana and I talking, touching, settling the past."

Cibrien nodded. "He speaks the truth. The need is

written."

Ryuichi rose to his feet. "Then you will stay with us. It is painful, but I see no other way. Ariana will not separate from us."

Daen shook his head. "So honored I am, invited into the fold once more." He walked past us and stepped into the church. When he drew in his breath, the entire building seemed to sigh under the weight of his presence. "Devils are not so black as they are painted, you know."

We shuddered as he walked down the aisle toward the altar. No one had ever appeared so out of place. Ryuichi caught my gaze. *You would have left me,* I heard him think.

Winger placed his hand on Ryuichi's shoulder. "There's a small office to the right, and beyond that a couple of rooms we can sleep in tonight. There's even a bathtub."

Wisps of that electric mist drifted around us as I followed Ryuichi into the office room and shut the door.

As soon at the bolt locked into placed, Ryu pushed me gently against the wall. "Do not leave me, Ariana. Do not ever go away with him." His forehead touched mine and the tears came again. "I have not been so scared before." He kissed me quickly. "I could endure a thousand executions, breathe the Nile waters a thousand more times, but I cannot endure your loss again."

"I love you, Ryuichi. But I hold another love for him, no matter the hatred you feel. This is not a romantic game for me. This is no contest."

"I love you as a man loves a woman, Ariana. Not as part of our quest. Never just that." He looked like a perfect work of art before me, all emotion and eloquence.

"Marry me, Ariana. Marry me and make us holy before God."

To lay with him without sin. To kiss those lips without fear of corruption. The temptation ached in me to say yes and run away with him into the night, but it was wrong. The ache in me was physical, residual effects of a lifetime long ago slipped through our fingers, but I could no longer tell if it meant much more than that.

As I struggled to form my answer, he apologized and embraced me tightly. "Forgive me for my weakness. Do what you must. Things will be right in the end."

•

I walked behind the church with Daen under the light of stars. Winger and Cibrien sat inside with Ryuichi, all rigid with tension and distrust, trying to ignore the situation and remain aware of it at once.

Daen took my hand as we walked quietly. "We've complicated ourselves, haven't we?"

I didn't know whether to hold his hand tighter or pull away. "I don't know who I should love or hate anymore."

"It's simple for me," Daen said, "The rest are naught."

"The more I remember, the harder it is to sort out the right from the wrong. I don't know when it stopped being clear."

Daen chuckled. "The entire soul-defining concept of reincarnation only works for mere mortals. For Urshu, each round in the flesh becomes more destructive. We begin to forget just enough to make the human desires become dangerous."

"See, take what you just said for instance. It makes such good sense. But my soul knows that any other way goes against the Plan."

The softness I recalled in Daen reappeared. "Ariana, we did nothing wrong. We did everything He asked. Everything without question. And what did He do? Tore us apart and tormented us."

"We could have been together again. It could have happened, but you chose a different path. He Who Never Sleeps—you know that's what you're called?"

"One of us had to stay alert. I can't stand aside and watch another end. Not another flood, not a fire," he said.

"But Daen, another end is building with or without you and you know it. It's why we've found each other again."

Daen remained quiet for moments. "I watched you sail away," he began. "Tell me what happened when your ship hit land. It was the only time we were truly apart. It's what I wanted to know when I followed you to Japan."

The quiet richness of his voice caused me to take his other hand in mine as I released my tale for him, face to face in the desert behind the church.

"We followed the stars across the night sky, through dark waters, guided by a smooth wind that I created myself. Ironic, isn't it? We seem to have worked together to separate ourselves, your power of the water, mine of the wind …

"When I arrived in what's now Egypt, the land was green and dripping with life. The Nile was narrow and clean, lined with grass and trees, fruit …" My concentration wavered. "And there were people scattered beside the river, some Asian, some black. Their blending had not yet started. I and those on my ship looked so starkly out of place.

"It was my job to record, to write. The One God demanded more than scrolls and carvings. He wanted a remembrance of our sacrifice and of his plan to carry throughout history. And so I built a monument to him on the border between Upper and Lower Egypt, a monument on the heart of the Earth. My God, Daen. It's so obvious that we were there to build the pyramids." I paused and drew in a ragged breath.

Daen wiped a tiny tear from my cheek with his warm hand and I continued. "But Daen, this wasn't immediately after Zep Tepi. The Golden Age of the Gods had passed by ten thousand years. What happened to us for all that time? Did we simply exist together in that place of white marble for so long?"

"I have no answer, Ariana. It's as if a thousand years were a day to us."

I nodded, trying to make sense of perplexity. "The pyramid building and our separation came after the second flood." I almost felt like laughing as the visions came and came. "Man has sought the riddle of the construction for so long. Ramps and pulleys, workers and slaves. How simple and primitive mankind has become. We used the heka! The heka from the force of our own powerful souls."

Our private aurora borealis grew around us. "We are energy after all. We just raised the stones in great waves of electromagnetic vibration. It really was brilliant. We marked the center of the earth and added architectural details pointing right at the stars. We mapped time. We mapped our place in time by aiming for celestial position. And if that weren't enough, we built the Sphinx. A great lion guardian to commemorate the sun's rise in Leo. And when my work with the pyramids and Pharaoh was done, I existed no more in Egypt."

"Until you returned to the flesh as the Priestess," added Daen.

We moved closer together and I rested my head against his chest. The beat of his heart was so real and so warm that I could pretend he was as human as me, that he would experience death and rebirth as I would.

He caught my thoughts. "My blood flows red as yours does, my hair will turn gray, and this body will die. This body I did not create. I came into it in a sense, was nearly born with it. That will have to be enough for us—for now. I am in love with you, Ariana, and I will wait and I will hope."

"Don't speak in such a way, Daen. We were the mates to your soul once upon a time. Now they believe you to be the enemy, but it's progress that you've stepped back into the rebirth cycle and out of limbo, if only this once."

The softness fled abruptly. "I care nothing for what they believe. And I have not stepped into the cycle. I simply claimed the body I wanted."

"Do you at least care what I believe then?"

"My entire purpose is to be with you and to prevent our separation. There is no evil in me where you are concerned."

"Then help me, Daen. Show me the soul I so remember."

He turned quickly and walked away into the night.

Chapter Twelve

Redemption for one
but not the other.
Misplaced melody
bound in chains
until the blessings run out.

We all awoke tired, cold, and drained of thought in the face of the impasse that had reached us somehow in the night. The five of us knew it as we met on the front steps of the church.

Cibrien looked at each of us in turn. "The Whispering is completely quiet after last night." He ran his finger along the bottom of his lip. "We all know that nothing is revealed out of place or out of time."

Winger nodded. "It feels like we're just waiting now. No surprise memories, no revelations."

"Charming though I find my present company, being with you for weeks on end is a thrill I'll just have to forego," Daen added. "Come with me, Ariana." He held out his hand to me.

Winger and Ryuichi started forward, but Cibrien stopped them with a hand lightly placed on their shoulders. "Daen knows she can't leave with him. He also knows that when the Whispering begins anew, we'll gather."

"Wise old priest," Daen said so softly that it was scarcely a sound. "When Egypt calls, I'll see you all again." With a kiss on my cheek, he said in my ear so that none other heard, "I'm living for the only thing I know, my love. You. There's nothing else."

Winger and Cibrien left together in the direction of Sedona, Daen left in another, and Ryuichi and I stood quietly in front of the church letting the wind blow dust around us for a very long time.

"I can't be your bodyguard much longer, Ariana," Winger had said. "It's high time you, Daen and Ryu worked this out one way or the other. You're going to have to make a choice."

And just as simply as he had said it, the angel thoughts fled. The psychic connection severed itself and the Whispering stopped. Not one of us sensed the other with anything more than the physical sight of looking at the other standing nearby. So when we went in separate directions, the weight of carrying one another's souls lifted for this first time in all of history.

Ryuichi and I stood together, just a man and a woman, alone with intense memories and in love with each other. I breathed more freely than I ever remembered, lifted clean of my burden if only for a brief while.

Ryuichi laughed, hugged me quickly, and laughed again. "Let's go to Egypt! Let's go as tourists before we never can again. Before the Whispering returns and the others join us, let's just go."

I nodded in agreement. "Yes, Ryuichi. The time has come for the builder gods to return to the cradle of humanity."

•

At first glance, Cairo had become the lamentable city described and despised in Ryuichi's lyrics. Then I caught the desert air mingling with flowing water, and as a poet once said, there's nothing like a scent nearly forgotten to make the heartstrings crack.

Here we were, home to our limestone, cobblestones, sandy times, silent nights, and uncertain magic. But, the mosques and churches around us looked aged in one aspect, and grotesquely new in another. *At least the One God is worshipped openly now*, I thought.

Ryuichi and I sat on the hotel room floor, held each other, and stared blankly out an open window. Was it all lost to us? We had returned to a living cemetery, to a giant monument covering up and wiping away an entire lifetime. So little of the place was recognizable now. Even the pyramids inspired great sadness in us with their crumbling stones, worn and defiled.

We saw baskets and jars on the street, a bit of clothing now and again, which might have been pulled straight from our memories. The Nile water had become filthy, the air thickened, the streets overcrowded—but there were little signs, tiny things that endured.

"Tourists. What a fool I was to say that," said Ryuichi. "We may not be able to sense the others right now, but we will always mourn what this used to be."

"Why don't we explore? We may find something to celebrate."

Ryuichi looked at me with serious eyes. "You know the place I need to see."

The next morning, we hired a car and driver to take us southward following the Nile as best we could. Several times we asked the driver to stop as we sprang from the car and ran to the banks of the river.

"There, with the pyramids on the other side of the water off in the distance. It looked like that," Ryuichi said.

I shook my head. "No, the angle is wrong. It's different." Then the slow reality reached us. The river had changed its course. A curve had straightened where once it twisted. A straight stretch now curved, only we had no idea where.

Ryuichi looked at me with sunlight liquid in his brown eyes as he tossed a handful of dry sand fiercely back onto the ground.

"You would think my mind would open up, here. Why can I not feel the exact place? Have I fallen too far?"

"There are other places to look. The memories will come as they will. We never know the trigger," I reminded.

We traveled in search of it anyway. For the better part of the month we journeyed down to Upper Egypt, back up to Lower Egypt. There were temples and obelisks, imitation artifacts, spices and souks. And for all those days, we talked of small things and walked without touching hands.

Do not look upon him, I thought I heard as another night fell. Was it the Whispering returned or only my imagination?

We walked silently near the entrance to the Great Pyramid, the way made clear to us for a bit of money to a guard. How many times had the tight passageway seen claustrophobia, trepidation, or the hope for unattainable mysteries revealed?

"Do you ever feel loneliness here?" Ryuichi asked.

My familiar answer came back to me. "Sometimes."

"Good," he continued, "Because I know you're beside me now, but I can't find you." He stopped at the top of the steep stairs leading deep inside the pyramid and his words were halting and dreamlike. "You make me question the training. I'm not sure I want to assume this role if it removes me from all intimacy."

Tears flowed of their own accord down my face. "Ryuichi, do you hear us?"

He nodded and whispered, "The wooden rails and the metal, the electricity in here—the energy is weakened."

I whispered back, "My Roman, if you do not take the high road to these powers, they will corrupt you. You will be lost to me."

Ryuichi took my hand and held it against his chest. "I have no power, Priestess. I have no pride. I have only you, the fading light, and the stones beneath us."

I felt we had stepped inside a dream. The cool granite pressed against my back and the pale, diffused light of a solitary bulb glowed. His face was all I remembered of the Roman soldier, all I knew of the musician-poet-priest. Rejuvenation of my soul with a look into him, for he had somehow caused time to stop with his beauty.

"Please, Ariana," he whispered with his lips brushing mine. "Forever and ever …"

All I cared for in creation was caught in his voice and the tremble of his hand in my hair. When we kissed, the world dropped away as a veil falling from the heavens. I was the priestess embracing the past and our sorrow. I was the scribe and the magnet and *his*.

Ryuichi's fingers lingered near the skin at my throat,

his breath came fast, but as the wanting nearly over-powered us, the spell broke and we knew in a look that we couldn't continue. The color of desire suddenly faded from his eyes and shock replaced it just as suddenly.

"You glow golden," he murmured while backing away to look at me.

"As do you," I answered. "Zep Tepi …"

"Illusions." The word fell strong and flat in the shadows, and Ryuichi and I caught our breath so quickly that it was audible. Daen's voice commanded through gritted teeth, "Or maybe reality. Either way, if you touch her again, you'll be in agony the likes of which … "

I put up my hand against his words and golden silver glimmering. "Did you follow me?"

Daen stood up imposing and idyllic, appearing like a breathtakingly beautiful ghost out of the darkness. "I didn't need to, my love. Egypt called and I knew where you would end up. Sneaking glances at the past. Shame, shame."

Ryuichi tucked his thumbs in the pockets of his jeans and looked at Daen with his head tilted ever so slightly to the side. "I know why you're here and it isn't Ariana. You want to bring back the memory with us. You long for it, too."

Daen laughed, bright and dark, cold and warm all at once in the splendor of the aura surrounding us. "Is that so wrong?"

I looked with understanding at Ryuichi. What was the catch?

Daen's laugh fell to a smile. "I admit. You think me something of a trickster. The devil incarnate even." He leaned in closer to us. "What does it matter if we can relive just a while of Zep Tepi or of the time after it?"

I raised my arms and brought my hands together in the sacred gesture of beginnings and endings from ceremonies long past. Ryuichi responded in kind and the Whispering flooded back to us in a roar—and we were swept away in it.

．

We were as we had already come to know, Watchers close to God with our feet firmly planted on a piece of earth now faded into antiquity. We stood on an island between Africa and Asia's edge, with waters of brisk blue and sunlight clear. This was not Zep Tepi; that time had gone. Here again were the pillars of white and the marble terraces carved into a steep mountainside above the sea.

This was our Eden, this mountain. The Watchers gathered here, stepping across the water on floating walkways connecting our temple in the center to another ring of land, and then to another even larger ring. Islands within an island.

A crystal tear slipped from Daen's tormented then-blue eyes as he spoke to us. We were all cut from the same unusual cloth then, with our eyes of blue and complexions fair.

"The angels divided themselves at Zep Tepi. We watched for nine days as they fell. Azazel, Rosier, Jetrel, and so many more … They're all hiding in a level to which we cannot descend. They corrupted themselves with the daughters of mankind until the flood washed it all away. And here we are again, summoned," he said.

Winger touched his friend's arm. "He Whispers to you that the waters will be unleashed?"

Daen nodded. "Not only the waters." He gestured toward the mountain behind us.

"Our island temple," I added, "the fire and the earth." I paused for a moment. "I do not remember how to lend much strength to the elements when He commands them. The flesh has weakened me somewhat this time."

"I worry," said Ryuichi. "Are we at last to perish and be awake as one in the form of the spirit?"

Winger jumped to his feet. "No. I can feel it. This time is different. The destruction is enormous and we are bound to it."

Daen's fists clenched, surprising me with a new emotion that burned almost tangible in the air. "This is not justice," he declared.

I rose to my feet as quickly as Winger had. "That is not for us to question."

Ryuichi also rose. "Why can we not question? Why must we watch?"

"Because that is our purpose," Winger said.

"We have done as commanded," Daen whispered violently. "We have done all He asked. The Fallen Ones have one another for comfort in their limited domain. These humans who have forgotten even their own souls have one another and the earth itself. What are we to have except our suffering?"

Cibrien stood from his seat on the white fountain. Silent until now, he spoke, "There is little doubt, my friend, that we will be separated. Who will record these events after they are complete? Who else will renew civilization?"

"I will beseech the One God," Daen said. With that, he turned and fled up the stone stairs along the side of the mountain, as many other Watchers stepped aside in awe of him.

Tears now flowed freely down my face as well. "This

is doom," I warned. "To question as he questions is to follow the Way of the Fallen Ones."

Daen's usual demeanor returned as the days passed. He was the one who accessed the Record most easily, whose strength calmed and whose wisdom assured us all.

The two of us would sit on the fountain together and watch the ocean sway below us, and we would smile at one another in the sunlight.

"Could you imagine anything so amazing as creation?" he would ask. "Every glorious minute is unique. Can you just imagine?"

"I can," I answered, "And then I can't." I pulled my thin skirt up to my thighs and tilted my head back to expose my neck to the sun. Daen lifted a strand of hair off of my shoulder and smoothed it back.

"I can imagine many things," he said.

I opened my eyes to find him staring at me strangely, and he quickly rose. As I sat alone, Cibrien and Ryuichi watched from across the terrace. Cibrien and I frowned at each other when Daen strode away and as Ryuichi suddenly turned and walked in the opposite direction.

Our peace was punctuated more and more frequently with currents of newly born emotion that we didn't quite comprehend. Winger and Cibrien never strayed far from me now, while Ryuichi sought out his music in solitude, no longer sharing with me as he once had.

Daen began to stay apart from us for days at a time. We had no knowledge of when the One God would ask us to do as we must, and so without Daen we swam in clear waters and memorized the scents of the lush flora around us. Who knew if we would be blessed with such aromas again? We talked together and made plans as best we could, chanting universal patterns and numbers until they etched in our minds, speaking again the history we knew from the Record as if it were a grand campfire story.

At last I grew weary of waiting for Daen's return one evening. As the sun dropped, I slipped away, retraced Daen's steps up the mountainside, and easily followed the Whispering to him. Rain began to slip from the sky and more than once the water washed my feet from their hold on the stone stairs.

Muddy and with robes torn I discovered the entrance to a cave tucked away on the green hillside. I called his name aloud, held back the vines with my hand, and stepped into the black opening.

As the plants shut off the way behind me, I felt petrified. Blue and white lights clashed against the walls on all sides of me, flickering scenes of the aberrant and the ruined—none of which Daen seemed to see as he stood with his back to me. In the unholy radiance, bits of a lower echelon split open, its contents spilling out inside this small cavern.

I screamed Daen's name and with it came the start of chaos and movements so fast I couldn't tell one from the next. The bluish white panorama whirled away into nothing, leaving darkness and the reverberation of enormous wings beating against earth. Unnatural gemstone colors reflected off feathers, scattering around a pair of luminous eyes that seemed to recognize me in a gaze that wouldn't be held.

I cupped my hands against the sides of my head and fell to the floor, my knees striking the dirt hard. The blast of the wings and an infernal shriek of energy threatened to burst my ears. Then the voice and its laughter rolled together like a low explosion through the cave, "Praying? For him?"

And then there was a silence all too sudden.

The place smelled of sulphur as I scrambled out of the cave for air. A red mist cloaked the moon above me in the night and the rain poured in a deluge from the sky, pulling parts of the mountainside with it as it raced to join the water of the sea far below.

"What have you done?" I screamed against the tempest. Daen put his arms around me and when he pulled me close, I pushed away. "You have gone against His will and you dare defile me with a touch?"

Daen grabbed me and forced me back into his arms, holding me there against my struggles as he spoke into my ear. "I begged of Him. I tried all I could, my love. It was in vain and He is without mercy. I will carry out this one final act of His will, and then I will choose an act of will all my own."

"What do you mean? What are you saying to me?" Hysteria rose inside me. "I saw you converse with the creature …"

As if time moved in concentrated, delayed measures, a torrent of water slowly seemed to catch us. We lost our footing on the side of the mountain, and Daen lost his hold on me. An embrace from which I had just fought to release myself, I now fought violently to regain. If I could only reach his fingertips. His blue eyes were filled with anguished terror and I noticed in the stained moonlight that his hair had gone starkest white.

"My love," I heard him say in words unspoken, "I will find you."

The flood twisted and threw us down the side of

the mountain in a river of mud and I lost sight of Daen. Winger appeared as if from nowhere and with one arm, hooked me around the waist just as I was to be carried off into the churning waters below.

Winger's eyes were turbulent with a power building in him. He shook me gently. "You have to channel it now. The wind is yours. Take it."

Hand-in-hand we raced across the inner ring of land to our boats in the harbor there. Winger had the power of the elements, the power of the One God, and its fierceness shook the whole of the mountain behind us.

Ryuichi joined us, catching me by my other arm. He, too, glowed with the same godly force. "Get on the boat!" he yelled.

Winger pulled me aboard and I wiped the rain away from my face trying with all my might to see the others.

Ryuichi stood beside us on the boat. "What is wrong with you? The time is now. The wind. Do it!"

I looked frantically around me. "Where is he? I can't see him."

Ryuichi's eyes burned with a power promising to ignite at any moment. "Listen to me. My fire will erupt from the mountain in less than minutes and it will consume us. You must call the wind and fill the sails with it. There are only three of us aboard and we are not enough to row. Do you hear me?"

"Yes," I said stupidly, tears running down my face. Why did I cry? What was this piercing new obsession I felt in my chest? And as the mountain began to spew glowing red lava, I caught the wind and with all my soul, blasted it against the cloth sails.

Bits of rock and ash fell beside us as the vessel sped out of the harbor. The mountain roared and the waves rocked, and I heard Ryuichi yell as Winger disappeared over the side of the ship. I thought for a moment to still the wind.

"No! Go on!" a voice called. "I have him." I looked up to see Cibrien pull Winger aboard his ship just as the wind took on a life of its own and jerked them away on a course far from my own ship's.

The air was heavy with rain and ash, and the sky so dark that all I could see was the red blaze of the moon and hell's inferno streaking through smoke where terraces of white once stood.

We had all summoned our elements well, fed them with energy until we could no longer bottle them. Then, as we were swept out of the harbor into the open sea, I saw Daen.

He stood straight and tall, alone on a ship with sails billowing white. His hands gripped the rail as our eyes met. I started to raise my hand to wave a farewell, but the gesture seemed inadequate and futile. His water and my air, conspiring to separate their masters. He was lost to me, carried to the opposite side of the world while I stood useless and overwhelmed by human emotions I had never felt before. How would I ever know what existed right then in his heart? How would I learn what he had meant outside the cave or what he had done inside it? And how could I survive not knowing?

•

The spell shattered against the present. Daen jumped to his feet and ran down the stairs until he reached the outside of the pyramid. "You love me still, Ariana. I know it!" he yelled.

Ryuichi and I followed him outside, breathless after the run down the steep stairway.

Daen threw his head back and laughed. "Oh, don't you worry, little pop-star. I'm not leaving. Not again, not for more than a moment." He leaned closer to Ryuichi, "Aren't human emotions a bitch?"

"Daen, just stop it," I said. "Stop. We need peace between us. Too many centuries have passed this way."

Ryuichi smiled as my voice trailed off. "Do you hear it?" he asked. "It is like some distant love song, like waking up from the sweetest coma. Again, there—do you hear it?"

I fell silent and listened in the Gizah night with my eyes closed as something like a melody floated through us and disappeared.

"What was it?" I whispered.

Daen stood with his shoulders back, his gaze toward the heavens, and tears glistening in his dark eyes. "He let me hear it."

Chapter Thirteen

Veils tear against temptation.
Precious love poems
Scratched out.
While the wrong thing
calmly waits.

I sensed that Daen was alive and well in Cairo, felt him examining the unraveling skeins of our existence. I don't know if it was the blended harmony of the heavens that we had heard in the nighttime or my awareness of his watching, but I felt cocooned in lightness and caressed by rose petals in the morning light. Yet in spite of his attention, his cursed promises to Ryuichi, and my elation, Daen had gone from us if for only a short while.

"He is in pain from hearing what he turned his back on. I would be, too, if I could never feel that completeness again," Ryuichi said over breakfast, accent slurring softly with the last bit of sleep dropping away.

I shook my head. "We know better. God doesn't tease that way. There's something to salvage in his soul or the music wouldn't have touched him so." I sipped my coffee, which was too thick and strong to drink any faster.

Ryuichi banged his cup down on the table. "How can you think this?" He pushed the unbuttoned cuffs of his white shirt up to his elbows.

"How can you not?"

"You know what he did in that cave. He met with some thing that fell, and he learned the escape of rebirth from it."

"Yes, I know. He told me himself that he took himself outside the cycle."

"He laughs in the face of everything holy."

"Maybe not," I said meekly. "I don't think he ever completely fell from grace."

Ryuichi looked at me with inky black brows drawn together. "Why was your forgiveness of me not given so quickly in your temple, Priestess?"

"That's not fair."

He leaned closer across the small table. "He is not even human, Ariana. He is not a Watcher or a man. He is a godless, loveless piece of energy on its way out of life."

"What's wrong with you? You sound like Winger. I'd think that you of all people would recognize a chance at redemption when you saw it."

We sat silent for moments after that. Ryuichi was wrong. He had to be wrong. My vision was not so obscured by emotion that I couldn't recognize the spark of divinity creeping back into Daen. Did I misplace my faith and hope for a wrong, unattainable thing?

Ryuichi studied me for a while. He was at his most focused when torn with intense longing and anger. I could nearly see the poetry flowing off his fingertips and he ran his hands through his silky brown-black hair.

"I have to write this music out of my head, Ariana. I'm sorry." He went back upstairs to his room where the songs could stream out of him, and I knew the dark lyrics would be fit for Ashes of Roses, not Ryuichi on his own.

I twisted my hair into a single braid down my back and set out for a walk through the bazaar. For a fleeting instant I heard a rustle behind me just before a breeze swept across my cheek. The airy silk scarves hanging delicately on a rack beside me didn't move.

I turned in a direction I hadn't originally intended and walked a little faster. I moved across the cobblestones and around the vendors, each pressing something toward me for which I had no use. When I felt the breeze caress my cheek again, I walked even faster down yet another side street. Brushed by angels' wings...

Out of the corner of my eye I saw a tall black man standing under the shadow of a striped awning with the words "Branch Road Café" drawn across it. I tried to concentrate on the painted words, but his eyes drew me.

He smiled as I approached. "Have we met, Ma'am?" he asked with a smoky inflection in his voice that I didn't recognize.

"No, I don't think so. I'm Ariana." I answered and extended my hand. There was something familiar about him.

"Negoso Greythorne at your service. I'm called Grey."

I dropped his hand. "Grey?" This was the same name carried to me in Daen's enduring voice only weeks before.

He laughed deeply and created a contagious merriment simply by doing so. "Not a name you were expecting? It's a long story."

"Oh, it's not that," I said. "I really think I should have been expecting it."

Grey narrowed his laughing, light green eyes, which seemed to absolutely glow against the warm, dark tones of his skin. "I'll buy you coffee. Come." He held open the door to the café and gestured me inside.

Could this be a coincidence? Perhaps this Grey was a smuggler, a con artist, or a more generic ilk of thief. Here I sat, a lone woman in a foreign country at a table with a complete stranger. Yet I felt I should stay.

"Did the Ministry send you?" he asked.

Why did the Record not open at moments like these? "The Ministry?" I responded in ignorance.

He laughed again. "I suppose that answers my question. Then you are not government, but a tourist in need of a guide?"

"Yes, that's exactly right. What services can you provide?" No harm could come from playing along with his assumption.

"Ah." He stretched out his long legs and put his feet up on the wicker seat of the chair beside him. "I know all the sites, the legends, the religions. Whatever the interest, I provide the adventure." He flashed a startling white smile.

He held no instantaneous recognition of me. That he felt a kindred familiarity of me was something, maybe even a tiny last shred of Grey the Ancient. Otherwise, the Gift in him was faded beyond retrieval. All I had to work with was an immediate comfort in one another's company, shared interest in this locale, and a meeting of divine coincidence. I imagined that he would only laugh at my imaginative tale if I were to tell him who he had been once upon a time. Nostalgic sorrow was mine while he smiled.

"I am an honest man, Ms. Ariana," he continued. "My father was British aristocracy. My mother was the youngest daughter of a man whose brother once guarded the Ark in Ethiopia, before it was moved away, that is. I would not bring shame to them."

I put my hand over his and smiled back. At the contact, only the faintest of glimmers touched me. I saw him walking on the terrace of white, though his features were nondescript and blurred and my vision was too weak to bring them into focus. Just imprints of an emotion stained into Time itself—that was all that remained.

"Are you busy this afternoon, Grey? I would like to hire you."

"Let's talk fees." He laughed again.

•

Early that evening, Ryuichi and I walked downstairs to the hotel lobby to find Grey already awaiting us. I had told Ryuichi, "The Gift has fled him. But I'm sure he's the same man Daen mentioned." Neither of us knew whether to celebrate the discovery of him or mourn the memories lost in him.

Grey radiated a human warmth and earthly peace the likes of which Ryu and I could never find in our nearly human, Watcher-corrupted states. He embraced both of us vigorously. "My employers," he declared with enthusiasm, "come. I will show you to the best Mexican restaurant in Cairo. We'll have no trouble at all getting a private booth."

On some level, we envied him.

It was impossible not to slip into an animated conversation with Grey like old friends reunited. Ryuichi and I stole glances at one other, alone in our childlike excitement for our companion. I could tell from Ryuichi's eyes that he was convinced I was right.

"So," Ryuichi continued between bites, "do you ever remember hearing a story about a Roman soldier who was executed in the Nile?"

Grey shook his head slowly. "I don't recall hearing anything like that. Romans. There's of course the Anthony and Cleopatra tale ..."

"... which has been told to death," I added with a laugh of my own.

Grey took a hearty sip of wine. "Well, so I am not dealing with meager amateurs. Ah, something more exotic. I do remember a tale of a Roman soldier who was said to have become a priest. Went against all the rules of propriety."

We hung on his words. "Where was he priest?" I asked.

"Temple of the Moon and Sun, or something like that."

"Sun and Moon," Ryuichi and I corrected in unison.

Grey wiped his mouth with the back of his hand. "So it was, so it was. They say that temple never existed. A myth."

Ryuichi pressed on. "Did you hear anything else about the Roman?"

"Only that he committed a great offense to the goddess Isis. Some say Nephthys. Who knows?"

"It doesn't matter," I explained, "those aspects were one and the same priestess anyway."

Grey set down his glass. "Just who are you people? You're not tourists to be sure." His lively green eyes narrowed slightly.

Ryuichi smiled. "No. We are trying to be, though. We lived here once before, but it was long ago."

I added, "And I'm a writer now."

"Ah." The growing confusion lifted from Grey's face. "A writer. So this is research then?"

"Absolutely," I answered in what really wasn't a lie. "We're looking for any piece of information we can find."

Grey leaned forward in a conspiratorial demeanor. "Well, I don't usually tell clients this part of the story, but I think you'll appreciate it. The story goes that Isis—Nephthys—whoever—was so distraught with the Roman priest's betrayal that she wept out the tears of her heart into the stars where Thoth captured them. He sealed her tears in a box, where they formed words that would become a key to the knowledge. That is, if those who discover them can read their meaning. Egyptologists don't actually think a document like this exists, but who knows?"

My entire body went cold and Ryuichi held my hand painfully tight. "What knowledge would the key open?" he asked.

"That's where things get more mythical," Grey continued. "There are supposed to have been Seven Sages, Builder Gods—I've heard a dozen different names for them. After the great flood of Noah and their separation, they each recorded something in a magnificent book. I don't know what they recorded, so don't ask. Anyway, each book was locked away inside a box of purest gold. The gold box was then placed in a silver box.

The silver box was put inside a box of ebony and ivory, which was placed inside a wooden box. The wooden box was covered in bronze, and then again in a layer of iron. It was all locked up tight with another layer, a seal that supposedly looked like a serpent."

"So there are seven boxes like this?" Ryuichi asked.

Grey finished another bite and nodded. "Seven. Hidden at seven sacred places around the world."

"I think we should start with the key. The document. Could you start researching this part? See what else you can find out. Maybe see where folklore places the Temple of the Sun and Moon?" I asked.

Grey agreed and we parted ways for the evening. But, as Ryuichi and I turned to walk upstairs to our room, Cibrien and Winger rose from their seats on the dusty steps. Newly arrived from the airport, their minds were already turned to topics other than travel. Our connection and the Whispering had flooded back to us with a vengeance after such a short-lived reprieve.

Cibrien uttered darkly, "And I saw when the Lamb opened one of the seals. Behold …"

Winger put his arm around me as we all walked together up to my room. "Seven seals. We were sitting here listening to your discussion," he said. "I don't know how we were, but every word reached our ears as if we were sitting right there next to you."

Cibrien continued, "Here's a theory: it's biblical. Revelation of St. John. End times. Makes a person wonder, doesn't it?"

"The seven seals," Winger said again as he kicked his boots off under the bed. "That doesn't feel right to me. Like this isn't the final end time, just the end of another cycle between now and then. Besides, wasn't Jesus himself the only one found pure enough to open them? We definitely don't qualify, guys."

"Wait a second. In Revelations, God has one book with seven seals on it. There weren't seven separate books," I said.

"Besides," said Ryuichi, "if we wrote the contents of those books, then we have already seen them. How terrible would it be to see them again?"

Layers of the old high priest enfolded Cibrien. "Possibly the plan was to separate the books into seven parts when He separated us. Maybe they're to be brought together into one again, just as we've been."

"As in the heavens, so below," Winger said. "Remember? Maybe there are two sets of seals, two of everything. God has his copy on the nightstand, and we have ours down here."

"It makes no sense," Ryuichi said. "We have it all wrong. It is not about the seals. But at least I get my wish. We get to do something besides Watch."

I rubbed my temples. "The truth is, we don't have a clue what we're supposed to do next. We're just being led along at the moment. Like finding Grey; that was no accident. So we can either sit here and drive ourselves crazy trying to guess the will of the One God, or we can just relax and follow the Whispering. I'm tired."

•

One book, seven books—the details didn't matter. We decided to let the inklings come as they may. We would follow one to the next and see where we were led. Cibrien went with Grey in search of the lost key. Together they sifted through countless piles of artifacts and scrolls to which they gained access only through Grey's connections at the Egyptian Ministry of Antiquities.

While Grey and Cibrien became academic recluses, Winger, Ryu, and I rented horses at a stable near Gizah and rode down the path of the Nile. We stopped constantly to walk near the water in first one direction and then the next for anything on the horizon that might look familiar. As the day wore on, we wore out.

Horsehair clinging to Winger's jeans seemed the most natural occurrence on earth, but for Ryuichi it was particularly unpleasant. Though he had cast aside the stylish clothes of the Japanese gods of rock, the appearance of his shirt and jeans was always classically fashionable somehow. Picking away hair, Ryuichi decided to turn back to the stables early, leaving Winger and me to the search. I hadn't seen Ryu in a mood so foul for many months.

"How long has he been like that?" Winger asked as he watched Ryuichi's horse kicking up dust into the distance.

"A few days. I know, he's really been on edge since we came here."

"Something doesn't feel right. Just now I thought I actually caught a whiff of sulphur. Can you imagine?"

The hair stood up on the back of my neck. "When Daen, Ryu and I were in the pyramid, were you and Cibrien able to see what we recalled?"

"Every second of it. Like watching a movie."

"When I found Daen in the cavern with the Fallen One, there was sulphur in the air."

Winger touched the back of my hand to still me as he strained to listen. "That's what worries me." After a silence, Winger's fingers left my hands. "Seems the Watchers are being watched," he whispered. "I'll be damned."

I thought I sensed with a hearing that wasn't quite physical the distant rustle of something leaving our presence. I wanted to call out words of ceremony and shout, "Be gone!" to the sound that wasn't a sound. I was the lion at the gate once more and the threat of the thing invading my temple had returned to me.

"We can't let Ryuichi leave our sight again," I said.

Winger and I rode fast to the stables, but no matter our pace, Ryuichi had been there and gone.

"Cibrien," I called out silently in fast thoughts, "Cibrien, meet us."

And when we arrived back at the hotel, Cibrien was pacing at the foot of the stairs, consumed with a focused seriousness of intent that Winger and I had never seen.

"I heard you call," he said. "I felt my head would split from the strength of it. And just now our little rock star marched right past me up the stairs without so much as a glance in my direction."

Winger's blue eyes narrowed to slits and his lips drew back over his magnificent teeth. "Ryuichi—" he began, shook his head back and forth, and then bolted up the stairs three at a time while Cibrien and I ran behind him.

Winger threw open Ryuichi's hotel room door and stood there in the entry. "I knew something didn't smell right."

Closed curtains draped the room in darkness and a single light glowed from somewhere inside. The odor of sulphur was nearly visible. Cibrien and Winger stood in the doorway and blocked the room from my view.

Though Cibrien's eyes held warning, I pushed him gently aside. Standing in the center of the room was my

Ryuichi, and in his hand was the shine of a flame balanced above his palm without scorching his flesh.

"Ryu, what are you doing?"

"Priestess, what a strange name you call me. Come, see what I have learned."

Icy fingers tore down my back. Maybe it was the way he held his body or the changed manner in which his facial muscles showed expression, but the Roman in Red, Anubis from my memories looked out through Ryuichi's eyes. He was the same beloved man, but a man who had not yet redeemed himself from his great fall. In fact, he stood poised on the verge of repeating it.

"Roman, extinguish it now," I commanded.

The flame sank into nothingness in his grasp. "I see the High Priest is with you." He nodded deeply and gave a greeting of respect to Cibrien. "Is it not amazing, Priestess? Do you see the power we can achieve?" He was manic in the aftermath of the spell, walking back and forth across the room. His rolling Japanese accent was no more. In its place was a speech so long unheard that it seemed unreal.

Winger addressed him. "Do you remember me?"

"I do not. How is it you enter the temple without the blessing of Nephthys?"

Winger looked to me and back to Ryuichi. "I have the blessing." He shrugged at me and continued, "I am here for training."

Ryuichi drew himself up to full height. "Yes, you have the Gift, but you are not here now—wrong time." He clasped his hands over his ears wincing in pain. "*Yamero*. Make it stop." His familiar Japanese accent lulled across those last words.

"Cibrien," I begged in panic, "do you remember the

rites? Do you?"

Cibrien grasped my hand tightly. "The words escape me, but the will is there. Feel the command strongly enough, and it will flee."

The two of us concentrated while Winger held Ryuichi's arms tightly at his sides. Our prayer flowed over Ryu and bathed the room with protection. There had been a time in history, when a single command from my lips would have been sufficient to send the beast scurrying from our presence. But now so much was lost.

We concentrated with a force that consumed the room until at last we felt the sensation of something shrinking from us, of something slipping backward across the ceiling and into the ether.

Ryuichi collapsed to the floor as Winger caught him under the arms. I raced over to him. "What's happening to you?" I asked. Ryuichi's eyes fluttered open briefly before he slipped into an exhausted sleep. Still, I wasn't certain if the one looking at me was Ryuichi or the person he had been so long ago.

I stayed with him in his room as the moonlight rose and spread across the bed. He was fitful and burned with a sudden fever. I sat beside him and wiped his forehead with a cool cloth, kissing him now and again, and only partially understanding his symptoms.

He spoke inside a delirium, "I would hand you the knife myself this time. I swear I would—just to be here."

"Shh," I soothed, "I'm here. Can you open your eyes?"

He breathed deeply and the olden thought passed through me that the poetry of the universe danced inside him even while he slept. I kissed him again and as his lips began to move against mine, I pulled away.

He smiled. "How far have they gone?"

My fingertips slid down off the edge of the bed. "Who, Ryuichi?" My body refused to move. Air refused my breaths. "How far have who gone?"

He looked at me strangely. "The others, Priestess. Who else could I mean?" He leaned up on his elbows and examined his flesh for a wound he would never find. "Have I slept for so long? Or have you used some healing spell on me?"

"Close your eyes, Roman, and rest. I will return."

Walking as calmly as I could from his view, I shut the door behind me and ran to Winger and Cibrien.

"I can't reach him," I gasped. "He's gone back. I mean he's not here with me." I sank to the floor.

Cibrien studied me for much too long without speaking. "They've taken him back to the place in which he nearly destroyed himself."

Winger sat beside me. "The sulphur. We should have known. there would be enemies to find us."

"I'm scared," I whispered. "I'm really scared. I don't remember how to fight them. Cibrien, we can't even recall the words."

"I can recall some still," Cibrien answered. "Just remember that the more we fear, the stronger they grow. Remember that negative energy becomes a gateway for them. They feed on our anger and our fear, Ariana. This much I know."

"I can't lose him. I won't. And if I have to shove aside all my feelings to get him back, I can do it."

Winger rose first and led us back to Ryuichi who was pacing the floor when we entered the room.

"Priestess, Nephthys, Isis," he greeted. "Forgive me, I know not how to address you." He didn't seem to even see the two men standing in the room beside me.

"Do you know where you are, Ryuichi?" I asked.

"In the middle of Egypt herself. You saw to that." He walked forward and struggled with the want to touch my hands, but refrained from touching the priestess that he saw me to be.

"What year do you think it is, Ryuichi?"

"Why do you address me by that name? Has it something to do with my training?"

I sighed and looked in resignation at Cibrien. "No, my Roman, it does not."

What was I to do with him? He required my full attention back in a life that I longed to see with him, but reality defeated me. He expected training and magic reborn inside him. What were we to do?

It was with relief that I heard him say, "I have lost more blood than I thought. Forgive me, Priestess. I will sleep more now."

Cibrien shook his head. "I can only think that the Fallen Ones couldn't have touched him if he didn't so long for what he lost."

"His mind is stuck, Cib," Winger said. "He's as good as insane right now."

"No," Cibrien answered, "He's not insane. He's just locked inside the Record and we have to get him out."

"I'm worried," I said, "that if I try to remind him of who he is now—if I try to coax him back, he'll get upset. The more upset he gets, the more energy he breeds and the stronger the Fallen Ones grow."

Winger's eyeteeth showed sharply as he tossed his head back in exasperation. "You're right. The more confused he grows, the stronger their hold on him. Just the way they held onto him when the Roman army came back for him. Just the way they sealed his fate in the Nile."

"I can play along with him," I offered. "I remember enough to reenact it all."

"That's dangerous," Cibrien cautioned. "You might slip through the tear in Time's fabric and stay there with him."

"I admit, that doesn't sound all that horrible to me."

"Which is exactly why it's too dangerous."

"Well what am I supposed to do? If I try to talk him back to us, I lose him. If I stay there with him until we figure it out, you could lose me. I'm taking the risk."

Winger's eyes flashed and I put up my hand in protest before he could say a word.

"We don't even remember the rituals," I continued. "At least my way will buy us time to bring some memories back, and if I'm mentally in Ancient Egypt with Ryuichi, and you watch our training, you could bring us both back."

"I was there, too," Cibrien chided. "We'll take turns with him."

Chapter Fourteen

Fingertips slender in the night.
Seeking touches at bloom.
Like bright, mournful petals
The answers fall.

Ryuichi rose now and again from a sleep that was our only blessing. When his eyes opened and he walked the room, he stepped into a world invisible to us. I feared he was fading away from me. Where he saw the holy of holies, we saw merely a dusty rug on the floor of a small hotel room. But mostly, he slept and fought the ungodly force that pulled him backward in time.

At the first opportune moment in which he was alert, I entered his play, an actor on a stage I couldn't see.

"Priestess," he greeted with the long unseen gesture of old that sent shudders through me. "What shall we do this day? Am I to come into your service?"

"No, Roman," I answered as Winger watched my performance. "You have not yet completed your training with the High Priest. You must know this."

"Ah." He laughed aloud and smoothed back the flow-

ing robes that were not there. "Shall we simply walk together this day then? I will meander through the city by
your side and observe the works of Isis."

Winger murmured, "This oughta be good." He
winked at me as I shot him a wide-eyed look of re-
proach.

I backed away as if my legs were pulled back by a
force not my own. "Get Cibrien. I can't do this. I just
can't."

So Cibrien, with an essential lack of desire to return to a time finished for him, stepped into my role on
the invisible stage. He went through the motions with
Ryuichi, in no danger of becoming absorbed into them.
From time to time he would roll his eyes in our direction to remind us just what magnitude of chore this task
was becoming.

"What are we doing?" I asked Winger. "Nothing
makes sense to me. The Whispering is muddled. Grey
keeps delivering notes and maps and stories. There are a
hundred of them. We could dig up half of Egypt and still
not have a clue what we're doing. It's ridiculous."

Winger nodded. "I know. I know, damn it." He put
his arm around me as we made our escape to a nearby café. "We've made up theories about Armageddon,
seals, Watchers ..."

"... and we haven't hit on a single true blue thing,"
I finished. "And what's worse, I think we're losing
Ryuichi."

As we turned the corner, a hand clamped down
on my shoulder. "You two are hard to catch up with,"
gasped the sweetly accented voice. "You glide over these
old cobblestones."

Grey reached high over me and caught open the

door to a small Greek restaurant. "You have to try the baklava. It's heaven."

Winger and I followed his smile to a back table bathed in golden sunlight. Grey's green eyes and dark skin glowed like the rich colors of a fairy tale and it was impossible not to warm to him.

"There is sadness on your face, Ariana. Winger, I can never read his face," he teased, "but yours is so full of sadness."

"Well, Grey. It's just that we've asked you to bring us all this wonderful information, thinking that was the answer. But, a lot has happened and I'm wondering why we're here and what we're supposed to do."

To our dismay, Grey laughed. "People take themselves much too seriously. Sometimes we search so hard for meaning that we can't see we've already found it."

The heavy feeling in my chest was lifting away by the second and Winger nudged my leg under the table.

Grey continued, "Right now is exactly what you're supposed to do. Right now you are among friends. At the end of your life, you will remember what you've experienced and with whom you experienced it. Everything in between is just—details."

"I've been such an idiot," I half-yelled. "Sorry guys, I have something to do. Enjoy the baklava."

I ran back the way I had just come and sought out Cibrien with a vitality I was thrilled to feel again. "We've been so blind," I called out down the hall.

Cibrien greeted me with a finger against his lips. "Quiet. You'll wake up Sleeping Beauty." He tilted his head toward Ryuichi.

"Taking ourselves too seriously. Sins. We've been rolling in a new one—pride. Don't you get it? We've gotten so wrapped up in this grand mission that we've almost become arrogant about it. Oh, poor us. Oh, where has the Whispering gone? Oh why haven't we been given the keys to the universe?" I threw my arm up over my forehead in dramatic effect. "I'm disgusted with us. We've completely forgotten that this is about the will of our old One God. No wonder we're so lost. We've been wallowing in our own sense of self-importance and misery ever since we came back to Egypt." Sin after sin after sin—my old words came back to me.

Cibrien slapped himself on the forehead. "You're right. We haven't behaved well. God's plan will unfold for us. We just threw aside the listening—and our faith with it. We tried to take the power on for ourselves."

His eyes showed that he was greatly disturbed that he had started down a path followed by the Fallen Ones so long ago, that even a High Priest of his training wasn't immune to the corruption.

"We may as well have sent engraved invitations to the Fallen Ones saying, 'Hey, here we are. Pick us off one by one. We're very preoccupied with trying to outguess God and we'll make lovely targets.'"

Cibrien crouched down on his heels for a moment and then bounced up. "Go in and get him, Ariana. Go draw him back. No matter the outcome, it will be right."

Ryuichi himself had said, "... your outcomes are never wrong. They happen exactly the way you plan—if you have any priestess in you still."

The One God spoke to me again and in my mind's eye I saw Winger, protector that he was, spring to his feet inside the Greek restaurant, knowing my intention. I went into Ryuichi's room before my warrior brave could reach the hotel.

The click of the door rang hollow as I shut it against the present, and locked Ryuichi and me away in our nightmare. "Priestess?" he asked.

"Ryuichi, I need you to look into my eyes," I pressed with faith complete once more.

He was still my Ryuichi dressed in a simple shirt and jeans, sitting on the edge of a bed in Cairo. The same strange odor hung in the air and the hum of a quiet vibration touched my hearing ever so slightly.

He looked at me with the glimmer of his soul in his eyes. "Again with that name, Priestess. What part of the training have I missed that this name meets no connection with my understanding?"

For the briefest, darkest, fleeting moment I couldn't see him. In front of me stood my Roman-turned-priest, hair silken and robes flowing with the subtle magic of music and old ways caressing his very being. Oh, to hold onto him, to cling to that beloved image. A whiteout of vibration cloaked the fake image as I shook it from my mind. Was this my heaven or my hell?

"My name is Ariana now and you know me well."

The room shimmered and I fought to focus on Ryuichi's face, tried to force my vision to cling to a feature that linked him to the present century.

"I'm slipping into lunacy," he whispered, sliding his hands against the sides of his head.

"No, my beautiful Ryuichi. You're not." I ran to him and threw my arms around him. "Wake up. Come back to me."

A dull ache clenched my chest. I knew I stood on a pivot in time itself and that the aching was spinning me away with him in a lost direction.

Remember the Fallen Ones, those who are behind

this, I told myself. But when I stood back and looked at the man I held, he was the Roman soldier and I could feel the soft fabric of his garb between the tips of my fingers.

From somewhere behind and beside my Roman, a light began to penetrate the shimmering energy. I stood together with him in the middle of white nothingness as a glow like an orange and crimson fog emerged. I knew immediately what it must be—the eternal flame burning inside the Holy of Holies, the centermost tribute in our temple to the One God. We had knelt together and prayed there, trained there, loved there once.

The temple walls materialized around me, blessedly familiar in all the cool, pale stonework that had been decorated elegantly and without the gaudiness so admired by Pharaoh. A mirror caught the light of the fire in that old trick and illuminated our sanctuary. I felt the thin fabric of my clothing hanging silken around my body. The skin of my arms was dark and smooth with each delicate gesture.

"This period isn't right," I whispered. "1999 has long since passed and the new millennium ..." What was it I thought exactly? "Akashic loop, eradicating reality. In which moment have I landed?"

I breathed deeply of the ancient scents, the spices and the Nile, clean smoke circling up toward the sky. Fine golden threads wove through my robes beside a stream of thinnest purple flowing down each side of the cream-colored cloth, and I could feel it all brush sumptuously against my body. Then I looked up at my Roman and saw that we stood on the stone steps before the altar.

"Forgive me," he had said. And when my sight

cleared, the first image I saw was the look in the eyes of my Roman as his soul reached out through a glance and walked with mine.

His hands twined through my hair, pulling my lips toward his in a kiss that awakened the passions of a priestess the way none other ever could. I embraced and consumed the strength of the Roman as he pulled against me, his body powerful with a soldier's training, his spirit dancing in harmony with and against creation itself.

The agony of need blinded me as he lowered me onto the altar steps. "Until the day I die in this life and in every life after, my heart is yours," he murmured as his fingers slid around my thighs. I knew clearly somehow through this haze of need that I would not relive this sin.

"No." The single word filtered through the air into my ears, though I had not spoken it. "No." Consciousness drifted over me as this word not born from my self, yet carrying such intimate pain, tapped away at my mind.

"Ariana." The muffled voice picked up strength as the Egyptian dress vibrated around my body and the scents of the temple weakened. "Never again. Never!" It was a sharp call shattering a glass veil, a summoning with a greatness of command such as I had never heard.

Daen's strong arms slid under my knees and lifted me to my feet as Ryuichi rose to his own. The glamour of the scene around us dripped away in slow distress, not wanting to be sent back into the void.

Ryuichi and I looked at each other in a recognition not there in previous moments. "Ryuichi?" I asked.

"Yes." He nodded.

Daen grew tall and imposing, forming a glamour of his own and forcing into my mind images of the cemetery statues of archangels and swords. He Who Never Sleeps. The words weren't lost to him —they never had been. He knew the ceremony, had watched me perform it from his hiding place between worlds so many centuries ago. With the force of his being and a spoken language so potent, the shimmering melted. And that sound, that flapping of invisible wings and crawling of lesser things, roared its outrage and shrank from us.

Then all was calm. Should we breathe? Speak? We simply stood again with a frayed carpet and dusty floor under our feet. The hotel room door hung in ragged, wooden shreds from its hinges with Winger and Cibrien just outside.

I turned to Daen. His black hair was damp with perspiration at the temples and his eyes glittered with moisture. I put my hand softly on his forearm. There were no words, nothing ever uttered in all of creation that would suffice.

He pulled me against his broad chest and pressed his face down into my hair. I waved Winger out of the room and he disappeared with Ryuichi and Cibrien from my view.

Daen composed himself and pushed me quietly away. "I couldn't let it happen again."

"Daen ..." I began. I had begun to forget, to underestimate the power of Daen held quietly in check.

He silenced me with a look. "I did it for myself, Ariana. To see it again would have murdered me." He started to reach out for me again and thought better of it, a sign of conscience. Did God's voice reach him once more? "All I ask is that you give me another chance in this life." His voice came warmly, smoothly, and without rage. "I'm crazy about you, you know." He winked, breaking the tightly strained emotion between us.

I laughed now. "I promise nothing."

His eyebrows arched. "We'll see."

•

Ryuichi sat cross-legged in the felucca, its billowing white sails reminiscent of those that haunted our memories. We glided silently down the Nile until finally he said to us, "I have achieved nothing. If Daen hadn't come when he did, we would have repeated the same mistake."

"It was an illusion this time," I said.

Daen stared at Ryuichi intensely. "You know he means that the same intentions were there. The same sins."

Winger looked at the toes of his boots. "Who's to say it was a mistake in the first place. I say it was fate."

Cibrien agreed. "Fate the first time. Games the second. The Fallen Ones just found a snippet of the Record that would trap two of us in lust, and they used it."

Daen snickered, "A broken Record, playing over and over."

I rolled my eyes at him. "Let's not give more energy to this than we should. We're back and we're together. Finally."

Winger's tense muscles told me that he'd either like to stand or toss Daen over the edge. "Whose fault was it that we ever separated in the first place?"

Daen's eyes took on a dull glow. "Why that would be your precious One God's." He gave a signal and the boat's owner steered it back ashore.

"Enough," I commanded.

Ryuichi put up his hand before I could continue. "Yes, it is enough," he whispered.

Unexpected yet so clear how a tone with its simple nuance says more than the words actually spoken. Winger, Cibrien, and Daen all stepped from the boat and stood together awaiting my response, the fallout from dread turned real.

Fear slowly began to creep through against the numbness as Ryuichi took my arm and led me away from them. I prayed silently to God, Jesus, Michael, Gabriel—knowing full well I wished in vain.

"I am going back to Tokyo."

Libra falling from the sky. The balance turned and twisted out of sorts. Had I not dreamt those symbols once? Had I not prayed even then against omens? And yet it had come to pass as though I had no power over it. It was as if I could actually feel the magic, the words of our souls dry up and blow away like grains of sand strewn about the cosmos. Orion's hourglass broken and tilted.

I sank backward, thankful to find a wall behind me. Ryuichi cupped my shoulders with his hands and pressed his forehead against mine, his eyes closed as he spoke.

"I would do anything to have you, Ariana. You know I love you beyond reason," he said.

"Then why have you decided to leave me?"

Still he would not open his eyes. "Because you have had me all along, Priestess." Tears threatened and choked his throat as he opened his eyes to look at me. "But I have never had you."

I wiped the dampness from under his lashes. In all innocence and without intent, I had hurt him so unforgivably. Always in my heart was a tiny core reserved for the role of a Watcher, filled with writings, Whisperings and Daen. Those things consumed that same space Ryuichi needed to occupy. Only I couldn't give it to him, not yet. But at last, our slate was somehow clean. His betrayal in Ancient Egypt and my heart's betrayal of him now made us equal in pain. He would no longer walk in search of forgiveness and I admired the calm new strength I felt in him.

"Settle it with Daen. Settle it," he insisted as he kissed me softly. "I need to find a new dream to follow, but I cannot give you up until I know you are with him."

"And you can't be with me until you know I'm not," I finished. "But I don't think a time will ever come to pass when I'm not with him. I can't see it, Ryu."

He nodded gently, breathing in my words as they left me, twining his hands through my long hair to hold me closer.

"I would shut out the memories if I could," I said. "I would shut the floodgates on the Whispering …"

He silenced me with a kiss that sent an ache of longing through my entire being, missing him before he was gone. Tears streamed in earnest down both of our faces, mingling as I opened my mouth under his. I was inconsolable, spirit crushed with the taste of him on my lips and the touch of his chest under my hands. His last bit of resolve wavered—I sensed that it did, that I could talk him out of his decision with enough force of will. But what kind of selfish, vile creature would I become by doing so?

He searched my eyes with a final gaze meant to capture me in memory, freeze this moment in the Record that he might see it again someday. And then he turned and walked away.

How long I sat on the dirty ground up against that wall, I don't know. After a time, I remember Winger with his protective arms and saddened blue eyes helping me back to the hotel. Always my guardian, my defender. Of us all, Winger kept his role purest. He certainly executed his purpose better than me. Better than Daen. Better than my lost Ryuichi. Of that, I was grateful.

I watched the online Japanese magazines for signs of Ryuichi, and after only a week came the announcement of a new solo single and the possibility of a tour. I craved a picture, a quote, anything in which I might divine a message. There was nothing.

When I had no more tears to give, Daen came to my room and sat on the corner of my bed. I knew that Winger was aware of his visit, but my situation was changed. My blessed friends would now leave me alone with Daen, alone without intervention or advice though I knew the pull to intercede must be strong in them. They hadn't said so, but I suspected their opinions of Daen still mirrored Ryu's.

"Grey stopped by today," Daen said. "He's got Winger and Cibrien on an archeological dig."

"I'm sure the timing worked out well."

The expression in Daen's dark, dark eyes begged me to look at him. "Ariana ..."

"I don't know my own heart anymore. Do you have any idea how amazing that is to me? I've run on instinct and that little voice from the One God my entire existence, and now I'm met with confusion when I listen inside myself."

Daen said quietly, "Irony is wicked sometimes. The Voice has been silent in me for so long, I wondered if I'd imagined it all along. But one night in a pyramid with my rival and I suddenly begin to hear music in the stars again."

"I'm weary all the way through," I told him. "I don't know what to tell you that I haven't already said, but I have hope for you. I always have."

He brushed the back of his hand across my cheekbone. "I have to admit that the little pop-star surprised me. I didn't expect him to concede defeat."

"Defeat? This isn't sport. I'm not the blue ribbon prize."

Daen's eyes glimmered like light striking pools of ink as he pushed himself back off the bed. "The hell you're not." He did look imposing when drawn up to his full height. "You're the only prize I've ever seen in all of creation that was worth competing for."

I rose to my feet, refusing to be towered over. "I wish I could hate you. But even when you say something as arrogant and male as that, I can feel the source. I know the meaning even when the words obscure it."

"That's because we're bound, my love. Bound and tied and molded together by heavenly inspiration. We just got so far off track that you can't recognize it anymore."

I was properly, unreasonably angered and glad for it. Any feeling at all was preferable to the void I'd felt since Ryuichi left.

"We didn't get off track. You are the one who took yourself outside the cycle. You are the one who flew in the face of the One God and the angels and my entire purpose."

I held his intense gaze for long moments, taking great satisfaction in knowing I was probably the one person on the face of the earth who could do so. I wanted to raise my voice, wanted him to yell back condemnations about the Roman soldier on the altar steps and fight until I came alive again.

Instead he bent down and whispered in my ear. "Oh no, Ariana. I'll not be the tool by which you pry yourself out of this slump. You shake this inconvenient little mood aside for yourself and when you're up to it, find me. Call my name and I'll be there." His hair smelled faintly of cinnamon and rainwater. How was it so that even his very scent held on over the centuries?

I made a sound of exasperation low in my throat and wished desperately for something to throw at him as he walked toward the door.

"Daen?" I yelled.

He turned and raised an eyebrow at me.

"Damn it. I'm calling you now."

•

I was both uneasy and pleased to be alone with Daen. The sound of the road under my feet, the blur of his shadow touching the ground beside me—it all induced the excitement of unknown adventures unfolding. I nearly laughed at the impression of anything about Daen seeming new to me. Being with him was like coming home again after a great, winding journey.

We walked around Cairo, the maze of narrow streets never ceasing to give us new routes to explore. We were terribly powerful together when we chose to be, and sometimes even when we weren't aware. Our combination parted crowds in our path so we could move freely. Street vendors hesitated with their sales pitches and invariably approached whoever walked behind us. Over the years, I had forgotten the impact, the dark effect …

Daen was always careful not to touch me, and I knew anger toward Ryuichi bubbled inside him. Though we spoke very seldom at first, sometimes I sensed that Daen would like to dunk me in the Nile and baptize me clean of Ryuichi's touches, few and limited as they had been. He wondered if only then would he be able to take my hand or pull me close without sensing some imprint of Ryuichi there.

I continued to search the Internet for Ryuichi in the evenings. He had started his own Web site with its contents in complicated *kanji*, Chinese characters, which I couldn't begin to read the way I could the phonetic characters of the Japanese alphabet. I ran my hand over my laptop's screen trying to pick up a sense of meaning, but still there was nothing. The farther he delved into his revived solo career, the faster he slipped from me. How I hungered to go to him and stop our disintegration.

Daen and I rented a car and set out across the desert to Mt. Sinai. It was as if we had been transported back across time ten years to those days before he left without a word, to that year of suggestion and shadow when I had longed only for the concrete. Here we sat again, side by side in a private symphony of souls. If a strong emotion swept through me, he felt it. If a thought truly consumed him, I heard it. The connection so finely tuned was no less for our separation. Made from the same bit of ether, we had used to think. My mortal mind spun. I simply couldn't reconcile my bond to Daen with my attachment to Ryuichi, nor was I willing to debate it.

"You've thrown up a block." Daen shot me a piercing look.

"Gotta have privacy from time to time," I answered.

His knuckles grew pale around the steering wheel. "I don't. Fire away. Ask me anything you desire."

"I wouldn't know where to begin." My voice seemed to trail away strangely, even to my own hearing. The wind picked up the sand quickly and whipped it upward with the same whirling energy I felt inside. Child of Water, Child of Wind …

"Wind and water. I caught that much," he said. "Care for a little rain?"

"Let's not play there, Daen. I'll take your invitation. I want to know about something Winger told us not so many weeks ago."

"Ah," Daen began. "You want to know about the wolf. It's simple, Ariana. I took my spirit and I entered it into the animal."

"But why?"

He smiled and shrugged. "Whyever not?"

"You murdered my brother."

"Animals are not capable of murder. Only human creatures do that." He paused with thoughts I couldn't hear, then continued, "It was fascinating really. There was no pull of conscience, no decision-making behind an action. My whole existence was pared down to what was true and real. In the most primal fiber of my being, Winger had to go from you."

"If you had no control over your action, how could you have targeted Winger and spared me?"

"Some shred of love, some essence of it for you. I don't know really. Nowhere in my life's energy is it written that I should hurt you. I don't believe myself capable of it."

"Then you were still responsible, even as the animal." Then a slow realization crept over me. "Daen, you said you lost the pull of conscience when you were in that wolf's body."

"Yes."

"That means you still have the pull other times?"

"I suppose."

"That's where God Whispers—there inside a human conscience."

"Don't get your hopes too far up. No creator makes a thing without leaving something of himself in it. That's all I feel, I think. Just the leftover pieces of Him inside me."

I smiled in spite of myself. "Come back inside the cycle for real, Daen. I believe you're salvageable if you do."

"You make me sound like a damaged car part." His strangely indefinable accent loosened and rolled when amusement relaxed him.

"I'm serious."

"Oh, I know you are," he said.

"Live out this life. Die a natural death. Don't take your spirit out of its proper dimension—and then go where I go."

"Ariana, my love, if I were to die I don't think I would be directed to the same place as you."

"So what's your plan? To continue on as He Who Never Sleeps?"

Daen raised his black brows nonchalantly. "Why, yes."

I squeezed my eyes shut tightly and opened them again. "New subject," I suggested.

"What can you possibly ask that you don't already know about me really?"

"Tell me what happened when you hit the Yucatan—

after the boats had carried us apart during the flood."

Daen gazed forward at the road ahead for a while, not knowing where to begin I suspected, not wanting to stir up the anguish I knew accompanied such memories.

"We struck land in a place that looked as if no man had ever existed," he said. "The weeds and plants were like a wall between the ocean waters and the land. But, I was strong. So were the others who had climbed aboard my ship as it drifted away."

"Other Watchers?"

"Other Watchers who began to fade and sleep aboard that very same boat, forgetting so quickly. I think they were never part of the core. They were disposable in their roles, I believe—like Grey. I realized that the One God never worked his power through most of them the way He had through you and me.

"Anyway, how we were not weakened by the long voyage is purely His mystery. Mere unprotected humans would have died from so many weeks at sea without food or water. So, we cut through the flora, climbed over rocks, and came upon a village so primitive it was laughable. None of the advances from our ringed island had touched this world.

"Picture their faces when they saw me emerge from the jungle. My beard and hair had grown long and gone very, very white. You remember my eyes were blue then, and the contrast to their own eyes was striking. They were a wiry little folk—all withered like leathery raisins from the sun, dark-haired, dark-eyed. And I was white skinned. They thought I was a god. Perceptive group, come to think of it."

I shook my head. "You set them straight, right?"

"How could I? And why should I have? It's not like I was given the power to communicate in their strange language right out of the boat. They threw down their sticks and spears, and knelt on the ground at my feet. When I touched one of them or tried to speak to one, he would fall prostrate. Face down right into the dirt just because I acknowledged him.

"I let them feed me and give me shelter, but how could I live in conditions like that? I'm talking caves, huts … Things definitely had to change, so I started teaching them."

"What did they call you?" I asked.

"Quetzalcoatl at your service." He laughed. "At least that was one of my names I ended up becoming in later eras. I'm not sure what I was called while there—some variation of the same."

"You didn't stay?"

"I did. For a while. I had promised that for this last time, I would teach and spread the wisdom of the One God. Doing it out of self-preservation just made the role all the easier and the first thing I needed was some real food.

"These people lived on what they could grab off trees or club in the head. Snake is not a tasty appetizer and I don't care for berries. I found a few kernels of maize on the floor of the boat and planted them. They'd already gotten pretty adept at carving spears and digging out pit traps for animals, so meat wasn't an issue. I sent a few of the Watchers off into the wilderness to see what they could find, and by the time the corn crop was starting to grow, they had returned with all sorts of unusual seeds. Fruits mostly. We could plant fruit."

I pictured Daen in flowing robes and sandals, tilling

the earth and finding calluses on his palms for the first time.

"After what we had been, it was hard to start anew. I remember. I had to do the same thing in Egypt. I wonder what they came to call me after I left," I mused.

Daen nodded his head. "You probably gave birth to a new goddess for the history books. I'm sure you were more deserving of the title than I was. I taught to better my existence. You taught to better civilization, to civilize the ignorant."

"Was that a stab at humility I just heard?"

"More like my recognition of you, Ariana." He looked at me with those black, black eyes and continued, "It took one night in particular for me to realize I was doing His will in spite of my self. I had intended the destruction of our island to be my last service. But, when the crops started to grow and they understood that I was bringing a new source of food, they all gathered and built a bonfire in the middle of their village. They wanted to thank the resident god for his generous miracle.

"I remember the moon in the sky and the crackling of the wood on the fire. And then the screams started. They dragged this girl in front of me with arms bound behind her. Her long hair was caught up in one of their fists so that when he pulled back, her throat was exposed to the blade. Exciting in a perverse way. A dark part of me wanted to see what would happen if they ran the knife across her flesh, but the greater part of me won out over that impulse.

"She was beautiful with arms and legs sleekly muscular, body glistening with oil in the firelight. She made me ache for you, Ariana. I craved you in a way I had never imagined possible. I had fallen so far down into the flesh that human desires were finally bursting through me with reckless abandon. If you had been near me in that instant, I would have thrown you to the ground and taken you without a second thought. You would have had no defense. I was no better than primal for a moment.

"With all these new emotions surging through me, I lunged to my feet and yelled out for them to stop. I tossed the knife away and did the only thing I could think to do. I reached out, removed the flower they had tucked behind her ear, and took it for my sacrifice instead of her blood.

"They tore down their sacrificial altar the next morning just to appease their local god. I'd seen the blood-stained stones just outside the huts before, but I'd never realized they were used for more than cleaning out whatever animal they killed on the hunt."

I breathed in deeply. Dusk was falling across the desert road and Daen turned on the headlights. "You changed their entire system of worship with one action."

"My insane lust for you drove me to react so strongly. Ironic, isn't it? Sin driving out another sin.

"The next miracle happened during harvest. When I was showing the tribe how to reap, I noticed something shiny in the soil, a sparkle in the black sand that separated itself along the edges of streams. Little specks of glitter here and there. That's when I realized I had been living atop a wealth of gold and silver. Metals to build with. Metals to forge finery, eating utensils—all those things I'd sorely missed."

Daen's tone changed. "I think I see the monastery up ahead, so I'll make a long story shorter than I'd planned. After I found all that silver I also realized how much rock was around the place. I put all my energy into building a respectable city amidst the granite and vines. Step temples and pyramids to rival the ones we'd had before. Houses with a system of running water and sleeping arrangements that got people up off their dirt floors. You should have seen how artistic these people became once they had the knowledge. And I even got people to start bathing just by doing so myself. My surroundings were starting to feel comfortable, but every time I stopped building and teaching, my mind went back to you. Ariana, you have no idea what our separation did to me."

"I do know, Daen. I tapped into that part of the Record once." Had I ever heard such honesty from him? At last he shed the attitude and revealed himself in the open for me.

"With all the unlikelihood of actually finding you, still I had to try. My soul screamed for you and when I closed my eyes at night, I could see you. Sometimes the color of the clothes you wore sprang into my mind. Sometimes it was something you held in your hands. You created so much when you landed in Egypt that first time. I was in awe just watching how you could wield such creative force and never claim it for your own."

"Creation was never ours, Daen. You know that. Everything we did and can do now as Watchers is the result of a gift from the One God. The old teachings taught us so. The power is His to grant or withhold."

Daen steered the rattling little car up to the outside wall of the monastery and turned off the engine. "You almost make me want to find faith again, my love. Almost."

We stepped out of the car, enfolded by night and thankful to stretch our legs in the coolness. Beyond the monastery in which we would stay was Mt. Sinai itself with the same soil and rocks that had once rolled under the feet of Moses. Within the earth-toned building, encircled by a low stone wall was the plant alleged to be the burning bush.

I pointed the bush out to Daen as we walked past. "That plant leaks an oil that has been known to burst into flames under the desert sun. Something so rare is the perfect backdrop for a divine vision. Can you imagine?" I spoke in whispers, not wanting to disturb the sacred stillness around us.

Daen set his jaw grimly. "I prefer not to imagine any more. My reality with your One God was enough."

Our hosts led us quietly to a single room with two small beds and no bathroom.

"They think we're married," Daen said. "Or they wouldn't have tossed us in here together."

For a moment, I saw an image of Winger's face. He was out on a dig with Grey and Cibrien, yet he knew as he always did whenever I slipped into a questionable situation. I willed one of our inexplicably fast "angel thoughts" to him, trying to relay that I was fine, that Daen was the consummate gentleman he'd promised to be.

Daen tossed his bag down on one of the beds and looked at me strangely. "I felt that," he said. "Warrior with his Gift of the Wolf —just an overprotective voyeur, if you ask me. Not even he could drive fast enough to protect you from my evil advances if I made any."

I nodded absentmindedly and set my own bag down

on the floor. The old stirrings were taking shape in me, prompted by the click of the door to our single room. I remembered the medieval bed with its carved posts and fur coverlet. *I for you, you for me, twining through eternity.* The careless words of a childhood poem reached my mind. An iron gate swung open to a rose garden. I saw the silky veil of the bed curtains wave in a draught that flowed in through a loose shutter.

Walking down the hallway to the bathroom, I physically shook my head to clear the rich images. I took care to keep my eyes wide open in the hot shower. Should I close them, the memories might come back—or even worse, I might open my mind to Daen while undressed. I thought of Ryuichi and immediately an empty sadness swept over me as if something were missing that I had not yet discovered gone.

When I entered the room, Daen was already inside. He lay stretched out on his bed, his body taking the full length of it as he rolled over onto one side and propped himself up on one elbow to watch me. He wore only the loose bottoms of his blue and white striped pajamas. Bare from the waist up, the dim lighting in the room glowed against his tan skin. He looked like a bronze sculpture, carved to perfection, designed for my eyes alone. I brought the warning from my long-ago vision to my mind, even though it didn't apply to him. *Do not look upon him. Do not look ...*

Daen rolled onto his back, put his hands under his head, and laughed with great feeling. "You know you're in trouble when you have to recite mantras to keep yourself in check. Where did you get that little caveat from anyway?"

I crawled under my covers and considered for a moment before answering. "It was what the general told me just before they executed my Roman."

Daen rolled back up onto his elbow and peered intensely at me through the darkness. "No, he didn't."

I sat up in my bed and looked at him. "What do you mean? I heard him myself."

"You must have heard someone else say that. The general never said a word."

A shiver shook through my shoulders and rippled across the back of my neck. As I had told the others, I would know a lie coming from Daen. I knew in my very soul that I would. And there was only truth around him.

"I don't understand what you mean."

"Ariana, I watched them toss the bastard into the river. You looked at the Roman filth once and walked off. Those soldiers never said a word to you and no one else was around."

I felt ridiculous, stinging tears swell up and blur my vision. "You were watching in spirit form, Daen. Did you say it to me?"

"No, love. It wasn't me." His voice was genuinely gentle as he felt a wave of my pain strike his chest.

Daen slipped into the bed beside me and pulled me tight against him while I sobbed. I wanted to say things about eternal love never being denied, about the beauty I thought I knew in Ryuichi's soul. For the first time I had to admit that even I could never see the innermost part of Ryuichi's heart. But my spirit ran close enough to his to recognize the flaws he would enjoy acting on and the distance he still had to climb. Somewhere in me grew an inkling that during all my closeness to him, I had been protected by more than Winger.

There was only one answer, the only thing I knew to

be true. That simple warning so strongly felt—it was the voice of the One God speaking to that place deep inside me. It could have been none other, unless the Fallen Ones had spoken, watched me as long ago as my trip to the Japanese music store. I hadn't sensed them there, hadn't caught the scent of sulphur. But would I have recognized it then?

Daen kissed my hair and whispered, "Do you remember the old lesson, Ariana? One knows the nature of a tree by its fruits." He looked into my eyes. "So with man and his actions."

Chapter Fifteen

*Wind laughed and whipped
the sands without permission
slipped from the tower.
Fallen Ones pushing
the tides of time.*

I awoke at four o'clock AM, innocently as it's possible to do when nestled in Daen's strong arms and breathing in the cool magic in the Sinai air. Daen awoke with the same heartbeat as me, with the very same breath as if our bodies were one.

"Raison d'etre," he murmured against the top of my head.

"What?" I asked quietly.

"Reason for living, more or less."

I kissed the back of his hand as his arms held me tighter. "When you say such things to me, it's hard to think of anything else."

"Ariana, all the love I've ever felt or given has been meant for you."

I sighed and pushed a wave of feeling toward him. I needed to explain to him the intimacy, the connection, the longing and the poetic beauty I felt for Ryuichi. I needed him to feel how right I felt at that moment in his arms and how torn to shreds my heart was because of it.

"Thank you for that. It helps me." He wrapped his long fingers around my hand. "You have many mates to your soul. You will love them all and they will all love you exquisitely. I'll bet you don't realize that when we look into your eyes we see a mirror of ourselves, hints of God, scenes of our history kept locked inside you—and we see such stunning beauty in the secrets of your soul that it nearly kills us to not have you with us in some way. But each of us is drawn to you in a different way and when one of us mistakes the nature of his way ..."

"You think that's what I've done with Ryuichi? Mistaken him for something he should never have been to me?"

"And what he's done with you. The two of you were lovely together so long ago. Before lust crept into him, you shared music in the stars and poetry in the seasons."

"I miss that so much."

"I don't know how to get that back for you, Ariana. Just remember that with all that ties you to Ryuichi, it's nothing compared to what we share. It's not even close."

Just as I had done for him, Daen pushed a current of emotion back to me and I accepted it. Golden and full of light came a sentiment straight and pure from the heart of him. The sensation of his love wrapped around me with a passionate, familiar sincerity that knocked the breath from me. I was suddenly aware of the scent of his skin so unchanged over the centuries.

"Daen." I closed my eyes with a tremble. "We need to get out of this bed. Please. Now."

We showered, dressed in layers, and began our hike

up the face of the mountain long before the sun started to rise. The hike must have continued for hours, but I didn't notice. With each step I sunk into a deeper state of thought, my mind revisiting each touch Ryuichi had ever given, each word spoken. The brilliance of him was without question to me. The Gift I had seen in him was true and real, the Whispering strong.

He was as we Watchers had all become when we entered humanity. We were tempted and imperfect. We came in shades of gray sometimes. But Ryuichi's betrayal, no matter the reason behind it, had also been as real as his love for me. We were not the villains in this game we played—no more so than any human at least. Not villains, only the once glorious Watchers who slowly fell asleep in the flesh and now fought to awaken. Each of us stood from time to time on the edge of being lost or of finding new blessings.

Daen and I sat together in silence at the top of the mountain and watched the sun come up in the horizon. We slipped back into that silent knowing we had redeveloped ten years before, but this time it held a completeness and comfort. I had found my concrete proof of Daen and for once, didn't long for the words to be spoken aloud.

We drove back to Cairo that same day. The journey was a long one with scenery that changed little over the hours. I slept off and on, waking to study Daen's profile. Even after the time we had spent together, some part of me still registered disbelief that I could truly be looking at the curl of his dark lashes or the perfectly masculine face that made him seem invincible.

I saw Winger summoning me as best he could. He wasn't strong in that way, but knew I always saw him clearly and waved me homeward with a thought. Cibrien sat beside him, lending his strength to the summons from their camp atop the sandy earth.

"They've found something," I told Daen. "Something important."

Daen nodded. "Any idea what? The choices are many in this country."

The sending faded from me. "No. I can't find them again so soon. But Winger says we need to get back."

"You mean he says you need to."

I sifted through the message Winger had just sent. "No—I think he wants you there, too."

"Far be it from me to deny Wolf Boy his request. We'll get back to the hotel in Cairo fairly late. How about we sleep there tonight and go out to the dig site in the morning?"

•

I slept like the dead and so the morning came all too soon. I sensed that Daen still slept deeply in the next room at the same hotel. I hated to wake him. He would need all his energy to face Winger and Cibrien together at the dig. My laptop sat on the table across from the bed daring me to turn it on. I had avoided Ryu's abandoned room, but the need to feel some small part of him again was great.

I went to his Web site and found samples of the five songs on his new "maxi-single" there. Pieces of his thoughts, telltale signs of his life always found their way into his songs, I thought. He had invited and beckoned to me once through his mastery of this art. He could move me to tears with a note and trigger a memory with a word.

With a click, I downloaded the first song and listened

as the music streamed to my ears. My chest pounded with anticipation and then I grew numb just as quickly. Could this be my Ryuichi? The familiar magic in his music was lost and the lyrics fell with a din on my ears. Where was the man I knew in this dreary mix of notes? One after the next I listened to his fingers coolly striking piano keys, to his fluid voice calling out meaningless language in a higher key than he had ever used with Ashes of Roses. It was all so unnatural and scarcely him.

I flipped off the power switch and sat back. I hadn't even bothered to check the online gossip magazines for fear of what I might find. No one other than Daen would completely understand the disturbance in me that Ryuichi's vacant music had generated. I simply could not feel the darkly poetic allure I had grown so used to in his music. No message. No Whispering. No life left in that one, select area of temple training he had mastered. I feared for him, missed him.

When we were ready, Daen and I drove to the campsite from which Winger had summoned. "You never finished your story," I said. "What happened to you after you starting building a city for the tribe?"

"As I said, I started seeing you everywhere. And so I set out to find you like I'd promised."

"In the boat? What about supplies?"

"Yes, we repaired the boat. Patched the sails. Filled it with necessities. Several of the Watchers stayed behind. Only two others accompanied me. The women in the city wept as the wind caught the vessel. The air caught the sound of wailing and carried it over the waves to me. I could still hear it even after the shore was gone from view.

"But I'm tired of storytelling, Ariana. It takes something from me to bring sound to words so casually this way."

"You never reached me, Daen."

"No. We set sail in the right direction, but the confusion set in somewhere along the way and we took a turn to the south instead of the north."

"Where did you end up?"

"We came ashore near a great mountain range and began another adventure of teaching and building. Smelled of sublime influence, the whole thing did. Divine deception. Again I was the god among men and again I left—alone this time because I knew what I had to do."

Grayed ocean waters and the red morning sky passed through my mind. When the rocking overtook the boat that evening, Daen had not been in his body through that ancient technique we all knew and never imagined to use for such a purpose. He had slipped outside the cycle at that very instant and watched the sea erase his last connection to it. Daen had been true to his word.

As we came upon the site from which Cibrien, Grey, and Winger had beckoned, wind whipped the sand up against our car and we sat there until the abrasive flurry passed.

"Did you do that?" Daen asked.

"No." A sense of unease passed through us. At the mouth of a tunnel dug down into the earth, a set of pale green tents fluttered and jumped. Digging tools, once propped upright against the sides of vehicles, slid with a thud to the ground. "I have the sense we're being greeted."

We waited inside the car until Winger appeared at

my window and knocked his fist against the glass. With a cloth pressed against his nose and mouth, he waved for us to get out and follow him into the tunnel.

We ran inside after him, shaking the loose sand from our hair. Winger pulled away the cloth and said, "I'm glad you came when you did. We don't have much time to talk."

"Why?" I asked as we followed Winger down the hole into an excavated room where Cibrien awaited.

Daen sniffed the stale air and narrowed his eyes at the former High Priest. "Where's Grey? Wolf Boy here eat him?"

Cibrien looked as if he were tempted to unleash his wickedly sarcastic temper on Daen and then pushed the urge aside. "Grey went back to Cairo. Wouldn't stay. He said he felt evil in the room after what we found."

"Or what found us," Winger corrected.

Cibrien moved crates around the room in a semi-circle and gestured for us to sit. "We'll have to remember the temple training. Remember that only the One God is omniscient. Devils aren't. One can't be with all four of us at once and they can't know a thought blocked tightly in our hearts. And remember the lesson you once taught so well, Ariana. Know to bring up a defense without anger or fear so that it doesn't breed dark energy and invite more evil to us."

I had so often seen the youthful, obnoxious side of Cibrien reborn in this body that to witness my old friend's priesthood surface came as a jolt to my senses. But he couldn't have been more serious.

Daen breathed in the air again and looked into my eyes. "I think they're saying we need to brace ourselves." The stench of sulphur burned past us so quickly that I wondered if it had really been there. Then the sound of sand grains cracking underfoot filled the small room.

"So they made it."

We turned to see a woman at the entrance to the site. Bright red hair, silky and straight, hung far down her back. Very slender and almost timid, she moved her body toward us quietly until she was close enough for me to look into her light gray eyes. Was that the Gift I saw there? Or was it something else designed to appear as it?

"Ariana," she said in a soft voice, "I'm Tiran. I've been waiting for you."

I stretched out my hand to shake hers, but she seemed to genuinely not see my gesture as she turned too eagerly toward Daen. She made no effort to touch him, nor did he her. She quickly turned back to me.

"I thought there would be one more of you," she said in that calm, airy tone she struggled to maintain.

"Whatever could you mean?" I asked.

She narrowed her eyes at me. "Oh, I mean I thought there were five of you on this dig."

Winger stood. "Well, you did meet our guide, Grey. He would count as number five, now that you mention it." He was masking Ryuichi's name, blocking him entirely from this woman, this Tiran. I did the same and to my great surprise, felt Daen immediately follow suit.

"I meant five in addition to Greythorne." She smiled prettily. "But I see I was mistaken."

Cibrien rose to his feet to stand beside Winger. "Tiran here heard about our research and thought she would come by to introduce herself, offer her archeological services."

Winger bared his fangs as he leaned back to study

her with a smile. "We do appreciate your dropping by. Daen and Ariana have just come off a long drive, so I hope you'll understand ..."

"Say no more," Tiran interrupted. "I just wanted to say hello to the rest of the group. Have a great evening." She gave a small nod and disappeared back out the passageway.

We waited without breathing until we heard the sound of her car's engine fade in the distance, and then we all let out a collective sigh.

"Friend of yours?" Winger asked with a snarl in Daen's direction.

"Bite me, Mountain Man," Daen responded coolly.

"She looks so innocent," I said. "But the aura around her is controlled, threatening even. What is she?"

Cibrien hopped back on top of his crate and sat cross-legged. "Did you get a small sense of the Gift at first?" he asked me.

I nodded. "I did, but I wonder if it was a glamour."

Cibrien mulled over the possibility and said, "I lean toward two choices. First, she's just a local archeologist who has been attacked and possessed by a demon-type trying to imitate us. Or second, she's a former Watcher who has forgotten who she was, got curious, turned ... I don't know."

"Or," Daen said, "she's something else." He crossed his arms over his broad chest.

Though he kept his emotions hidden, I touched my hand to his wrist to calm him. That misty, electric energy the bunch of us generated together began to dance in colors around the cave-like room.

"She's somewhat like I am now, but I don't know how she did it. Or how they did it, I guess." Daen laughed a little. "Damn."

Winger breathed in through his nose. He never had much patience for those in whom he placed no love. "Spit it out."

"I think one of the Fallen Ones has possessed a body so perfectly that its natural soul has been virtually pushed aside. Except she achieved this recently—when the soul was fully in place in an adult body. Nothing like I would have done. Or could have. That body must be around thirty or so. Same as us."

Cibrien listened without expression. "So how do we exorcise it? How do we cast it out?"

Daen chuckled. "Cast out the demon of a perfect possession? Good luck. The victim would have had to be willing. She wanted it."

Winger grinned. "We can always kill it."

Daen held his gaze. "You could try. You don't get it though, do you? For a Fallen One to have taken hold, it must have been invited. And not long ago, either. It moves awkwardly inside the woman's body, as if the flesh makes it clumsy still. Why don't we try to cast it out and see what happens? Could be fun."

Winger looked at me with his ice-blue eyes. "How you can listen to this son-of-a-bitch and still think there's some shred of redemption left for him is beyond me."

Daen interrupted, "Heard of mercy? I've been told it's a cornerstone of your belief system."

"Don't start down this road," I warned them. "I can't stand for another of us to run or be forced out, regardless of his current popularity."

Cibrien said, "My concern is what to do when Ti-ran comes back. She doesn't know about Ryuichi and she doesn't know how much we remember. For all she knows, we have snippets of intuition and maybe a dream here and there. But, we could be as asleep as Grey is."

"And we can't dig while she's here, but we can't not dig either. It would make her suspicious," Winger added.

I breathed in deeply just to be sure some telltale trace of sulphur didn't hang in the air before I spoke.

"What scares me most is that I know she has to be in contact with other Fallen Ones. Sure, they can't read minds, but they certainly can hear what we say out loud."

Daen nodded. "I know them, and I wouldn't be so quick to bet they don't know about your pop star. Remember his little slip through time back in the hotel room? Think he got that way all by his lonesome? They're just wondering where he is. That's all." He paused and clenched his jaw. "They'll be visiting soon. Count on it."

"Of course they will," Cibrien agreed. "We're not exactly Watchers anymore—we're humans with Watcher knowledge. And when they see humans strong in good spirit, they think they've found a great prize to corrupt for their side."

That we were under attack or soon would be was a certainty. But, the question circling through my mind was, which Fallen One had become flesh in Tiran? One of such strength as to lure Daen, like the one named Rosier? I remembered that name strongly. Something of a higher order, a more powerful ilk? Something lowly and fit only for spying?

"Delicate sensibilities aside," Daen began, "if she gets in the way, we could kill her without moral repercussion. I know how much you all care about that."

For once Winger nodded. "It's just a body filled with one of those things. Not like we'd be murdering." His voice trailed off like a breath, transformed into a semi-echo in the room. "And I don't think I'd have been too fond of her anyway."

Daen sat down hard on one of the small crates and rested his forearms on his knees. "So what could make Negoso Greythorne run scared? Wasn't Tiran, was it?"

"Nope." Winger bent down and lifted a dusty gunny-sack off the ground from between the crates. "We found this."

Cibrien chuckled to himself. "It was inside a plain stone box with a curse on the seal."

I shook the reason for Grey's fear aside once I realized what it was. "We always did that thing with the curses." I waved my hand to brush away any doubt hanging in the air. "Kept the unworthy away."

"Except for now," Daen muttered dimly under his breath as Winger lifted a tablet out of the bag Cibrien held.

Our eyes narrowed as we gathered tightly around Winger, struggling to absorb every detail of the carved relief at once. I scarcely believed something that sprung from what could have been only yesterday to me, was now balanced in Winger's hands as a dusty relic from so long past.

"Cib, it's one of yours," I whispered.

"I know."

Cibrien ran his hand along the tablet, across the figures of two goddesses side by side, one of darkness and malice, the other of light and life.

"I had art in me then," he said, "sculpting and painting. Shapes, colors, measurements, vision … That was my mastery. I wonder is it still?"

"But what does it mean? This carving, I mean." Winger grew impatient—he so rarely did with Cibrien.

"It's ironic that this should be the piece that found its way back to me," Cibrien answered, "because it shows something I'd long since forgotten. See the goddess on the right? Music, colors, beauty—they're all hers. But the one on the left? She sees none of these."

Winger shoved the tablet back into the bag and set it on the ground. "Can you see colors, Daen?" He folded his arms across his chest and waited, blue eyes flashing eerily in the dusk.

"What I see or do not see is none of your damn business."

"Speak, you son of a—"

Daen smiled brilliantly, wickedly. "You first. I'll make you a deal, Wolfie. You tell them what happened when Ariana and the artist formerly known as Roman Rubbish stayed behind in Japan. Tell them what happened when you tracked me. You tell that, and I'll answer your question for all to hear."

I think we all waited for some sign of an expression to cross Winger's face, the movement of a single muscle, the twitch of temptation in fingers that longed to reach for his knife. But there was nothing to read. Even the eyes that shone too blue were quickly shielded from all emotion.

"Maybe you'll both be ready to tell these things someday," I said as softly as I could. "But not today." I took Daen by the hand and walked with him to the opening of the room where we paused by the makeshift steps. "Think you guys can get Grey out of hiding?" I asked.

Cibrien nodded and stared after us as we disappeared up the stairs to the sandy world outside.

"I don't like this division," I said to Daen once we were safely inside the car.

"I don't mind it. You and I aren't divided. Who cares about the rest of them?"

"I do. And so do you, I think."

He sighed and reached to turn the key in the ignition. "I do see colors, Ariana. Sometimes. I did vividly at the beginning. But that evening when the sea swallowed my boat and I took myself beyond its grasp, that's when the colors faded away. Except when I come near you. Then the world is vibrant again. And sometimes, ever since that night at the pyramids when the Music let itself be heard, the colors slip back for no reason at all."

"Thank you for sharing that."

"You'd have guessed it anyway." He turned away from me for a moment, gazing out the car window across the endless mounds of sand that surrounded the small opening to the dig site.

"It's interesting, isn't it? When a feeling goes away, we say it fades. Just like a color. The color of our emotions goes away."

"Not if 'our' is us. If I were poetic—the colors of our love never fading … Might be worth writing down." His voice trailed off low and deep.

"What happened between you and Winger?" I would ask but once, then never mention it again.

As I thought he would, he replied, "That's not for me to tell."

"Ok then. What about music in general? How does it sound to you?"

"I hear it. I appreciate some of it. But they can't, my

love. They can't. When the notes blend beautifully like a dance of sound, it escapes them. Yet some types of music you might find unpleasant, those they can follow."

"Must be grim to be them."

"You've no idea," he said. The gold flecks in his black eyes looked like pure light sinking into great depths.

"No," I agreed, "I don't. And I don't think you do either."

The corners of his lips turned in what might have been a smile. "My hell has been entirely unique."

I waited for a moment in silence, sensing a struggle in him, watching his hand reach for the ignition and then fall be to his lap.

"What is it?"

"We can't drive off just yet. Damn it." His hands were clenched into fists now. "I didn't want to help them." His gaze drifted back toward the opening of the dig again.

"If that were true, we'd already be on our way back into the city."

I sat still and breathed, tried to grasp at a rational thought inside the stream of emotion he sent my way. Then it hit me. He hadn't been in on past conversations, had missed our theorizing about the key and manner of the seven books, one book, seals—whatever would be opened. And we had never thought to ask.

"Trust me, love. I would keep it all to myself were it not for Tiran showing up, or with more creatures like her probably on the way. Better Wolf Boy and the smart ass get their hands on it than them. At least you and I will benefit. We'll be together."

I didn't need to speak.

He growled. "Don't get me wrong, I don't know where the damn thing is. I just remember what it looked like."

"You saw the key? It's not just a map? A document?"

He held up his hands to demonstrate. "It's a small golden triangle. Short spikes of different lengths attached on the back. A design of two hands with the tips of forefingers and thumbs touching like in that gesture you used to do in the temple. The whole thing isn't any bigger than an inch on each side. Hell, it could be sitting in the museum and no one would even know what it was. It looks like jewelry. You used to wear it on a chain around your neck, and I never saw you do it, but I imagine you set it down so the spikes matched the holes in the side of your book—"

"My book? Is that what it opens? The myth is just a way to reclaim all the writings I've buried."

"Well what did you think it was?" His eyes narrowed. "Ahh ... Cibrien making it harder than it needed to be. Hocus pocus and Revelations crap no doubt."

I gasped. "You dare to call it that?"

"No offense meant." He laughed. "Alright, offense meant. But, it's just so damn funny. We aren't at the end times. Yet." He opened the car door. "Come on."

The wind whipped through the sand, lifting it in swirls that looked harmless until they struck us. I knew I caused this. My frustration with Daen spilled over. He took my hand as we bent low and crept back down through the passageway.

Winger turned and set a brush down on top of a sandy crate. "I knew I smelled something. Just wasn't sulphur."

"Daen has some things to tell you and Cib." I put my hand softly against Daen's arm to urge him forward.

Cibrien straightened his back and wiped the sweat

off his brow with his shirtsleeve. In the odd lighting, his narrowed hazel eyes almost wanted to be green. He didn't say a word.

"The myth Grey told you harebrains about—I can help decipher it."

"Go on," I encouraged.

"Ah, damn it all to hell," he growled. "You're all going to be in danger if you don't find what you're looking for and get out of here. I can't risk Ariana."

"So help us then," Winger said with a too-calm smile.

"The key is literally a key, a small golden triangle Ariana used to wear around her neck. It opened a sort of padlock to her writings in Egypt. The book was rigged so that if she didn't use the lock to open it, the writing inside would be destroyed. There were supposedly narrow vials of liquid in the spine and cover that would burst and eat away the words if a person forced it open. Everyone knew the story at the time. I don't know if that particular key opened any of the other six books, though. I wasn't really Watching." He unsuccessfully suppressed a laugh.

"So there are seven books then. Seven total? Not just one with seven seals?" Cibrien sat down further in the shadow and his eyes became brown.

Daen nodded. "Seven that I can recall off the top of my head. All booby-trapped. Scattered and hidden in those places Ariana lived around the world, those sacred places …"

Winger's lips stretched across his teeth, but the smile was gone. "So if we're just looking for Ariana's writings, what's the urgency? She already knows the words. We all know the gist of whatever's in those books."

Daen laughed darkly. "Historic value. The story of

mankind wrapped up in one neat little package."

"That's not all," Cibrien whispered. "We may know what's written, but the Fallen Ones don't. They're trying what Daen suggested, to stop our One God from 'cleaning house.'"

"They're looking for information?" I asked and then it dawned on me. "Information. Evidence of a timeline I might have written. Signs I recorded. And they probably want the Watchers separated, too. The enemy camp rendered useless. They could chart their own future, rewrite history. And did you ever stop to think of the things I could have written. Cib, when you and I ran the temples, we knew things ..."

"That information that the Fallen Ones would like, isn't it something like what Daen wanted?" Winger asked.

"Clueless as always," he shot back. "I came to Tokyo that night for Ariana. I didn't want to join your merry gang of renegade idiots. Where you were was of no consequence to me, but now—"

"It's different," Cibrien finished. "Because you know Tiran and the others will come, and Ariana will be their target. It's going to take all of us together to fend them off, and you know it. You're stuck with us."

"You mean we're stuck with him. I wonder how Daen will like admitting that we need Ryuichi back." Winger lifted the brush from the crate and sat down where it had been.

"I don't think we need him back right now." My voice rang flat and far too soft inside the hollow of the small room. Everyone sat up straighter and looked to me for the words that would come next. "We might not need him. We might not want him back. I don't know where his inclination lies."

"Don't let your recent nearness to this bastard cloud your judgment, Ariana. Think back ten years."

"Winger." I held up my hand. "I know, all right? But this isn't about Daen. I can't reach out with my mind and find Ryu anymore. Can you? That's gone. And I downloaded his latest song. It's completely empty. Empty. Like he's gone dead inside. Like he's written something only the Fallen Ones could understand."

"It could be grief," Cibrien offered.

"His music thrives on longing, Cib. The stronger the emotion, the more potent the song. It's what connected me with him and led me to him in the first place. No, it's like his temple mastery isn't operating on the right level. And then there's—never mind."

"There's what?" Winger stood, blue eyes peering through the faded light toward me and Daen. The sun would soon set, slide away from the opening of the dig and leave us in total eerie darkness.

"The warning from the music store. 'Do not look upon him.' I could have sworn the Roman general said it at his execution. I thought it had come from him when I approached the cage on the banks of the Nile. But I can picture that man's face and his lips never moved. Daen was there watching and he says those words were never spoken."

"Do you swear it, Daen?" Winger moved a step closer and stopped, throwing his hands up in front of him in disgust. "What am I asking? What would he swear on?"

"On my love for Ariana," he answered. "What else sacred is there left to me?"

"That leaves only two choices," I continued, refusing to be distracted. "The warning not to look upon him was either a divine Whisper, or a message from the Fallen Ones. Neither option sounds particularly good to me."

"But Ariana, you do still hold love for him," Cibrien said in a tone that told me it wasn't really a question.

"Of course I do. And when he's supposed to, I think he'll be able to come back."

Daen made a noise low in his throat. "Depends on what he's coming back for."

Cibrien picked up the stone relief and ran his fingers gingerly across the faces of the goddesses chiseled there. What memory the caress carried to him he pushed aside with apparent effort. I could see a fragment of the future hanging in the air, revealing itself only to him, High Priest of old with his mastery of color and shape. He looked from me to Daen and back to Winger before covering his treasure and hiding it away from the world once more.

"Someday, when the time is different, I'll ask Grey more about the Temple of Osiris," he said. "Or about its Keeper. Maybe there's a 'legend' about me to be told."

Chapter Sixteen

He who never sleeps
Takes no sanctuary in dreams.
Swims through swords
sharp sea of remembrance.

"Miss Ariana! So good to see you again." The hearty voice with its lush accent caught me off guard and I turned.

"Grey." I stepped forward and took his hands in mine before leaning in to kiss him on the cheek. For an instant I thought he might have at least a sense of déjà vu toward the gesture, but it passed in the hustle and bustle of the street, and was gone.

"I heard you and Daen had returned. My apologies for not meeting you at the site, but I trust you understand." His green eyes were vivid as stained glass in the sunlight, so full of constant joy that I almost envied his lack of remembrance. Was that the road to peace?

"I do understand. And I also wonder if some things should stay buried."

He nodded toward the hotel only a block behind me. "Where are you off to this morning?"

"Just walking. But in this city there's no way to wake up early enough to avoid the crowds."

Grey's expression showed his disapproval. "A young woman should not walk through certain parts of Cairo alone at sunrise. As in any large city, it has its bad elements."

He had no idea how bad, I wanted to say. Or how good. I couldn't tell him that the moment I drew my first waking breath, Daen had wakened in the next room, matching me heartbeat for heartbeat. Or that when I left the hotel, Winger's warrior senses had called him to attention. Or that even with the protection around me, I no longer strayed alone more than five minutes from our nest.

"I'll be more careful," was all I said. "Were you coming to get Cib?"

"Him. And Daen as well. Ah, I see your escort has arrived." He nodded and walked on toward the hotel.

Winger tugged his brown suede jacket around him, still pulling his clothing into place as his boots clunked down the narrow sidewalk toward me. He and Grey shook hands and spoke for a moment before Winger continued on to me. He shoved his strong hands into the pockets of his jeans.

We turned and walked together in silence, watching the street vendors setting up, the peddlers taking position. I recognized all their faces by now and they had finally given up their efforts to sell their wares to me. They had never approached Daen or Winger as far as I'd seen.

"Didn't feel like spending the day on another dig?" I finally asked.

He shook his head and I caught a flash of those

white, white teeth. "There was nothing for me to do there. I think the effort is futile." He reached out and took my hand.

"I'm starting to think so, too. The dreams are starting again."

"You have those every time you're about to leave a place. What did you see this time?"

"Mist. And stones. Ivy."

"That's all?" With his free hand he adjusted his jacket around what I suspected was his hunting knife hidden beneath.

"Yes." I gave his hand a quick squeeze before letting it drop away from mine. "I wish there was more."

"What you said about Ryuichi worries me." Winger peered far off into the distance, not really seeing the buildings in front of us. "You're quick to forgive Daen, and his transgressions are worse."

"Ryu is welcome back whenever he chooses. You know that."

"But does he?"

"I think so." The wind picked up and I stopped the draft immediately, tucked a blown strand of gold-hued hair back behind my ear.

"It's confusing," he said, "knowing who to choose, or whether to choose either of them at all. If you make a covenant with the wrong one—"

I interrupted. "I haven't chosen, if that's what you're asking. But I do know without a doubt that what I felt for Ryu has slipped. It's like my feelings were heightening only because they were a replay of that time in Egypt, you know? Maybe they were never real. Or misplaced. But they kept us together long enough to trigger the right memories."

"All I know is that you screw up, and you're Grey. Back in the flesh way too many times to remember a damn thing. Or to relate to those of us who didn't screw up. We lose *you*."

"I wish I'd gotten that across to Ryu better." I swirled a dust devil across the bottom step and let it dissipate.

"You told him he was wrong when he held fire in his hand in Egypt. But you've been practicing your tricks, I see. And at the last Age, we did a whole lot worse with our elements."

"It's different. We used our elements when we were supposed to. Not to build our egos and summon dark things. That's what the Roman—Ryu did. We're not supposed to take a power like that and whirl it around just for fun."

"No, never just for the hell of it."

He winked at me as we sat down on the front steps of the museum. The sun was up at last, but not yet strong enough to warm the cold stone steps. We'd walked farther than I'd realized and I felt a twinge of apprehension. Winger's muscles grew tense, though he didn't move.

"It's all about the intent, I suppose." I looked behind me toward the large front doors of the museum. Morning was fully upon us and the air was warming.

Winger's gaze followed mine. "You have the air, and the earth is mine. I didn't know what I could do until I tracked down Daen that time. I want to tell you what he meant back at the dig site, Ariana. But not now."

He stood suddenly and slid his hand inside his jacket, waiting, scanning the area around us carefully with senses honed sharper even than my own. Then his eyes rested on something.

In the crowd, still a street away, a glimpse of shining

red peeked out and then was hidden. Winger took me by the hand and pulled me to my feet. Slowly we turned and walked down the steps, moving in a direction to take us away from the red.

I didn't need to look behind to know what followed had not lost sight of us. Winger and I walked around the block, backtracking to another side street deliberately chosen for its mass of people. As we turned the corner I dared a glimpse. Tiran wasn't alone. Beside her jogged a man, tall and willowy with pale hair the color of moonlight.

"The sulphur scent isn't with them," Winger said as he guided me through a maze of people, stands, and old bicycles. "There's nothing in spirit form floating around them. Yet."

"Are they gaining on us?"

"Yes." He tugged me roughly down the street. "And they don't want to talk nice."

"You could take 'em, O Great Protector," I teased.

He groaned but smiled all the same. "Yeah, but they'd call for backup once they got us cornered. Cibrien and Daen couldn't get to us in time. Besides, wouldn't wanna give away all our tricks at once."

"We have tricks? Plural?" I glanced over my shoulder again, breathless now and worried for the first time. Yet something new, or old, was expanding inside me out of necessity. Something dormant was coming to life.

"Just a little farther." Winger plunged us into another crowd and then made a quick turn down a narrow alley with brickwork walls on either side. I felt the faintest brush cross my cheek and raised my hand to touch the caress that wasn't there. The sugary cool aroma of flowers passed briefly. We weren't alone.

The footsteps behind us seemed magnified, each one echoing toward us as Tiran and her strange companion rounded the corner and glided into the alley.

"Now," Winger said as we neared the end of the passage. He stopped suddenly, let go of my hand, and spun around to face them. The morning sun glinted frighteningly off his teeth, his compelling blue eyes. And then the air behind us carried a rumble with a swirl of dust stirred from the mortar in the walls. A tremor shook the ground, but not all of it, like an earthquake concentrated on a few square feet of space.

The air hung heavy with the musty scent of earth long undisturbed now called to action. With a moan, the walls shifted and trembled, and then the bricks began to fall. Tiran's smooth white face contorted in anger as the wall flew outward, hitting the ground in front of her and the man, stopping them cold in their tracks.

"I've been practicing, too," Winger growled.

I grabbed my guardian's hand again, not risking separation as we fled the pathway that yawned open wide at the end, transformed into a marketplace in a public plaza. Perpetual motion thrived in the enormous square, a throng so dense and active that we couldn't have run if we'd wanted. Elbow to elbow with strangers, we maneuvered our way.

"I only bought us a few seconds," Winger warned. "We're the only two with light-colored hair in this mess. They'll spot us."

"Take off your jacket," I said as I removed mine and rolled it into a tight package that I clung to and held against my stomach. "I think I may have a trick they won't even see. If I can pull it off."

Winger shrugged out of his suede and held it firmly

in front of him, too. We both wore white T-shirts underneath and the color blended smoothly with the neutral Egyptian clothing surrounding us.

"Keep walking slowly and don't look back," I instructed. From Winger's expression, I could tell that Tiran had just emerged from the alley and stood surveying the multitude.

Training of the temple, come to me.

"Isis in the sun, Nephthys under the moon," I whispered. The glamour, I had used it routinely and at will once. So long ago. The feeling shimmered deep inside me, a strength and energy so softly there beneath the surface. I struggled to bring it outward, strained to lend all my force to it, but still it hovered just out of reach. Then that now-familiar touch like the kiss of an angel child returned against my cheek and took the struggle from me. I breathed deeply and when I exhaled in relaxation, the cloak—my "shell" as the Roman had once called it—returned.

"Do not let go of my hand," I commanded of Winger. "To break contact is to break the spell."

"Holy hell," Winger breathed out as he looked down at me. "You've darkened."

"So have you."

Once the glamour was in place, the effort was minimal to keep it there. Winger and I strolled casually, hands clasped, away from the souk and its controlled chaos. If Tiran saw us at all, she would see an Arab man and woman with deep complexions and dark brown hair.—no one who could have possibly been us.

On and on we walked as the morning sun ripened. The illusion's internal shimmer carried me along as if the energy I used to generate it somehow encouraged the creation of more energy along the way. No one supposed for a moment that we were travelers, visitors, hunted. The senses deceive.

We were near our hotel again before Winger spoke and let my hand drop. "That was interesting, Ariana. How long have you known you could still do that?"

"About fifteen minutes. How about you?"

"Moving mountains?" He grinned and swung his jacket over his shoulder. "Since just before Cib and I left Sedona. I'd bet my eyeteeth we all have a little something special left over."

We stopped just in front of the hotel. The screeching brakes of a rickety Cairo taxi and the grind of its tires against the curb prevented us from continuing inside. The taxi doors flew open as Winger moved his hand over to the knife now visible at his side. I exhaled as Cibrien and Daen leapt from the vehicle.

Daen slid his arm around my shoulder and led me quickly inside. He leaned down low, his lips near my ear. "We need to pack this afternoon. There can be no more nights in this place. They know you're here." The scent of cinnamon and fresh snowfall wafted from him in spite of the archeological dust clinging to his shirt and hair. We continued upstairs to his room.

Cibrien turned the deadbolt on the door behind us and locked the chair across while Winger tugged the drapes shut across the windows. The view from the street below into our room was gone and only the light could find its way through the heavy cloth. Cibrien gestured and the four of us sat down in a circle on the frayed rug in the middle of the floor.

"Gee, guess what we did today," I said.

"It's nothing to laugh at." The child-like enthusiasm

and youthful energy were gone from Cibrien's face.

Daen's eyes met mine. "Grey left. I don't know if we can convince him to return. Not after today."

"You had visitors today?" Winger's question was more of a statement.

Daen nodded. "Their stench was everywhere—all over the site. We aren't going back. Not like there's anything more there anyway. Grey started praying to whatever ancient god would listen and drove like hell away from the place. Of course they let him go. They don't even know who he once was. But Cib and I knew most of the old words, and we were strong enough."

"We had Tiran," I said. The tone in the room was enough to sober anyone. These men feared for my safety more than even I had the sense to.

"She had a friend," Winger added. "Tall, pale."

"With clear eyes," I said. "Did you notice that? His eyes reminded me of peeled grapes. Or those glass bricks they use in building medical offices."

Cibrien shook his head. "Could be anyone."

The frantic colors began to hum and snap in the room, looking as if God had crushed a rainbow in his hand and blown all the glittering bits out in the air around us.

"We're burning too much energy here," I warned. "Calm it down."

"They were testing us," Winger said. "Seeing what we can do."

Daen leaned forward and peered into Winger's eyes. "And what exactly can we do, Wolf Boy?"

"As if you don't already know." Winger flashed a dazzling smile at Daen and then clicked his teeth together.

Daen chuckled low in his throat.

"But our Ariana here still has a few surprises, doesn't she? After Daen and I got rid of our guests, he felt you darken. Just like you used to do in the temple. Fair as Isis in the day. Dark as Nephthys in the nighttime. I taught you that, you know."

"And what can you still do, High Priest?" I asked.

"I have the art in me still. The command of shape and color has not yet eluded me. I also know most of the words to the rituals, and maybe something else. I don't know yet."

"It seems I've got control of dirt and rock. Yay, me."

"Listen to the humble Wolf Boy, selling himself short." Daen raised an eyebrow as if daring Winger to continue. When no one spoke, Daen gave an exasperated sigh. "And Ariana. You can still do that temple glide. I remember your movement without noise or witness, so I know it's true. Then there was the darkening and lightening today. The mastery of all things written. Control of the air. We can all separate from our bodies, project—"

"Which I don't think is safe to try now," I interrupted. "Not with the bad guys lurking in that same level."

"What can you do, Daen?" There was no sarcasm in Cibrien's voice. None at all.

"I am He Who Never Sleeps. I recall everything. And you already know my thing with water."

"You all have so much of the Gift," I said. "I'm not sure I'll ever understand why the Fallen Ones are after me."

"My love, truly you don't know?" Daen asked.

"You're the magnet," Winger said.

"The scribe," Cibrien added.

Daen's dark eyes held mine. "You and your writings

are what draw the Ancients together. Time and time and time again. Without you, how would we ever find each other? How would we ever find it within ourselves to care to?"

"You're the heart of us," Winger said softly.

The room was entirely hushed for moments. My blessings were most poignant when the situation turned dimmest. I looked from face to face around the circle. Winger with his bravery and a warrior's embrace. Daen, old stones and golden sunsets, chivalry drowning in darkness. Cibrien with a mix of olden wisdom and vibrant youth. The terror that a single shred of harm might befall any of them twisted deeply inside me.

"If anyone suggests a group hug, I'll hurt him," Daen said and we all exhaled at last. For the first time in so many Ages, the four of us laughed together.

"Where do we go?" I asked.

"I don't know," Cibrien said. "We can't stay here. We don't know when they'll attack. But they will. They'll try to test us or trap us. They'll want us to lead them to the keys and the books one way or another. Then they'll want us to join their side or die."

"Join us or die," Daen said low under his breath and then chuckled to himself.

"We need sacred ground," I said. "If my temple were still standing we could wage a defense there. They couldn't cross the threshold of power there."

"We could go back to Sedona," Winger suggested. "There's protection there."

"Ariana, my love. The castle? I found it, remember." Daen's voice began with a low resonance, repeating what he'd insisted on telling me before. "The iron gate. The rose garden."

"Yes, I know."

"The one built on ground blessed over seven centuries," he pressed. "The castle, our fortress. The one sitting where the numbers align in exactly the right place under the heavens and the geography is perfect and safe."

"Yes." Adrenalin pulsed through my blood.

"I bought it, remember?"

"Go on." I stood and Daen rose to his feet beside me while Cibrien and Winger watched.

"I left something out," he whispered. "I rebuilt it stone by stone. Each pane of glass. Every heavy wooden door. The hidden passages. Even the rose garden and that damned rusty gate you so loved. It looks just like it did seven hundred years ago—with a few modern adjustments." He leaned down closer, his face near mine. "Where do you think I was all those ten years?"

I gasped as the pieces fell into place. "Did you always know it would come to this? Is that why you did it?"

Daen laughed out loud. "Hell, no. I just did it for you. It was supposed to be a gift, but you know how He is about divine influence. I'm discovering I can't do anything without it coming back to some extraordinary purpose. I really am cursed, you know."

"Forget it. I'm not going back to that area," Winger said. "I built that damn stone ring not too far from there. That was enough of fog and drizzle for me."

"Oh lord above. So that was yours, Winger. We wondered once." My hand flew to cover my mouth. "I buried one of the books there inside Winger's megalith circle. Daen and I were there together when I did."

Daen frowned. "You still remember that?"

"Right down to your name, Nicholaus."

Winger's senses were on alert. No foul scent tainted the air and the hallway was free from footsteps outside our door. But the information we spoke aloud and the plans we debated were sensitive and precious, too valuable to treat without the greatest of care.

Cibrien stood and walked over to sit cross-legged on Daen's bed. "There's no choice then. The Whispers couldn't be clearer. Daen's castle it is."

"Ariana's castle," Daen corrected.

Winger literally growled in defeat. "Well, at least we'll be out of this infernal city. After Tokyo and Cairo, I'm starting to feel—dulled."

"How are we going to fund this?" I asked. "Will what I saved from my writing contract and what Winger made from his last wilderness tour cover airfare? We don't have Ryu or his millions with us anymore."

"I will cover it," Daen said. "And after we get home to Britannia of Old, believe me, there'll be no shortage of coin."

We packed in great haste and left the local hotel that had become our temporary home for so many weeks. Not one of us doubted the Fallen Ones knew where we stayed. They had carried Ryuichi back through the veil into a temple memory there. Those rooms had already known the scent of sulphur.

We blocked all thoughts from our minds, sending up a barrier on all sides in case some dark sentry hovered near. But it takes much effort to remain in that state of blankness, much more than to concentrate deeply on a thought, and so we didn't speak. We couldn't. We simply walked out the front door into the noonday brightness when our departure would be least anticipated, before the enemy had time to meet and regroup.

The more expensive the hotel the better, Daen suggested and then secured two adjoining mini-suites inside a great modern tower for the four of us. There were no suites with four beds, and Winger wisely argued against any one of us left alone in a room. We hoped the security at the door of a luxurious retreat would be tighter, and the rooms in which to hunt us more numerous and confusing. I laughed to think that of all the things to do, the Watchers were buying time.

As long as Cairo bound us to her, we had no choice but to remain. The key I had once worn around my neck had not allowed itself to be found. I wondered if we shouldn't leave without it. Cibrien agreed that we could leave when either the key or the book was found, but while both remained dangerously behind for the finding, our escape was not to be. And yet I longed to see our castle again.

When night slid across the hazy sky, it was with grave reserve that Winger finally left Daen alone to share a room with me. He lingered for a moment in the doorway that connected the two suites.

"Cibrien asked me to help track down something lost. If it works, I think we'll have a way to find your key. It's funny. Before long we'll have a key to open writings we don't have from Ancient Egypt, and writings from Britannia of Old with no key." His eyes shifted to Daen. "Touch her and die."

Daen grinned wickedly as the ornate door clicked shut behind Winger. "Now I have you all to myself."

"I've begun to suspect I'm divided amongst you all."

Daen shook his head, shaking a strand of inky black hair down across his sunkissed forehead. "I'm going to take a shower."

I sank down onto one of the oversized beds and took in my plush surroundings with a pile of downy pillows stacked behind my head. Even the ceilings were gilded around the edges and painted in languorous scenes thought up by the old masters. Copies, yet opulent just the same. The furniture was upholstered in thick velvets, the curtains held back by thick golden ropes with tassels.

The rush of the shower stopped and the muffled sweeping sound of a towel pulled roughly from its rod came to me. Daen emerged from the bathroom wearing a gray cotton T-shirt and jeans. I rolled my head lazily to the side to look at him. His dress had become far more casual now than in any time I remembered. His skin glowed with the fading effect of the heated water. The tones of his wet hair had been deepened until they took on a subtle blue cast under the warm lighting.

"What have you added to the castle?" I asked as he sat on the edge of the bed. Surely he had put even the decorators of this lavish room to shame.

"My adjustments?" He tugged the T-shirt off over his head and inched closer to me. "Indoor plumbing for one. And electricity."

I propped myself up on my elbows. "Electricity is good."

"I think so." He leaned down close to me, so close I could again see the golden flecks layered in his eyes, each individual lash, the faintest shadow gone unshaven from his chin. The scent of soap mingled with that of his skin, and a droplet or two of water slid from his hair to his neck and ran in small rivulets down his magnificent chest. The tips of my fingers ached to trace the path the water had made. The air between us hummed.

"Why do you hold back, my love?" he asked.

"For a million reasons, all of which you know."

Daen sunk an elbow into the soft bed on either side of me, his body dangerously close, bare skin only separated from me by the smallest of spaces. He lowered his head until I could feel the steady warmth of his breath near my collarbone.

"What if I said I'm going to make love to you, Ariana?" His lips found the tender flesh between my neck and shoulder.

"Am I to have no say in this?"

"There's much you can say. You can say 'yes.'" The words tickled along the curve of my throat. "You can say my name. Again and again." His kisses punctuated each sound. "You can say that I shouldn't stop, my love."

I gasped and opened my eyes for a moment. The air surrounding us still hummed, and now it held a dim light that enshrouded our bodies, silver and gold combined.

I ached for him. He trailed a fingertip over the swell of my hip.

"I won't." I sat up swiftly and he rose with me, matching me movement for movement and not relinquishing an inch of closeness. We each looked calm and unruffled were it not for the wild gleam of desire lighting our eyes, the heat of exquisite memories that called out to be reborn. If I closed my eyes, I could almost feel him inside me, taste him …

"Choose to be with me," he said. "You know I'm where your heart lies. And don't misunderstand. I don't intend to corrupt you. I intend to marry you. In a church if you'd like, with Him as witness looking on from above. Harps and flowers."

"But you have stepped outside the circle, Daen. What happens when I'm old and gray? What happens when this body shrivels and dies? What will you do then? What if I come back into the flesh again? What if I'm not granted the memories next time and can't appreciate what you are to me?"

He wrapped his strong arms around me and held me securely. "You're afraid of me? Afraid to be with the one creature who protests destructive plans? Who stays as I wish, not as something else wishes?"

I pushed him far enough away for him to see my eyes. "You aren't the only creature. There are the Fallen Ones and an even greater evil—all of which seem to feel as you do. That's what scares me. If I join with you, how am I to know that I don't sacrifice the role I've been gifted? I don't intend sacrilege or blasphemy."

"If I agree to slip back into the cycle, to be born in the flesh, my recollections will fade away as surely as yours have. Little by little you and I will drift away. It would be an existence worse than hell, Ariana. Think of it. Born again and again, completely as humans and always with the inkling that there's someone out there somewhere whom we're supposed to find. Except we'd never be able to find each other. And if we managed to, we might not recognize what we'd found. We'd just keep drifting. Endless. Empty. Not even suicide could cut the pain. It would just continue on forever." He drew in a deep breath. "You could slip outside the cycle with me."

My muscles jerked suddenly as if of their own accord. "You can't mean that."

His gaze held mine steadily and I saw in his eyes the light of swimming emotions. "You would still be a Watcher. Of sorts."

"Not if it goes against the natural design of my body—or my soul."

"There are many things that have grown apart from what they were originally, my love. Not all of them are evil. If something absolutely isn't meant to happen, the One God does not let it happen. That is one of the greatest truths I know."

"But, Daen," I whispered, "there are levels to which you can't ascend now. How can you bear being separated from all that is holy? And what if you stay outside the cycle and then I don't get cast back into the flesh again? I'll be in a level you can't even see. Have you thought of that? We would be separated forever. Permanently and without hope. The pain there is even greater."

He smiled. "You love me still."

"I love you still."

His lips found mine, sweet and urgent, caressing and claiming all at once. When the kiss deepened, a thousand shards of magic broke around us. The loveliest aromas passed fleetingly yet lushly through our senses. Colors we could only imagine and never quite remember flooded around us, dancing in and out of the silver-gold shimmer we generated.

With trembling fingers he lifted my shirt free and laid against me, skin to skin. Absolute trust touched my heart and I knew he would not take this temptation past the point of return. I felt a sweep of emotions carried together with volumes of thoughts he'd conjured somewhere along the way. In deft movements, our clothing was shed, and he rolled to his side and pulled me back against him.

"I would not cause you to sin, Ariana. Can you bear for me to simply hold you through the night this way?"

"No. You'll have to go soon," I breathed. "At least across the room to your own bed."

"Will you call for Winger? Even by accident?"

"I have blocked him. For now." I moved my hand back and forth in front of me, watching the metallic shimmer follow it. "I don't think Winger needs to see this."

He laughed and kissed the top of my head. "When we finally come together, Ariana, can you imagine the strength of it?"

I shivered in want. "Yes."

"Ryuichi was never like this for you." It wasn't a challenge, wasn't even a question.

"Not even close. Even the physical attraction to him is gone, Daen," I said very, very gently. "I think we had to exorcise the unfinished feelings that carried over from Egypt. I'm certain now that the residue of the time on the altar steps, mixed with our present plutonic love, turned into the start of a relationship that wasn't supposed to be. You were right, Daen. The nature of his way with me was mistaken."

"Will you tell him you've chosen me?"

"But I haven't chosen you. I can't be with you until we figure out a way to be together. So far we're striking out. But I will tell him I haven't chosen to be with him."

"You have chosen me. You just don't know it yet."

Chapter Seventeen

Telltale signs
of Time's imprisonment.
With a charm and a fade,
we war.

When the long night dissolved, I went to Cibrien and at first asked nothing of what he and Winger had delved into the evening before. In turn, I shared nothing of what had passed between Daen and me.

"Cib," I began, "does your mastery of art and color still hold?"

"It does."

"I want to send a message to Ryu. I can't risk calling or writing a normal letter. None of us know what might be watching over his shoulder."

"And you wonder if he has turned."

I nodded. "Can you paint something? A note hidden in a puzzle of color?" Fallen Ones couldn't see color.

"I foresaw this request. When I held up the relief back at the dig site, I saw it." Cibrien brushed a piece of brown hair across his forehead, away from his eyes. Cut with a razor's edge in the hotel spa, it was both stylish and careless at once, modern when the depth of his gaze showed that the man himself wasn't.

"If he can read through the colors, it will tell us much. I remember those color-blindness tests from my eye doctor's office. Something designed like that would do."

"And what will I convey?" Cibrien's hazel eyes glittered.

"Tell Ryu he must come to the place of my fullest time with Daen. He'll know where that is. Tell him I have not chosen him. But tell him he must come anyway."

"Should I write that you've chosen Daen instead?"

"I haven't done that, Cib. You know it."

"Do I?" Cibrien brought the bottoms of his feet up to the edge of his chair and wrapped his arms around his knees. He was all expectation.

I smiled without mirth and walked out of the room. As the door clicked shut under my hand, Cibrien unzipped his small duffle bag and took from it a set of paints and a small brush. Time would press him to complete such intricate work. We had only days at best before the wicked winged things found us, before one of us slipped and became so lost in thought that the block thrown up against them wavered, weakened.

Daen chose for our travel plans, our escape route, to remain unwritten and unspoken. He coolly made arrangements in secrecy, in haste. Not even I dared look over his shoulder as he worked. Winger eyed him suspiciously; poignantly uncomfortable that our physical safety had been left to the devices of one he felt might betray us at any turn.

But betrayal was not on Daen's mind. I would have

perceived it, were it so. Instead I saw flashes of the castle when Daen's longing reached in that direction. The images could have been memories lifted straight from the Record were it not for the subtle changes that caught my attention. The rose garden always came to me, overflowing with the mingling of blooms and rain-dampened soil that filled my senses with sweet, soothing, fragrant reassurance.

Off the great hall, the kitchen had been connected to the building—no longer an outdoor oven here, a pantry there, a dining area upstairs … The adjustments made me laugh. Stainless steel modernity, shining copper-bottomed pots, and colors that managed to be vivid and tastefully muted all at once. These things swirled before my mind's eye and were gone.

Still Cibrien painted.

Still Winger paced the halls. He sat absently sipping café au lait downstairs where the front door met with his line of view.

Still Daen covertly made arrangements and then counter-arrangements until no one but him could know which way he planned to take us when at last the key was found. He had turned our suite into his office with the hotel phone and my laptop at his disposal. Winger and I had used our credit cards at Daen's instruction, and purchased useless tickets for a long flight to New Zealand we would never take. Where the rest of the money came from, Daen wouldn't entirely explain.

"The centuries have given up opportunity aplenty. A dragon with his hoard has nothing on me," he said with a chuckle low in his throat.

I was in a gilded cage while they each worked. My writing flowed too quickly, not filling nearly enough minutes of each day. Listless, I slid into a chair next to Winger and watched him pretend to sip his coffee.

"I would practice my powers if it wouldn't draw them near," I said.

"Do you know for sure it would draw them?"

I shrugged. "It used to sometimes. When things weren't done right."

"Well, can you practice and keep the block up?"

"I don't want to risk it. I'm not the High Priestess I once was. When we get to our haven, I'll practice to my hearts content. Not until then." I leaned closer and gazed intensely at him, though his icy blue eyes were fixed on the people walking casually through the lobby. "What did you and Cibrien work on?"

"Cibrien has a particularly unusual kind of talent. He'll tell you about it when the note to Ryu is done."

"He'd better work fast then. We aren't going to find the key sitting locked up in this glorified mausoleum all day. We need to get out and hunt for it." I clicked my fingernails against the polished tabletop. Suddenly the hotel and all its luxury felt pale and thin compared to the crumbling rooms we'd left behind, whose very walls were steeped in history and culture. "And just so you know," I added, "I hate being kept in the dark."

Winger's gaze finally shifted to meet mine. "If what Cib plans actually works, you can slap me senseless if we won't be able to leave in the next day or two."

"I'll take you up on that. And speak of the devil," I said as Cibrien entered the hotel café.

"You'd better not," Winger joked, "or he just might come for us."

Cibrien strolled over and tossed a small painting onto the table in front of me. I lifted the wet canvas delicately by its very edges.

"It's perfect. Very temple-like. And cryptic," I whispered. "I pray to God he can read it, though if he can, it will bring him pain."

I read the message again silently to myself.

By this Summons of the Ancients, you are called. The Magnet and Scribe has not chosen the Way you most desired. Yet if anything of the Priest, of Anubis, still rests in you, you will recognize and heed our call without hesitation. Find us at the place of her fullest time with He Who Never Sleeps. Come as near as you can. Reach out, and we will guide you in.

Countless tiny circles in a camouflage of colors floated over the square I held between the palms of my hands. Tedious, detailed, crucial, this masterpiece. In the bottom corner, Cibrien had painted a golden seal: two elegant hands shown from the back with tips of forefingers and thumbs touching to form a triangle in between. It was the gesture of our greeting and parting, a symbol from so long ago. In the background, visible through the open triangle were the stars of Orion's belt with the stars that marked the corners of the constellation's hourglass falling just outside the touching fingers. This symbol was ours again, reincarnated just as surely as we were.

"You're telling him you didn't pick him?" Winger asked.

I nodded. The tables around us were empty, the café winding down after the breakfast rush.

Cibrien ordered his own cup of coffee. "We'll see

what he does. I hope he's grown since the temple. He used to join the party only if he thought he was missing something, never when he could be useful."

Splotches of color stained Cibrien's smooth, nimble fingers. Even gnarled and cracked, they had once worked art to surpass that of the masters whose imitations I admired on my ceiling upstairs. His eyes were bright with life, but I recalled days when they were dim. Those fading eyes had seen the Roman soldier as I had, noted his faults, cared for him anyway.

"I still can't sense him, Cib. Not even in that way that's just a hunch and not the connection." I wished for Ryu's dark eyes, the inky hair falling on either side of a widow's peak, the lull of his voice. I missed my friend.

"When this dries, we'll mail it the fastest way possible," Cibrien assured. "And then we'll wait."

I closed my eyes for a moment and breathed. A low, powerful hum of energy passed over me. The water in my glass sloshed with its ice cubes clinking on the sides. And he had done this without even trying. I could see from Daen's face as he crossed the lobby to me that the aura he radiated simply—was. He did nothing to stimulate and create it.

"Bastard," Winger murmured and then said louder as Daen approached, "If you don't tone it down, you might as well send out a homing beacon."

"The arrangements are made," Daen announced. "And now I think it's time we all go upstairs and try to get the key."

"Why does everyone but me know what Cibrien has planned?"

"I don't even know how he knows it," Cibrien told me. "Unless you watched me do it when I was High

Priest?"

"Nah. I heard you and Wolf Boy talking about it through the bathroom wall when I was taking a shower." Daen laughed. "You Watchers. Always outthinking yourselves."

We left our coffee money on the cool, blue table-top and stood. A suspicion settled over me, an inkling of what Cibrien would attempt when we reached our suites upstairs. Now the reality dawned. Even as Priestess, I had not received the full gamut of the temple's intricately layered training. There were one or two tricks reserved for the High Priest alone, just as there had been those reserved for me. Even the old High Priest had had his moments of privacy that harbored secrets I hadn't suspected.

Upstairs at last, Daen and Winger locked the door that connected our two adjoining rooms and then slid one of the heavy mattresses up against it. The bed itself proved far too immense to move with portions so heavy that they may as well have been bolted to the wall. Against the heavy, ornate door that opened into the grand hallway, a barricade of tables and chairs fell into place under the crystal doorknob, deadbolt, and golden chain that stretched above them both. When we were finished, only the one bed remained as it had been.

Cibrien took a sip of water and exhaled as he set down the glass. I recognized the pattern his breathing took as he sat on the edge of that bed. Slow, deep breaths filled his lungs to the bottom and expelled the tension in his body a little at a time. He rolled his shoulders, tilted his neck from side to side.

"Ariana," he said, "you'll have to travel out with me. Winger and Daen will stand guard. It will take your thought strongly directed to guide us. I won't know the key without you. It wasn't mine. I don't even remember seeing it."

"I don't know where it is, either. It would make things simpler." I stretched out on the bed beside him, arms straight at my sides. "Do you really think you can carry it?"

"We'll see."

I looked at Winger and Daen who stood together, towering and glowering at the foot of the bed. Winger's arms were crossed in front of his chest, the planes of his face tight and defined. For a moment I saw not Winger, but my warrior brother before me. He was the one whose senses were sharpened beyond anyone's, the one so lost to the lore of the woods that he slipped beyond my reach from time to time.

Daen's fists clenched and unclenched. "One thing, my love. You sense one thing out of place and you will yourself back to me. Thoughts are deeds out there. Fly back."

His were the eyes I last saw before I closed mine.

I caught the rhythm of Cibrien's breathing. Inhale, exhale, relax, release … My arms and legs responded easily. Less of the soul attached there, I reasoned. The tension in my chest, my head eased in miniscule increments, coerced away into nothingness as I followed the steps I had gone over with my Roman again and again as he lay on my temple floor. Then my breathing was forgotten and the darkness behind my eyelids transformed into something else. A vibration. An overpowering whirr. An awareness. And then with a leap out of the flesh, I was free.

"Cibrien," I thought immediately.

Nothing.

"Cibrien?"

I calmed, gathering myself tightly while the impression of something like eyesight, which I so needed in this plane, slowly came into focus.

"I'm here," came the gasp from beside and around me.

Cibrien materialized steadily, growing from a thought to a shape, and finally into an altogether solid-looking version of himself.

"Try picturing the key." His astral mouth didn't move when he spoke. Daen's would have, if only for the sheer drama of it. Instead, Cibrien pushed fast, efficient thoughts to me.

"I can't hold static after the thought is made," I warned. "Think of me quickly—so you can follow."

Even as the idea reached him, I was gone. The impression of the small golden triangle crept into my mind and I was shooting across existence. I floated and soared all at once, passing over buildings and trees that looked familiar. I didn't see any of these landmarks distinctly, so great was my speed. But my mind caught an impression of everything and there was too much glittering information sweeping through me to hold onto or make sense of. A ripple of energy passed through my spirit when I knew for the first time that all the tidings and details I received on this journey were from the present. I wasn't slipping inside the Record. I wasn't seeing scenes from antiquity anymore.

My flight slowed and grew aimless. The memories hadn't surfaced in such a long time. They had blended with who I now was, hadn't they? I would have shivered. I fought to concentrate on my remembrance of the key.

I stopped. Faster than light or sound was the travel, and so was the halt. I hovered above cement steps that must have been warmed with the late afternoon sun. An alley in the distance, a street to the front, the grand scale and dark glass on the doors of the building in front of me told me where I'd returned. I laughed out into the universe for none to hear. Winger and I had been so close. The Cairo Museum.

I sensed Cibrien beside me and when I glanced over, saw the vague shape of him like an outline of gold pulsation. His appearance startled me at first; I was used to Daen's manner and style, his profound sense of artistry in detail. Odd that Cibrien's own unique mastery didn't carry over into this realm. His actions were precise and wise here, without the art.

Together we thought ourselves inside the very heart of the building. I might have gasped had I lungs and breath in them. All around me, the dug up and disturbed leered. Sacrilege to break the eternal rest of the dead—though I had known even when creating the mummies and artifacts that one day mankind would see them and learn. Oh, but they gleaned so precious little. Gone was the knowledge of the temple sect. Gone, the trappings and rituals of priest and priestess. Tattered and blown away like dust, my world. Gone. Only reflections in the Record and the trinkets I had hidden away were of consequence now.

I glided with Cibrien at my side. A security guard roamed the aisles and we were no more than unseen wraiths to him. In freshly wiped glass cases were beads and bits of shattered pottery, papyri and carved lapis lazuli. I would not have been so shaken were I not visiting the museum for the first time in this altered state without substance and time. The High Priest's own funerary rites seemed but a blink away, yet there sat a golden tablet carved in the centuries after his death. And here was a now-rotten scrap of linen my novices might have worn, clean and crisp in my memory as they fluttered away from the Roman.

Cibrien pushed a sentiment of thanks to me. The pyre and my insistence on it assured we would not bump into his shriveled time-blackened corpse in this place. The question of my own demise had not come to my mind in weeks. Suddenly I feared it.

Cibrien simply shrugged his form and led me upstairs through more displays, past the boy king whose exhumation had proven most profitable for Egypt. Our curiosity sated, I stilled.

"I'm going to imagine the key again now. Stay near." It came to me, the image of the gleaming triangle with its assortment of short, strong spikes gracing the back and waiting for the turn of my hand against the lock.

I snapped forward and stopped, my otherworldly vision knocked out. My ability to sense earthly aromas wasn't working sharply either, unpleasantly pointing out to me how ill at ease I was. Then something like dust and mildew came to me and passed. I concentrated on sight and knew suddenly that I had landed in a very dark place. I gathered myself tightly again, the glow of my energy illuminating the area around me. Soon Cibrien found me and added to the lustrous light source.

"It's the basement," he said. "Or a storage room."

"They don't know what it is, do they? To the museum, it's just some necklace they can't fit into a particular dynasty. So here it sits."

I moved close to the plain stainless steel and wood

worktable in front of me. Stacks upon stacks of paperwork and papyrus sat gathering age on the table's edges. But in the middle, arranged so that their chains lay in careful loops, a gathering of necklaces and bracelets sat waiting for me.

"Dear Lord above," I thought, "that's the one."

Cibrien followed my meaning and began to hum with concentration. Golden light poured from him. If he could carry it, if he could somehow bring it back across the threshold into the solid world in which Daen, Winger, and the hotel waited …

The brightness in the room increased. Something wasn't right here. There was too much light now, more than either Cibrien or I generated. I thought of the guard and the possibility that he had flipped a switch during his rounds. He had probably slipped outside to smoke the apple-flavored waterpipe hanging from his belt. He would stay for hours and watch the sun sink red in the sky, while we watched something else rise silver in that room.

Like a color turned inside out, a brilliant darkness materialized near the back of the room. Faintly blue-black and outlined in silver, an energy took shape with wings unfurling to span the entirety of the wall across from us. This creature was not as we were, neither human nor Watcher by design. It was at home in this realm and echelons lower, angel no more, Fallen One hunting us.

My training welled up inside me and abruptly dispelled the rising terror. I would give this abomination no more energy on which to feed.

"Neteru. Urshu." Its voice rumbled low and powerful like the growl of a demonic lion, features hidden in the metallic darkness. "I know you."

"It was you in the cave," I answered.

Baleful laughter ricocheted around us. "Foolish Watchers. Do not believe all you read. The end is imminent, but not yet the outcome."

I felt as if a vice clamped down around me. Cibrien was caught, too, and it was in both our primal instincts to struggle. Chaos unleashed around us with the leathery flap of wings, obsidian radiance, the whirl of sulfurous fumes and a deafening drone of laughter and long-dead language.

I cried out against the darkness, cried to the inspiration for those cemetery statues so grand and protective.

"You still pray for him. Why?" It demanded, remembered. More beings like him collected behind his wings, minions of a sort.

The roar overpowered Cibrien and me as the Fallen One who spoke to us swooped. As he neared, his eyes burned silver fire and the shape like a man's grew visible between the wings.

I felt it then, the saving grace of kind, strong intervention, like angels from some higher order arriving. Angels! Real angels! I heard the divine thought: *Slip into sleep and your body will reclaim you.* It went against my natural instinct to struggle, to fight.

A second later I awoke in bed, frozen inside my body until I felt the click of connection as my muscles came back to life. The bed trembled with Cib's return. My eyes opened, but our guardians were not at the foot of the bed as they should have been. The wood around the door adjoining the suites was splintered, the mattress once against it now flat on the floor.

Daen appeared, eyes flashing like black ice as he

lifted his hands off Cibrien's head. "Awaken, High Priest and lend support to my words." He had touched our bodies to help drive us home. If the divine cavalry hadn't arrived, his touches would have rescued us.

I jumped off of the bed to stand beside Daen. Tiran crouched low in the corner, fury marking her face as her red hair swirled about her shoulders. The tall, light-haired man with the crystalline eyes stood near the broken door, gazing absently through the twisted frame as if awaiting others.

"Rosier should have taken you," she spat at me.

"Rosier is no match," Daen countered. "I know him well." Whether his confidence was real or feigned, even I could not tell.

Tiran's voice changed to a purr. "Come with me, then. You don't desire what He desires. Or what the lowly Scribe beside you desires. Think of what you could create with all you know."

Daen grew sinister and still as the olden words came forth from his lips. He murmured the language of the Temple of the Sun and Moon, chanted in a tongue that had thrived before that. Cibrien's voice mingled with Daen's.

I knew this spell! I remembered with sudden clarity the song-prayer to expel such wretchedness. I added my voice to theirs. If the Fallen Ones had escaped the battle that must have ensued with our beloved guardians, they would not find a safe place to haunt here.

I stepped forward with Daen and Cibrien just behind me at each side. I raised my palms toward Tiran. "Blow wind, blow," I said with a smile. It was my dance from under the willow tree at the river's bend. Winger would be proud as the very air itself stirred to press the woman against the corner of the room.

"Winger?" I called as I held her in place. My friend gave no answer.

The clear-eyed man rushed toward the broken door, and at first it seemed he might flee. Then to my horror, another man and then another pushed through. I could not hold all four intruders, and instead let the air press Tiran harder up against the wall while Cibrien and Daen held away the Fallen Ones and caused these humans pain with their words. I could see agony on their faces, but still they advanced.

Out of the corner of my eye I caught a movement from just inside the bathroom door. I heard the sharp click of nails on the tile floor. In a blur of motion, an animal leapt into the room and without warning, went for the throat of the last intruder. There was a fierce grace in the beast, and it was wholly recognizable.

I jumped in shock, releasing Tiran to fall to the floor. Cibrien's chant died on his lips. Daen caught one of my hands and looked into my eyes with a somber expression that explained everything. Wolf Boy.

Silver-gray with long fur, the enormous wolf advanced on the second man. Tiran and her tall companion literally ran for their lives, so seized by terror that they would not stop to look back. The two strange men hadn't time to scream before the snap of their necks dropped them to the carpet. A clean kill, so little blood.

"Warrior brother," I whispered.

The wolf turned its head toward me and I took an involuntary step backward. Blue. Its eyes were blue. And they knew me. A visible shimmer consumed the wolf, like a glamour falling aside except that this glamour had held substance. In place of the wolf sat Winger, silent and serious, on the floor.

"I don't even know what to say," I said at long last. "How is this possible?"

Winger stretched his limbs and lifted himself stiffly from the floor to the bed. "It just is."

"I've never seen it. I've read stories about shapeshifters and werewolves—" I began.

"I'm neither," he answered. "I think it's like the glamour you pull around you when you darken and lighten. I've only done this once before now."

"Much as I'd roll over in ecstasy to have this conversation, we need to leave." Daen eyed the broken door warily. "Immediately."

I peered intensely at Daen for a moment and it crossed my mind to question him about the museum. The fact hadn't escaped me that mere days ago he had joked about finding the key there. And then it had happened. Even if he had known its location and kept it from me, which I couldn't fathom, where had we to go but with him? I wanted my castle. Then a second panic hit me.

"We were attacked before Cibrien could get the key."

"No." Cibrien smiled and sank to his knees on the carpet, the brightness of joy and exhaustion in his eyes. "I'll be able to travel in a moment," he said. "Just give me a moment to settle back into myself."

The back of Cibrien's hand rested against his thigh. Then slowly, his fingers uncurled from his clenched fist to reveal the gleam of a gold chain. As if it would no longer allow itself to be held, the chain slinked across his leg and landed on the floor beside him, pulling the charm along behind it. The smooth triangle rested upright, and I leaned down and swept it up in my fingers.

With trembling hands I separated the chain and lowered it around my neck. The triangle fell to that center place just below my collarbone. The short spikes touched my skin in a massage, smooth and polished rather than sharpened pinpricks. On the front the faintest of etchings showed themselves when the light was right, and I knew the symbol of the Priestess Scribe in those ancient runes. I also knew the key had found its natural home as it rested against my chest. That I had ever been without its adornment was the thing most unnatural.

"I think just maybe this key opens all seven books," I said. "Why would I have designed others with this one so perfect? Are you sure you don't remember that, Daen?"

Daen reached out and grabbed my hand. "We need to leave. Now, Ariana. I can feel them coming."

Winger nodded in agreement, his heightened senses never failing. I wanted to ask the details of the Wolf and what it had to do with Daen and the desert hills outside Sedona. I wanted to demand of Cibrien to teach me the carrying skill he had used, if it wasn't yet beyond hope for me. At least Daen's mind I thought I knew. There were too many ideas, too many dazzling displays of awakened power—and too little time. So, instead I flew into action.

We gathered our belongings at a run, tossing what little we possessed into our bags. It would be only a matter of time before the hotel staff discovered the bodies left tangled on the carpet and the twisted framework that once was a door. We had to be far, far from the city before the police arrived. I wondered what Grey would think when he heard the news, when our descriptions were broadcast throughout Cairo.

Down the back stairs we bolted, not caring to wait for the elevator or the possibility of becoming trapped in its confines. We paused in a rear hallway while I addressed the overnight delivery slip and stuck it to the envelope carrying Ryu's painted message.

"Don't check us out," Winger warned Cibrien. "It'll buy us time to get out of Egypt."

Cibrien nodded sternly, handed Daen his travel bag, and walked away with only the package in hand. We all watched from the distance as he calmly approached the concierge and with a smile asked him to take care of the delivery. He pressed some added incentive into the man's hand and then just as casually turned and strolled back to us.

Together again, we raced outside. "Alright, Daen. The show's yours now," I said. "Where to?"

"Do you have enough energy to lighten us?" Daen asked.

"Yes, but we'd all have to touch for it to pass to all of you. People will certainly remember seeing a bunch of foreigners leaving hand-in-hand." I looked from one man to the next, none of whom blended easily into a crowd.

Daen nodded. "Then you hold hands with Winger. The two of you are the only ones with family that could be traced back to you. Try for red hair or something. See if you can drastically change the height. I've seen you do it before."

"How do you know I don't have family?" Cibrien asked.

Daen smiled. "Am I wrong?"

Winger took my hand and in a heartbeat a shimmer

overtook us. The glamour took no more than a thought, no effort at all now that I had grown used to the trick. To the rest of the world we looked like an elderly couple, bent nearly double with age and holding fast to one another's hand for support.

Daen almost smiled again as he slipped on a pair of black sunglasses. "They won't find a trace of my name or roots anywhere anyway. Let them all see me."

Cibrien reached out and set his hand gently on my shoulder. "Give me the red hair then. I'll pretend I'm helping you two into the taxi. We're going to catch a taxi, aren't we?" A steady stream of the vehicles circled the hotel.

Daen raised his hand in response and a taxi stopped. Quickly, he caught up all our bags and tossed them into the trunk while Cibrien, Winger and I slid cautiously across the backseat, careful not to lose contact. Daen got in last and shut the door behind him. We waited for the word "airport" to come from his lips, but it didn't.

The last shreds of sunlight illuminated the sand and dust in the air that stirred up from the street, and when the sun fell from view, so did the tiny particles. They were like Rosier, possibly nearby and all around us, no less diminished though we could not see him.

Daen spoke to the driver in a stream of smooth, jovial Cairo Arabic. The vehicle sped down the crowded, narrow street. All the while, Daen and the driver kept up their lively conversation. We came to a halt in front of a train station.

I looked at Daen in awe.

"What? You used to speak it," he said. "There are advantages to not forgetting."

Cautiously as we could, we slid from the vehicle

while Daen handled the fare and our baggage. He gave a sidelong glance toward Winger and nearly snarled at the degrading burden of lifting Winger's bag. Winger laughed low in his throat and the sound did not suit his glamour-induced elderly physique.

There was nothing of glamour about the train we caught at the gritty station there in the darkness. The last train of the evening, sliding away across the horizon like the sun, someone said. It sounded romantic even if it weren't true. It slipped into the night on wobbly tracks, stark with its aging wear-stained seats and metal sides. A private sleeping car was ours and once inside, Winger and Cibrien were free to take their hands away from me and we blessedly looked like ourselves again.

Winger and I sat side by side on the tattered blue cushions facing Daen and Cibrien who sat across from us. A rickety table was bolted to the floor between the four of us.

"Where to begin, where to begin ..." Daen said as he propped his forearms against the edge of the table. Pipe smoke from passengers far back in another car crept in through the cracks and tinted the air a grayish-orange under the faint lights.

Cibrien kicked off his shoes. "There's the necklace, the Fallen Ones, our resident werewolf—or how about telling us where we're going."

"I told you, I'm not a damn werewolf," Winger snapped. "No more than Ariana is an eighty-year-old woman with a limp."

The steady turn of the wheels against the rails rocked us. The necklace hung peculiarly weightless against my chest. The lights of Cairo were slipping away far behind.

"Gifts," I said at length. "We could have been brilliant mathematicians or opera singers, but no. We're—this."

Daen leaned forward. "We'll have to use those gifts if we want to survive. I take it you caught another glimpse of Rosier?"

I nodded slowly.

"He can't harm us much in the state he's in. There's a lot of protection there and he knows it. You think Tiran is scary? She's nothing. Wait and see if Rosier comes into the flesh." Daen crossed his arms and leaned back in his seat again. "I knew him personally, and even I would prefer not to see that."

"If I were him," Winger said, "I'd claim a willing body. Then I'd form a very small, determined group. And I'd come after us."

"They'd have to find us first." I looked into Daen's eyes for concurrence. "And they'll have trouble doing that."

"We can't hide forever in this castle of yours," Winger said.

Daen narrowed his eyes. "You haven't seen it."

"Tell me about the wolf," I said softly to Winger.

"It's nothing," he answered. "I think it's an illusion like your lightening and darkening. That's all. But not nearly so effortless. I can feel it coming right from the center of me."

"How do you do it?" Cibrien asked.

Winger shrugged and leaned forward across the table. "In no way I'm proud of."

I placed my hand on his shoulder. Of little comfort, I suspected.

"Nothing born from hatred is." Daen's eyes bored into Winger's.

"If that's the case," Winger said, "then I suppose I have you to thank for my gift."

"I don't understand," I said. "Is this what happened between you and Daen when you tracked him from Tokyo? Is this what you didn't want to tell me?"

"In part." Winger nodded slowly. He sat up straight again before he continued. "I think I've always felt the wolf inside me. I mean—the teeth. Come on. It's always made sense. I don't know if this comes from Hopi training, or from some trauma stain on my soul from the day of the wolves on the bank of the river. Something in me has changed since Zep Tepi and it's just now coming out."

"Can you control it?" I looked at Winger with new eyes. He was always graceful and powerful. Primal with sophistication. Now he was even more so.

"Yes. I can control it. Hell, the only time I can even do it is when I'm threatened, or when someone I love is." He looked pointedly across the table at Daen. "Even then I think I can push the sensation down and away. I just can't bring it up arbitrarily."

Cibrien exhaled loudly and ran his hands though his unruly brown hair. "It amazes me that one of us spontaneously generated an ability that we weren't created with and didn't even train to bring out. Now, Ariana, what about your necklace."

I touched it. I couldn't help it. "It's the only key. Don't ask me how I know. I just do. There aren't seven of these scattered around the world. Just the seven writings. One key."

The train wheels clattered, the movement lulling us.

"Do you recognize it now?" Cibrien leaned closer to peer at its detail, but refrained from touching it as if it were a sacred relic.

"Absolutely. I think I must have made this myself and infused it with something magical that I can't even remember. It's as if a small part of me, of my essence, is actually fused with the gold. I'd swear it goes back to Zep Tepi."

"I don't like hearing that." Winger scowled.

"It fits me. It's come back to me. And it will help us. There's no doubt in my mind that Rosier or the other Fallen Ones will never ever open a book of my writing without this key."

Cibrien studied it at length. "Can I hold it for a second?"

I nodded and turned so that Winger could unfasten the clasp. When the metal left its nesting place against my chest, I gasped. Whether it was the sensation of cool air striking its place or the sudden absence of that weightless strength that caused the response, I do not know. Yet I was startled and at a loss when the chain slid into Winger's strong calloused hands and passed into Cibrien's.

The roll of the train had become nauseating, endless and nauseating.

"Are you okay?" Winger asked me.

"I'm fine." The night had grown too black outside. We were sailing into nowhere.

"She already had it with her in Egypt," Daen said. "Even as a child she hung it around her neck. I saw it there everyday."

"It's awfully cold in here," I said.

"What's wrong?" Daen asked. "I can feel that you're ill all of the sudden."

"I don't know." There wasn't enough oxygen in the

sleeping car. The smoke filtering from the guests at the back of the train was too much.

Daen grabbed the necklace roughly out of Cibrien's hands and slid it across the table to Winger.

"Put it back on her," he commanded. "Now."

"No. Not if that thing causes this."

"Just do it. Once she's had it on, I don't think she can go without it. I can feel what she's feeling." Daen crossed his arms in front of him tightly. "It's freezing in here."

"It's eighty degrees at least," Winger said.

Daen collapsed against the back of his seat. "We're bound, Ariana," he said. "But this is ridiculous."

I heard vaguely as Winger drew a deep breath. I felt his fingers at my throat. Not quick enough. I caught the scent of smoke in the air. Stifling. Cold.

Then everything faded away from me.

Chapter Eighteen

Haven flight
across a sea of
sepia memories.
Dawn blush, begin us anew.

With a single breath, in the same heartbeat, Daen and I awoke together on the narrow mattress inside the old sleeping car.

"I remember what else we used to do at the same time. Every time," I whispered and heard him moan in return.

The train's swaying had stopped and the oh-so faint glow of earliest morning light peeked in through the dirty windows. The smell of saltwater drifted through the air.

"Alexandria," Daen murmured against the back of my neck.

"Ariana," I corrected with a soft laugh.

He rolled over and pulled me into his arms. "You know what I mean, love."

"We're flying out of the airport here?"

His warm lips nuzzled their way down my collarbone. Dangerous. Delicious. I sat up quickly to avoid temptation. Unusually trusting, Winger and Cibrien were, to have thrown the two of us in together that way.

"Back to business then." He stretched his arms out over his head and sat up. "Hey you two, wakey wakey," Daen called out.

Winger threw back the curtain. "We're awake, damn it. And it's about time you came to. Cib thought we ought to let you sleep it off. The train's been stopped for a couple hours now. There's a car wreck or something up ahead on the tracks. But I can see the city and the coastline from here."

"It's almost dawn," I said as the room brightened.

Daen jumped down from the bed. "We have to get off the train and keep moving."

"That's it?" Winger said. "You two get sick and pass out cold. Then you spend the entire night talking in your sleep about things I sure as hell don't remember. Then it's just 'wakey wakey?' Like nothing happened?"

Daen nodded. "Never take that necklace off her again."

My hand flew to my chest. It was there, that tiny etched bit of magical gold, resting precisely where it should be.

Cibrien appeared with a smile. "Leave it to Ariana to build in a fool-proof way to hang onto a trinket. Wouldn't have guessed the charm would be strong enough to bring the mighty Daen down, too."

"It wasn't the charm," Daen mumbled. "It was Ariana."

"Get your things together," Winger growled. "As the crow flies, there are about two miles of sand between us and the nearest edge of town. I assume we're going to the airport here? Direct flight out?"

"If it's safe. If we get there and it's not, there are alternate routes booked."

I think the sleep following the removal of the necklace produced a kind of hangover effect in me. I was awake and alert, and yet I was not. Time slowed and sped up all at once for me. Daen experienced the same sensation and it bothered him more than he would admit. But the nearness of the necklace healed.

I remember swinging our belongings over our shoulders, slipping unseen through an open door, and trudging across the sand for well over an hour. Even in the fresh new texture of the morning, the Near East sun forced us into a slow motion trek. Gradually our scenery changed from tan nothingness to the crumbling paved back streets of Alexandria.

A taxi stopped for us eventually. The airport greeted us minutes later. The cool blues of the Mediterranean disappeared under sparkling light and then wispy clouds.

We were on our way.

Winger grasped the arm of his seat too tightly on the airplane, liking the method of the journey no better than before. The plane had taken off smoothly, yet still his nerves were on edge.

"These things skew my senses," he murmured and I heard it even though he was seated with Cibrien a row in front of me.

Daen breathed deeply. "I think a little rain storm is in order. You and I could conspire to ground every plane leaving Egypt if we wanted."

I nodded and stirred the wind far below on the ground, and with Daen's command of water, sent droplets of rain pelting the airport below. The desert didn't often see storms like this, even in the city of Alexandria sitting along the sea with its greater moisture.

"I think we overestimated ourselves," we said in unison.

Our burst of energy was short-lived and the storm would subside in no time at all. Perhaps we had bought us a few more minutes of distraction while the authorities in Cairo searched for people matching our description and the train conductors pondered the empty sleeping car.

We crossed the world and I could imagine a fading map made of parchment stretched out on the land underneath the plane, a dotted red line forming across it as we flew just like in the movies. Daen had connected and convoluted our journey like a master of illusion. We stopped in Athens, changed planes again in Frankfurt, again in Rome, and then again … Days literally passed on the run until finally the meandering took us to London. Our trail would be hard to find, harder to follow.

From the airport we took a bus, then another train. We rented a car and drove into remote areas where we returned the vehicle at the last possible opportunity. From that point, we were on our own. And we were on foot.

As the ground passed by in feet, and feet merged into miles beneath our shoes, we found we had advantages that others did not. When the wind grew too fierce, I stilled it. When rain threatened, Daen dried the skies. Strangest of all to see was Winger's power. A boulder blocked our easiest route and he shook it aside, the soil underneath it seemingly liquefied with his concentration well directed.

"Told you. Been practicing," he said with a grin.

On we trudged until night fell on that first day. Step by step we were not only disappearing from our enemy, but from civilization. Without tents, Winger built a temporary shelter from the branches, needles and leaves that blanketed the ground. We unrolled some sleeping bags we'd purchased earlier, and set them side by side.

"Careful not to leave your bodies," Cibrien cautioned. "It can be spontaneous in sleep."

"We know," Winger told him. "Believe me, we know."

"I wish Ryu were here," I said. "He could build us a campfire just by snapping his fingers."

"We don't need him," Daen said.

I turned on my side and looked at his profile in the dark. "Yes we do."

"What for?"

I thought for a moment. "It's safer with us all together."

Daen laughed. "For whom? Him?"

"For all of us," I answered.

"Aw, come on," Daen groaned. "The guy could dance in a teacup. What kind of protection could he possibly be?"

"I didn't mean that I need another bodyguard. Can't you feel it?" I asked.

Cibrien nodded. "I can. Ever since you put on that necklace."

"Do you think he got our message, Cib?" I asked.

"I hope so. Can you sense him?"

"No," I answered. "I haven't been able to since he left Egypt. It's still like he cut me off. Or he isn't even there anymore."

Winger moaned and flung his arm across his eyes. "Could we all shut up and get some sleep now?"

"Yeah," Daen said, "better store up on the sleep before the full moon comes around."

We acted like children suppressing our giggles with hands pressed over our mouths.

"Great, just great," Winger whispered.

Daen laughed out loud. "'night Mary Ellen."

Cibrien caught the joke. "'night Wolf Boy."

"Go to sleep, you bastards," Winger growled.

•

The midmorning sun hit the damp ground and heated it enough to send little curls of steam upward and around our feet. My boots rubbed on the backs of my ankles and Cibrien's backpack kept sliding out of position. Winger was the wise one with only his knife strapped to his side and a water bottle around his neck. He got by without the things the rest of us thought we needed.

"I don't have any idea where we are," Cibrien said. "Are we still in England?"

Daen raised his eyebrows. "I'm not sure I ought to say our location aloud until we're safely tucked away inside our hidey hole."

"There's no sulphur," Winger said. "And it's pretty obvious we're at least still in the United Kingdom somewhere. You could enlighten us."

"No chance."

We followed Daen deeper into rare woods only to come out again onto rolling green plains that would end in low mountains straight ahead in our line of vision.

"You must have picked the only place in this country left where you have to travel two days on foot to reach it," Winger said. "I approve."

Daen smelled the air before answering. "The first thing I did after the supplies were hauled in was eliminate the road. There was a small gravel lane leading in for fifteen miles or so off a larger road that people around here sometimes travel. It cost a small fortune to do, but I put in a damn forest of full-grown trees and bushes over the top of it. After ten years of undergrowth settling in, you can't even tell a road was ever there. It's all grown together."

"The place can't be too secret then, if supplies were brought in," Cibrien said.

"Doesn't matter. The history books would have record of the place anyway," I said. "It's been privately owned for centuries. Neighbors probably know about it, but they don't give it a second thought by now I'll bet. If it hadn't been so remote in the first place, someone would probably have turned it into a bed and breakfast."

Daen shivered. "That was never going to happen."

Cibrien adjusted his backpack again. "I almost wish I'd been born again between Egypt and now."

"But you wouldn't remember the chants and spells," I said. "Or anything else as clearly. We're all better off for it."

"I don't know. I may have traded a little memory to have lived in places like this," he said. The crisp blue skies soothed him no less than the rest of us, but I suspected that Daen held back the rain. The land was too green and too near the water to have remained without moisture for long.

Winger's focus hadn't shifted from Daen. "So you're saying that there's a section along where the old road was, where only trees separate the outside world from our fortress?"

Daen nodded. "That's the weakest section. You have to understand though, the castle is designed in the style King Edward I made famous. There's a very high stone wall several yards thick wrapping all around the outside of the castle. A few feet of that wall extend below ground, too. It makes the outer bailey fairly secure all on its own. Hard to dig under, hard to climb. The inner bailey is walled off with a second stone barricade."

"We'll need to reinforce that weak spot somehow anyway," Winger said, the wheels in his mind turning visibly. "What about the rest of the way around the castle?"

I smiled. "There's water along the entire front border of the land. And cliffs. Nothing but high, jagged brown rocks and cold black water. Very easy to defend. The water was too shallow there for ships."

Daen smiled back. "Your memory really has awakened."

"What's on the backside?" Winger asked with a gleam in his blue eyes.

"Those cliffs Ariana remembers wrap like a crescent all the way from the sea around the back. The other side is the weak point where the rocks taper off into those low mountains you see ahead. The only deterrent is that a person has to approach on foot more or less from this direction, and it's one hell of a long walk."

"They'd have a car at least as far as that main road went," I pointed out. "We couldn't risk abandoning one by the side of the road and drawing attention. They won't care."

"Still, fifteen miles is fifteen miles," Cibrien said as he paused for a breath. The rolling plains felt endless, but somehow, we had almost reached the edge of those mountains.

Winger surveyed the dense tree line ahead. "We'll have to work up a defense strategy when we get there."

"Don't worry, Wolf Boy. I have an arsenal in the castle even you can appreciate. Not to mention the laser alarm system all around the place. I figured we could put booby traps in together. Pits with sharpened stakes, snares …"

Winger's teeth flashed. "For a second, I almost liked you."

The grass was growing wetter by the minute and soaking through the leather sides of my boots. My hair, which had grown nearly to my waist, twisted uncomfortably around me in the growing heat, so I braided it as we walked.

"Guys—" Something sickening gripped me and I stopped in my tracks. I grabbed for the necklace. It was still in place.

Daen's brown eyes were in front of me in an instant. "What is it?"

The feeling passed. "I don't know."

"The Fallen Ones aren't anywhere near us," Winger assured. "We have them too well blocked. They don't have a clue where we are. And Tiran is probably still scouring Cairo for us."

I shrugged. "I felt ill, but it's gone now. Probably just the heat." But we all knew better even as I brushed the incident aside with that flimsy excuse.

Daen's eyes narrowed. "We need to get you inside the castle walls. Maybe that will help."

"You couldn't feel what I felt?" I asked.

He shook his head. "Too faint."

"We'd be subject to an air attack," Winger blurted out.

"Are you still back on that?" Cibrien chided.

Daen jumped back into the conversation. "The British Royal Air Force would shoot them down before they got close. You can't trespass into another's airspace these days."

"Gliders from the tops of the cliffs?" Cibrien suggested.

"Sure. And how do you propose they carry them there—"

I tuned out the conversation and just walked. Heel, toe, heel, toe. The muscles in my thighs were cramping beyond belief, but at least the sun was waning from its midday peak. I stirred a breeze around us to cool the beads of sweat from the backs of our necks. If anything, the necklace strengthened me as if providing an energy born from hope and wonder for whatever the future held. Neither gild nor flesh could wait to see what we could open together.

I was also beginning to remember the land on which I strode. The scent of the air and the color of the soil kicked up under our feet were familiar at last. My heart pounded as we began our ascent up the mountains, weaved through trees, turned to our right and began the final leg of the journey.

A ridge came into view ahead of us and I stopped. In a few steps we would look over into my once and future home. I would set eyes upon the place where Daen and I had lived, had loved, had left behind to travel to the stone rings and therein bury the writings I held inside a leather book.

We all stood back a step or two, just far enough away

from the edge that we couldn't see what sat on the earth below. Daen and Winger each reached for one of my hands, and held me tightly between them while Cibrien walked forward and peered over the rim.

"My God," he gasped. "It's magnificent. Ryu should have been here to see this with us."

The rest of us moved quietly beside him. Worshipful. Awestruck. The afternoon sun flooded into the canyon below us like strands of heavenly illumination pointing out a scene from a medieval history book come to life. At the other end of the property, the dark sea churned against rock.

"The engineer, James of St. George, needed fifteen hundred men with him to build it the first time. I just needed the memory of one woman," Daen whispered.

"How did you do this by yourself?" I asked in a whisper like his.

Daen squeezed my hand. "Priestess. Ariana of the Pyramids. Need you even ask?"

"The heka," I said with certainty as I surveyed the enormous gray stones fitted together with precision, the height of the glorious watchtowers.

"I'd like to make a flag with our seal. See our colors flying in the wind above the castle to declare it our sanctuary, our temple," Cibrien said. "But I suppose it would give us away too quickly and I'll have to forego the art."

"Paint our seal on linen or wool. We'll hang it as a tapestry in the Great Hall," I suggested.

We all leaned closer to the edge and looked straight down below to see the back of the castle. Inside the main body of the castle, surrounded by walls and courtyards, I could discern the windows of the solars, medieval bedrooms. From my solar, the view would be that of a great rose garden enclosed by an intricate fence and an iron gate to connect its ends. I pulled a current of air up from the side of the castle grounds to me high above on the mountain.

"I can actually smell the roses on the wind," I said.

"It's still blessed ground," Daen said. "Your roses bloom year-round and never die, even in the snow. I think they've been waiting for you to come back, too."

I closed my eyes. "Where the trees are over there, there used to be the castle town. I can almost hear the blacksmith's hammer and the noise from the birds that lady who lived by the tavern used to keep."

The colors stirred and danced in the air around us, crackling down the mountain and sparkling into the canyon, into the corners of my home. Our private aurora borealis was stronger than usual, stronger even than when Ryuichi was with us.

I pulled my hands free from the two men and gripped my stomach. "There it is again," I said. "That sick feeling. I think it's the Whispering."

"Don't try to hear it yet, Ariana," Cibrien warned. "Not until we get you into that castle. If what Daen says is true, and I feel it is, the place is built on one of the original sacred sites. Once there, you can let down the block."

I took Daen's hand again. "It's passed. And I know what kind of precious place our castle is. I remember its secrets. Let's go."

We followed the edge of the ravine around to the right, to the place where the old road once ran and the new forest now stood. We lost sight of the stronghold from time to time, yet at each place where we caught sight of it again, it seemed to loom ever larger. Slipping between trees we finally emerged at a clearing. Before us stood my castle.

The immense gate to the outer bailey yawned open for us. As we walked near I could feel the hidden aspects of the place. The air patterns moved in unusual currents as if to carry anything toxic up and away from us. The soil was rich and black, loaded with a mixture of metals and minerals the likes of which I could only guess. Any crops we wished to plant in that ground would flourish. A creek trickled through the place, and both inside and outside the gray walls, springs surrounded by lush green grass oozed crystal clear water. We couldn't be placed under siege in this place. We never had been. We had simply risked giving up such a wonder for the sake of hiding my writings where they were supposed to be hidden.

"But there aren't any phone or power lines," Winger noted.

"We have everything. Just wait and see," Daen said.

We stepped cautiously through the bastion gates. Everything was in place, everything constructed in painstaking detail just as I remembered it, right down to the angled holes in the towers for the archers to shoot through. Right down to the tan and gray cobblestones that lined the path in front of us.

The gates groaned under the strain of movement as the three men struggled to close them. From the outside, they looked like iron and steel over wood. But from the inside, they revealed that Daen had reinforced them with newer metals, some stronger steel than we had had so long ago, something that would have held up under any battering ram. Daen slid a series of thick steel poles in place across the back of the gates.

"Medieval deadbolts," he said.

We followed the cobblestones across the enormous open space toward the inner bailey. The outer bailey's emptiness seemed peculiar. Hay wagons, merchants' carts, horses, and a training field had filled the place with activity once. The mews and kennels had been somewhere, too. Over to the side?

Daen nudged me. "At least it smells better without them."

In one place, a long rectangular storage area had been constructed against, or into, the wall itself.

Daen took note of my gaze. "I have oil drums and spare belts and filters for the backup generators, about five hundred cords of split wood for the fireplaces, ammunition—"

"Only here?" Winger asked.

"No," Daen said. "There's another area near the inner courtyard and more supplies inside the castle in case we were to be cut off from one source or another."

"You said 'backup generators.' What's the main power source?" I asked.

"Solar," he said, "with a little added help."

And then we passed through the giant front doors at the heart of the castle and entered the Great Hall. A long, wood table took possession of the room's center, surrounded by heavy, splendidly carved chairs. Thrones, really. There had once been benches there instead. I liked the new style better.

Trestle tables stood stacked in a corner for those who would not be seated at the main table, as if one day we might have a gathering there of grand scale and all the Ancients would come into our sanctuary. At the head of the Hall was a gigantic stone fireplace and a smaller one sat tucked away in a sidewall toward its middle.

The details were so many …

A wave of nausea passed over me. "There it is again," I said. "I'm going to let it in now."

I slid slowly into one of the wooden thrones and rested my head against the high back. The Whispering swept into the room, safe to be heard and deliberately blocked no more.

Cibrien began to hum. "Can you hear that? It's music of some sort."

"I can't hear it," I said. "All I feel is this sickening emptiness. Like the Whispers aren't carrying a message but pointing out the lack of one."

Cibrien swayed. "It's a song."

Daen hummed along. "Hell, even I can hear that."

"That's not music," Winger said. "It's a mess."

The queasiness subsided and allowed a few notes to reach me. "It's Ryu," I said. "It has to be."

"Maybe his temple training has weakened to that?" Cibrien asked.

"No. When he was composing Hope for me, I heard it. He let me hear it along the way."

Daen breathed in and out. "I can see there's no avoiding the pop star pest, is there? Damn it."

Cibrien laughed. "What are you going to do when there are more than just Winger, Ryu and I vying for our Scribe's precious attention?"

Daen narrowed his eyes. "The same thing I've always done. Been better than all of you combined."

Winger laughed. "You wish."

"I *know*," Daen countered. "And I'm sick of the innuendo, High Priest. That's the second comment I've heard you make to the effect that other Ancients are out there awakening. That somewhere out there, floating around aimlessly in the mist, someone we haven't found is just waiting to appear. Believe me, they're all like Grey now. Fallen and asleep. Not even worth the search."

The red-oranges of a spectacular sunset kissed the cold stone walls outside. It seemed to me that the colors warmed the stones, though it was not so. Already the rain, held back for hours, was gathering in great storm clouds that bruised the sky in the direction of the ocean.

"I'm too tired to worry about any of this right now. I'm going to take a bath and go to sleep. I'll leave you to your fighting."

I turned from the Great Hall, ascended the grand curving staircase, and walked directly down the upper-level hall to my solar. I needed no instruction from Daen. I remembered it all so vividly that I could almost feel the brush of a long-gone surcoat and tunic against my skin.

I didn't tell the others, but the hum of the mutilated song still resonated. I heard it now, slowly flowing with the Whispers. Ryuichi. We needed him with us. He wasn't safe outside our holy ground, but neither would we be safe attempting to retrieve him. With that same otherworldly hearing, I knew Cibrien chanted the old protection rites around the perimeter of the land. I heard Winger and Daen in low, heated debate. Cacophony. Dissonance.

The noise was too much to sort through as I let the hot water flow from a gilded faucet into an enormous claw-foot bathtub. Air from the pipes sputtered into the stream. All new, the plumbing and modernity, all unused for months while Daen went to bring me home. I sank into the soothing water and rested, truly rested, for the first time in longer than I cared to think about.

The sounds in my head quieted until only Cibrien's melodic, measured prayer and the hum of the Whispering remained. Without the sound of arguing, everything was too quiet. Peaceful.

"Too quiet," I said aloud to myself as the images of movement through trees flickered through my mind.

I sprang from the tub and grabbed a thick robe off of the hanger behind the bathroom door. I ran downstairs in spite of exhaustion.

Daen sat with one of his long legs swung over the arm of a throne-chair. He was turned toward the stairwell. Expecting me. Waiting.

"Now that's precision," he murmured and his words echoed in the room.

"It's going to be dark outside soon," I said. "And he's too tired."

"He insisted."

"He did it when I wasn't looking."

Daen nodded. "Yes. To avoid the protest. With his— ways ..." Daen's voice trailed off. "He can cover a lot of ground in not much time at all. And he knows where to go. He built the megalith rings, after all."

I trembled in anger. "Winger did not have to go get those writings. It could have waited."

"Until when?" Daen rose and walked over the foot of the stairs.

"Until Ryuichi is back with us," I half-yelled.

Daen brow furrowed. He moved close enough to me that even in the muted ambient lighting of the wall sconces I could see the gold flecks in his eyes.

"Winger had to do this now. Right now. There would be no other opportunity without risking exposure. This isn't like you, exhausted or not. What am I missing?"

I clutched my stomach and sank to the bottom step. Pain rolled through me as bits of my own energy leaked away. I imagined that my spirit was bleeding to death through tiny pinprick holes that precious somethings once filled.

"What you don't realize is that it's not just the necklace I can no longer go without. It's any of you."

Chapter Nineteen

Flawed force,
Enchantments built
absent alteration
lest they not last
the Gathering.

Daen swept me up in his arms and carried me back up the stairs. That he felt he had to, annoyed me. If anything, I had grown stronger over the months, more attuned, more aware of my mission. The necklace hung strongly around my throat, but even that wasn't enough. The person I had once been had infused something strange into that piece of jewelry, and now it made me ill.

Daen continued on step by step and treated me as if I weighed nothing, as if holding my full weight against his chest were no effort at all.

"I can walk," I said and pulled the belt of my bathrobe tighter in front.

"You're going to bed. Then I'm going to get Cibrien."

"No need," I said. "I already called out for him and Winger. Winger isn't hearing me, though. Signal too weak."

"What happened?" Cibrien called from below as he sprinted up the stairs to catch us.

"Too many gone," I whispered as another wave of nausea gripped me.

"She means that Ryu and Winger being gone from her at the same time is too much. Their absence is affecting her the same as when the necklace was removed."

Daen kicked open the door to my solar as Cibrien ran forward to turn down the covers on my bed. Even that detail was the same.

"Oh, Daen. It's exactly right," I said. For a moment I forgot my impairment.

The bed sat positioned in the center of the room, its head flat against the wall to the left of the door as we entered the room. Along its heavy frame ran carved scenes of miniature wolves near the edges. Winger would have laughed.

Daen set me down somewhat unceremoniously on the bed. I knew without inspection that underneath me, the wood frame was interlaced with heavy leather straps, which were hidden by an enormous feather mattress, quilts, and a fur coverlet.

"I found it at an antique auction in Cardiff," Daen said.

"I knew it wasn't a copy."

"Ariana, do you remember making the necklace?" Cibrien brushed back the thin white curtains of almost transparent silk, which hung loosely around the bed for privacy. The two men sat on the bed next to me.

I looked past Cibrien and Daen to a large trunk, also built of cherry wood. It sat nestled at the foot of the bed and had been carved to match. A dressing table, mirror, and chair sat on the other side of the chamber. A smaller version of the Great Hall's stone fireplace was nestled in the wall between the bed and the door, just as it had been before. Even a familiar crimson hued tapestry covered the wall beside the window. If it hadn't been night, I would have run toward it to see my beloved rose garden and rest in the windowseat there.

"Ariana?" Cibrien repeated. "The necklace?"

"I don't," I said. "Why is my energy slipping like this? If I made the key, I made a mistake in the magic."

In my sleep, I heard Cibrien and Daen combine their energy and their words of olden times together for me. The prayers enveloped the room and though I heard them, I felt my spirit was sleeping somewhere frozen. I needed the physical presence, or even the soul presence of Ryuichi and Winger. Neither could or would know to travel in spirit to me. If they guessed my need, the risk of Rosier finding them on that plane would be too great. My protectors simply had to return to the castle before the life literally seeped from my body one tiny soul droplet at a time.

I awoke sometime in the night. Their chants provided enough strength in me to speak.

"Go to sleep," I told the two weary men. "I will hold like this for days I think."

Daen kissed my hand. "I'm so sorry, my love. I should have guessed that you would have placed some spell like this into the necklace. It must have been vital that the bunch of us not separate. You've always said so and I didn't listen. But you fixed it so that we couldn't."

Cibrien sighed from some dark corner. "When they get back, we'll listen to that necklace. It's the guide and you made no mistake in its making. You couldn't have guessed we'd get so stupid over the years."

"Promise me you'll sleep," I said.

I drifted fast into an off-center twilight state. Days and nights blended and I knew no concept of time passing. The air carried with it the scent of roses far below my bedroom window. I was never alone. Daen and Cib watched me always. After Cibrien's chants, I sometimes had the strength to open my eyes and peer about the room, but there were no colors to be seen and so I would shut my eyes again and sleep.

"Isn't there something to be done?" Cibrien asked. "I've tried every healing prayer and potion I could think of and they barely affect anything. I've never seen such a powerful hold from so small a trinket. And to think our Ariana was capable of that."

There were moments of silence until Daen leaned down and whispered in my ear, "There is one thing I can do, Ariana, to lend my strength to yours. But I will not do it unless you slip too far."

Soon, or maybe it was at long last, I could no longer open my eyes nor speak. Where was Winger? Why didn't he come? I agonized. He couldn't be that far.

I was aware whenever Daen and Cibrien were in the room. I heard their frantic discussions, as one trapped in a coma might. The soft fur on the bed caressed my warm skin and I could smell the roses wafting in through the window whenever Daen opened it.

This frozen state was hateful to me. I fought against it, struggled to relax or rage or flow with it. But nothing changed. I tried to work through the puzzle or problem that might have once been in my mind when I made the key. There was no loophole to be found in my spell. I realized my peril with sickening certainty, and Daen caught the current of that realization.

"Ariana," Daen whispered, "Cibrien and Winger would not allow what I have in mind. My cure is primitive, but it's also an act so sacred—"

I heard him swallow. His hand shook against my cheek.

"If you don't want this, please find a way to let me know."

I heard the heavy bolt, which crossed the wooden door of my solar, slide into place. The coverlet was no longer wrapped around me, I realized. The cool air met with my skin. Cool, seductive night air.

A coarse softness brushed across my bare stomach, and I knew it was Daen's thick hair. I imagined the blue-black strands, the firm beauty that lived in the shaped of his lips and fingers.

"Ariana?" His voice was a low, tortured whisper.

What I could not tell him in words, my body did with its response. My breathing grew ragged under the gentle kisses that spread liquid fire across my body. The heated moisture in me flowed with invitation in spite of this very final line I knew we crossed.

Sin, I thought. Salvation. Destruction. Whether the intent or not, the necklace and my design of it had driven this moment into reality. My knight from old walls now rebuilt had come home to me. My fearsome Urshu with hair whitened and eyes more brilliant than the sky had at last crossed the seas and found me. He had always been right. We were bound.

He moved low, taking no time to explore the small places that can simmer the pleasure. Instead he found the center of ecstasy itself and claimed it with a tongue made of pure velvet. I would have given the world to have the motion of my body again at my command. Each circling, each gentle suckle, each kiss was sublime pain. I could only lay in perfect deathlike stillness as Daen brought wave upon wave of rapture through every fiber in me.

I wanted to scream for him to stop, to continue, to take me fully as he had once done. I just wanted to scream. Yet it seemed the numbness deep inside my spirit stirred some. I could never live without this again, I knew it. Never.

"You feel that," he murmured against my core. "And I'm still outside."

I couldn't open my eyes or sit. But the flow of my blood was involuntary. It soared with the frantic pounding of my heart, gathered under Daen's tongue and burst back through me in climax.

He slipped into the bed beside me and slid his arms around me until all the exposed skin on my body lay pressed up against his. My breasts met with the solid planes of his chest. He lowered his head to them and slowly, deliberately made love to each until the sensation triggered a renewed ache between the thighs I would have willingly parted for him on my own.

"We're one, Ariana. My energy will blend with yours. Take my strength."

His silky hardness pressed against the curve of my hip as he held me. I could sense the desperate need in him, which went far deeper than the reaction his body had to my flesh. That, he could control if he needed to. But his spirit was dying of hunger just as surely as mine was. The warm cinnamon scent of his skin mingled with the musky smells of our desire. The heat from his naked body soaked into me and again, something stirred.

He pressed his lips against mine. "Come on, love. Move. Just a little. Tell me to come inside."

But I couldn't. Not yet. I would have gasped as his warm mouth moved back to the center of me. His kisses were sweet and undemanding, relentless with a precision that sent another climax rocking through me. The energy built. I was warmer, breathing, breathing—

My lips parted as I inhaled with a gasp under the pleasure.

"That's it," he urged.

"Inside," I breathed out. And slowly, my heavy eyelids lifted open.

He looked like a god, rugged and enormous positioned over me. Dark and fierce, a warrior in his own right, his eyes were soft and burning. And the colors! Gold and silver danced and sparked in the air around us. The room was vivid with bold colors turning bolder. The crimson tapestry fairly burned against the wall.

With strong, calloused hands he caught my ankles and widened the space there until there was room for him to settle between. He had laughed long ago and declared the rose petals in the garden below far inferior. Though he said nothing, I knew he recalled his own words as he eased himself deep inside me and stopped.

Daen drew a deep breath that sounded more like a groan, and he shuddered. Slowly he began to move inside me. The muffled scream rose in my throat and faded from my lips as each stroke carried me into him. I wanted to raise my hips to meet his; his movement demanded it. At last the muscles in my body loosened and I was filled with the light of his essence. Yes, I could move again if I willed it so. He had brought me back to life. I was real.

"Daen," I said, "let yourself come."

The length of his body consumed mine and he moved frantically, abandoning his measured restraint. My hips rose and fell, matching his passion in frenzied need. Perspiration dampened his hair at the temples and beaded on his bronze skin. I ran my hands down the ridges of his back, caressing and clawing my way lower to press and urge him. Our heartbeats and our breathing synchronized with the pace. Rhythm together. Identical existence. One.

Then, in the same moment, our bodies tightened and released together when his heat spilled. I locked my ankles behind him as our orgasm bowed my back and propelled him into me.

"Always at the same time," I murmured. I ached and spun, floated deliciously in the aftermath.

There were tears running down his face when I opened my eyes and looked into his.

"I love you, Ariana. I love you so that it hurts me."

"I have hurt you, haven't I? Oh, Daen. You shouldn't have done this."

I watched in horror as Daen rolled from me and lay flat on the bed beside me. The flashing metallic glow around us subsided.

"I'm fine. Just tired. I had to give up a little of my strength to get you out of that dark place you'd slipped into. That's all."

"That's all?"

"I'll recuperate after a while. But I'm worried that as I do, you'll weaken."

"Will Cibrien guess?" I asked.

Daen shook his sweat-dampened head. "I don't know. We'll both function well enough. Maybe he'll just think we're a little tired. Then again, they might all figure it out and try to kill me."

I brushed my fingers along the side of his face and kissed him deeply.

•

Sometime in the morning hours, I awoke to find Daen discretely gone from my bed though the scent of him remained on me. Cinnamon and snowfall. I could almost taste it.

I was still weak and the weakness was infuriating, more so because now I understood all I could have been doing. At least I was living and alert. Daen had filled the closets with clothing of several fashions, for men and women both, not knowing when he stocked them who would have need of them one day. With a fresh outfit in hand, I crossed the room. I could step from the bed, shower, and make my way down the stairs without help.

To say that Cibrien was surprised to see my rejuvenation would be an understatement. He helped me to a room on the first floor and well off the main walkways, a small room Daen had designed expressly for me and my writings. In no other place had my writing been born from me so smoothly.

The table and chair faced expansive windows, designed so elegantly with triangle-shaped crystals in their corners and old-fashioned latches. I could see my beloved garden from the seat, could sit surrounded by bookshelves filled with the works I so cherished. There I could remain for hours amidst my selection of paper and parchment, quill and ink or ballpoint pens. Daen had missed nothing.

Daen checked in on me from time to time, but mostly whenever Cib was away. We didn't dare risk the possibility that in one glance, the old High Priest might look from one of us to the other and guess our secret. Already though, Daen was strong again and I was more feeble. It was a delicate balance of energy we had to maintain without somehow transgressing into a repeat of Daen's exquisite remedy. Our situation had to remain this way and I had to remain alert until Winger and Ryu returned and the spell of the necklace was broken.

"I have to hold my own," I told Daen. "We can't do what we did again."

"Sure we could. And as often as you want."

"Daen—" The heat simmered underneath the surface and coursed through the air between us. Lust permeated the room.

"Why, Ariana?" He stepped back to read my face. "Ah. Because it was out of necessity, you can justify what you otherwise think sin. Once."

"If there had been any other way—"

"There wasn't. Your conscience is clear."

I stared out the window at the drizzling rain hitting the greenery.

"My conscience isn't clear. I wanted you," I said.

Daen smiled. "You might try thinking of this a different way. We made love on sacred ground, blessed by a High Priest and many others. You saw the colors merge with us. Under the olden ways, we are married."

I sat up straight in shock and then relaxed again as the tiredness caught me. "Under newer ways, we are not."

Daen kissed the top of my head softly, innocently, and yet I felt the caress through my entire body. Somehow in that instant I was tired no longer. In fact, I felt wholly myself again, stronger even than that.

"Now that you know what you've been without," Daen whispered, "you can't leave it alone so easily. Neither can I."

"I'm going to try."

I peered out the window again. Only something so extraordinary as what I was witnessing could have drawn my eyes away from Daen. The rain landed on the soil and then rose again in great curtains of steam. The wispy clouds grew and billowed in front of my windows until I could see nothing except dewy whiteness rising and rolling past.

"Look at that," I said. "It's like someone set fire to the ground itself and only the rain puts it out."

Daen straightened to his full height. "Damn it to hell, Ariana. Look at that? Look at you. You've got more energy back in you than you've had in weeks. And fire, you say?"

Daen turned and bolted from the room. I threw back the chair from my table and rushed to catch him as he pulled open the doors to the Great Hall and stepped outside into the mist. Cibrien came to my side.

"You're better," he stated.

Fire? I thought in panic. *Could it be?* I reached out with the Whispering, listened and called. There was no response for me, not even the vaguest hint of one. And yet the fog swelled up from the earth.

Daen glanced back at me before disappearing into the grayness. I could hear his feet strike the cobblestones for a moment before they were muffled and disappeared. Cibrien stood stiffly beside me.

"Use the wind," he said. "There's no diminishment of your strength now."

I stood tall inside the mist and raised my arms. The

power in my body overflowed and surged, wicked—had I allowed myself to enjoy it. The words came forth from my lips and the air moved for me. With a smooth gust I swirled the fog away, high up and away to clear the view in front of us. When it parted, Cibrien and I could see Daen, large and imposing as he was, kneeling over something smaller and fallen on the cobblestone path ahead.

"Ryuichi," I whispered and began to run. Already the fiery heat he bred had dwindled, and the rain simply drizzled again.

The three of us gathered around him, a sunken shape on the path, wet and worn with travel. I looked expectantly at Daen.

"You've got to be kidding," he growled in response. Then in spite of himself, he lifted Ryuichi and carried him over his shoulder and up the grand staircase into an awaiting room.

"He's not dead," I said. Ryuichi had become frighteningly thin. His inky back hair was unkempt and longer than before, his lashes resting against gaunt cheeks as he slept the sleep of utter exhaustion.

"I'd say that was too bad if it weren't for you," Daen said.

"How did he find us?" Cibrien asked. "I thought after he got the message he'd head for London and summon us from the airport."

"Maybe he couldn't call out," I said. "Not any more than we could on the way here."

Daen grinned. "On the bright side, at least we don't need Wolf Boy to hurry back."

Cibrien nodded. "At least I know what to attribute Ariana's recovery to. I had wondered."

Daen and I didn't dare exchange a glance. Instead, I went to the bed and sat beside Ryuichi. Though I saw with my own eyes that the man, my Roman, lay before me, I couldn't sense him. He was like a mirage, empty and ephemeral, shut down so completely that I had to wonder what of him remained. Yet he had controlled his element to draw our attention to him in the rain outside.

"Did either of you leave the front gates open?" I asked.

Cibrien nodded. "I didn't sense Rosier and wanted to leave a way for Winger to walk back in. I was watching."

"Not well enough," Daen snapped.

"There was nothing there," Cibrien snapped back with hazel eyes hard and challenging.

Daen looked from Cibrien back to Ryuichi. "I might agree with you on that."

"After Winger returns," I said, "we keep those gates shut tight. No one passes. Not even one of us without the others knowing."

Daen tucked his hand under my elbow and guided me from the room while Cibrien watched over Ryuichi. I cared for the spent man on the bed as would a sister to her brother. Looking at his sweet face had kindled none of the mistaken emotion that had threatened us once.

"Thank the One God for that," Daen said. "I want to show you something just in case."

He took me upstairs to his room, which I had known was beside mine, and pushed aside the dark blue tapestry that hung with its edge snugly against the corner. And then he pushed. Slowly, the stones moved inward under his weight and he stepped back.

In front of him loomed an opening in the wall, an

empty space from which flowed a torrent of cold heavy air scented with touches of earth and dampness. Daen bent down and stepped through the opening, the tapestry swinging down behind him. He reached back to hold it aside for me as I stepped through to join him.

"I remember now," I said. "There were escape routes. Passageways."

On the other side of the stone portal was a flat step just inside the wall. The faint light from the fireplace in Daen's room showed the other side of the wall in front and a winding series of steps below until he let the tapestry fall back. We were caught inside a vast darkness until I heard the flip of a light switch.

"Upgrades," Daen said with a smile.

"More supplies below?"

He nodded. "And there are two tunnels leading from the room at the bottom of the stairs. The first ends up near the creek. There's a wooden door there, very hidden by stones and grass. Water seeps through the tunnel walls at the end and you'll have to push hard to open that door. Another door off the same tunnel lies deep in that garden of yours."

"Where did you put the second tunnel?"

"All the way under the property. If you take the turn you'll end up under the altar in the castle chapel. Go straight and walk all the way out under the walls toward the sea. And Ariana?"

"Yes?"

"Don't tell Ryuichi about the tunnels, whatever you do. I don't know where he stands. I can't feel him any better than you can."

Chapter Twenty

Know yourself, Ancient.
You, genesis of mystery,
whose beginnings
disclose your end.

Winger arrived the next morning while Ryuichi continued to sleep even still. Whereas Ryuichi had stumbled into our stronghold, nearly destroyed by the journey, Winger had flourished alone out in the open. His blue eyes glittered with the sun and air. His skin glowed from the exertion and his fang-teeth flashed when he wiped the blade of his knife off on the wet grass and slid it back under his jacket.

After he crossed through our gates, the men locked and barricaded every opening. I waited for Daen to use the heka instead of pure muscle, but he never did. And when they were done, we were sealed inside for as long as we needed, safe from Rosier and the Fallen Ones should they ever find us.

"The little pop star found us after all," Daen told Winger. "And he's completely off."

Winger shook his head. "I'm amazed he got this far

without a limo. I had no idea he was here."

"That's how I found him before," I mused. "Lost and exhausted." On the banks of the Nile …

"An adventure guide, he ain't," Cibrien said with a laugh as he walked with the rest of us around to the garden.

We sat on four stone benches arranged in a rectangle under rare blue skies, and let the perpetual roses ooze their magic aroma around us. Winger unhooked the buckle on the strap that fastened a worn bag across his shoulder and chest. He held the bag in admiration for a little while before extending it out to me with both hands.

"This is yours, I think," he said.

I took the bag and set it down on my lap, half afraid to open it, half savoring the moment. As my hand touched the opening, I looked up to see a figure clothed in dark jeans and a white dress shirt emerge around the side of the castle.

"He's awake," I breathed out.

We all stood as Ryuichi made his way over to us, lithe and potent as before, yet strikingly thin. His warm eyes glowed amber against too-pale skin in the afternoon as he reached the bench beside me and sat down next to Cibrien. Silently, we all took our seats around him.

"You got our message," Cibrien said at last.

Ryuichi nodded.

"I'm so glad you came," I said when he said nothing. "We need you here."

Daen glanced at me quickly in warning. He was right. None of us should reveal too much before Ryu spoke, before we knew more.

Ryuichi smiled sadly. "Do not worry. I am still on your side."

"How do we know that?" Daen asked. "I mean, come on. I heard your latest CD."

Though I braced myself for Ryuichi's reaction to the insult, he only nodded in knowing. "I cannot hear the music right now. I almost could not see the color in the message. There was a thing around me. In my house. I could not sleep without attack. Then I remembered the temple training and I put up the block. I came here. I can only hope they did not follow me."

"How do you feel now?" I asked.

"Better," Ryu said. "I slept and ate in peace. And it does my heart good to see you again."

I slid to the end of my bench and threw my arms around him. His bones were fragile under my embrace. Cibrien patted him gently on the back in welcome, but Winger and Daen sat silent and observing. I could see no trust in their eyes.

"We've been through a lot," I said at last, and pulled away from the embrace.

Daen smiled and fixed his gaze on Ryuichi. "Yes, we have."

Ryu looked slowly from Daen to me as a realization crept over him. He always knew such things where I was concerned and I was both relieved and horrified to find that his ability hadn't changed.

"You said you had not chosen," he accused. "The message said so."

"I hadn't," I said.

Ryu leapt to his feet and stood near me, trembling as if he would scream or fall down in sobs at any moment. Winger, Cib, and Daen rose, ready for whatever was coming. Except Daen already knew.

"You slept with him," Ryuichi spat. "You gave yourself to him."

"That's no one's business," I said. "We're here for a purpose that doesn't concern what happens between me and Daen."

"The hell it doesn't." Winger's eyes blazed. "The hell it doesn't," he repeated. He turned toward Daen. "How long after I left did it take you to make your move, you son of a bitch? How long?"

"It wasn't like that," Daen said. "There was no other way."

"Oh God," Cibrien said. "That's how you recovered. It crossed my mind but I thought it couldn't be. The Ariana I trained in Egypt would never have allowed it."

"Well I did allow it. I was slipping fast and it worked."

"Recovered? What do you mean you were slipping?" Winger's jaw clenched and his hands were fists as he looked at me, at Daen.

"The necklace had some tricks of its own," I explained. "Now that I have it on, none of you can leave. With Ryu gone, I was weak. But Winger, when you also left I started to fade. We can't be separated right now. I programmed it into this key somehow when I forged it. I can't take it off and I can't be without all of you or it literally drains me to the point of death. So we'd better find a way to get along and do it fast. I'm trusting in all of you."

"That's the key?" Ryu asked.

I nodded and pointed to the bag sitting flat on the bench. "And that's the first writing we've managed to collect. It's the one I remember burying."

"But how could you let him touch you?" Ryu asked.

"Why did you do this to me? He tricked you. He used you. Don't you see?"

"Didn't have a damn thing to do with you," Daen said. "Never did. I tried to tell you that, but did you listen? No. It's always been more than sixth sense and incense for Ariana and me. It's never been more than that with you."

"Daen. Enough," I commanded.

"You think because he made this castle for you that you can trust him," Ryu said. "He bought you with it. He made you trust him with it. But ten years are nothing for someone like him. He never dies. He never forgets. He plays with us and you let him. You have trapped me here."

"Trapped you?" I asked. "You were summoned and you came freely."

"I did not know the circumstances. I could not feel you."

"And that doesn't bother you just a little?" Winger said. "What happened to your connection with us?"

"I was fighting too hard to survive alone," Ryu said. "Everything will come back. Winger, we were friends before. What has changed?"

"We're being hunted," I said, "by the same things that sent you through into the Record back in Cairo. They attacked us there. That's what's changed."

"I do not know how I can stay in this place. I cannot look at you each day and know that he—I cannot. But there is no way I can leave now or you will become ill. This is a nightmare. I wish I had never made a song or a video. I wish I had never found my Ariana."

"Can't you put your lovesick, love-scorned ego aside for just a minute, pop star? You're missing the bigger picture here," Daen said.

"We're being *hunted*," I repeated with emphasis. "We're all in danger."

"If we put up our blocks and do not leave our bodies," Ryu said, "they cannot harm us."

"It's gotten a little more complicated than that," Cibrien said.

While they hesitantly explained to Ryuichi about Tiran and her companions, and about our newly rediscovered abilities, I picked up the bag and strolled back across the garden, away from the group.

Daen watched me curiously, but didn't move to stop me. He caught my thoughts, knew that I had to be alone for the first time in this life when the key around my neck would touch the lock on the book hidden inside the sack. The metal hung lightly, floating around my throat toward its purpose.

I walked into my writing room and shut the door. Through those beautiful windows, I saw the four men stop talking and begin their walk into the Great Hall behind me. Solemn and serious they looked, chastised and small in their competition over me. I wondered for a moment at where the true strength in our group resided. My focus was where it had been even in the moment of the Roman's execution or in Nicholaus' revelations to me inside the rings of stone. I was the Magnet and the Scribe. Those things came first and it was my fate that they always would. The One God had arranged it so very long ago, I was sure.

I sat down at my chair and pulled the bag away from its contents. A worn journal with a tattered leather cover slid out onto the polished wood table. I flipped the book over in my hands and examined it. There was no lock, no clasp at all and no apparent use for the design of the key hanging around my neck. The leather itself seemed to have sealed over the years. The weather had not penetrated it. Human eyes had not looked upon it. Until now.

I breathed and purely on instinct, held the book tightly to my chest and felt it press the small pins at the back of the triangle pendant into my flesh. I inhaled sharply under the sensation of pleasure and pain mingling as a drop of my blood rolled down the chain of the necklace and touched the parched leather.

And then the leather casing fell aside.

The first notes of divine music filled the room, and the colors we Ancients tended to generate together exploded around me. A breeze stirred the collection of loose pages in my hands. I recognized my own handwriting as it had once been, precise and clear in bold black ink strokes. Preordained. Fearsome.

When I set the papers down on the table again, a separate bundle of papers peeked out and I lifted it. There, immortalized in crimson red wax on the back of that letter, was the crest of the castle in which I sat. Nicholaus' crest. Daen's. Mine.

I sat for a moment and questioned whether to call the men into the room. But somehow, I couldn't. After more than seven centuries, I pressed my thumbs against the wax and cracked the seal. With shaking hands, I brushed the red flecks aside and opened the stiff papers. I drew in a long breath and read silently of my own words.

Lady and Scribe,

If these writings have again come into your hands, my hands, then I can assume the Ancients have Awakened. I know only the vaguest images of what we once were and that I am compelled to write.

Are there more like me and Nicholaus? I know not. You will doubtless recall much more than I, for even as I set ink to this parchment, the things I should know are faded beyond my reach. Though some things, I recall still and strive to record for your eyes, should Fate and the centuries prove kind enough to allow me this.

This tome holds the history of my life here with Nicholaus. Tomorrow I will bury this message along with it. I have tried to convince Nicholaus to return to the Ways of the Watcher with me, though I fear too much has passed and it may be impossible. One more life in the flesh, and I may not remember those Ways myself. Already I know not from whence I came nor where I have been. I do not even understand how Nicholaus and I have found one another this time, except that it seems inevitable. We have had many conversations, yet always he holds something of the truth away from me.

Mayhaps you will find our answers in the other writings, which I—we have left scattered behind. I can guess where they might be hidden, but again, that true recollection is beyond me. I have the sense that they hold many secrets and that this volume, by comparison, is failing and weak. It is barely worthy of this astounding lock I will place upon it so that none, save you, can open my words.

The lock? I think it best to explain the key. It returned to me one summer when the merchant's cart carried with it all the wares we desired from across the dark waters. I purchased the colored lavender and orange sugars brought by crusaders all the way from Alexandria in the land of Egypt. Will that city still stand or the land itself exist when my message again sees light? I wonder.

There are secrets I can reveal, and those of the key, handed to me along with the colored sugar, are such. Would that I knew what I have written in the other books! Nicholaus believes I once designed the key, though I feel nothing when I wear it about my neck. When I leave on the journey to bury this writing, I will send it with my dear friend, the merchant, back to Egypt where it should await.

The merchant told me that the knight who sold him this necklace was all too glad to be rid of the thing. He had heard tales in Egypt, stories that the gold had some essence of life imbued in it at its forging. I believe it so. I knew the necklace to be a key at once. My dreams tell me that it will guide me one day, that in the proper time it will not let me stray, for I have built it to set me straight in times of peril.

I can tell you to trust where it leads and go where it urges. I can only guess at the command of the spell I must have placed over it, or the effects it may come to have on me one day. Like this Whispering I sometimes catch, the necklace key comes from a place of goodness. It will also open the books of sacred writings with the rules and words for all the power we knew. No one else must ever learn these things.

Such writings must be greatly hunted, such knowledge coveted. Be aware when the time draws nigh.

Find the books. You will know where. With the Awakening, you will have memories from the lands in which you dwelled. Use the knowledge therein to protect yourself and those you love. My final warning is thus: Do not lay with Nicholaus. I fear to do so will enhance the spell of the necklace too severely. We are already bound too tightly.

You have Awakened. Gather. Fight. Would that I could say more.

As I now am,
Devon of Wolvshire

I folded the note back the way it had been. Only the crumbling red wax on the table betrayed my invasion of it. Then I placed the message and all the other papers back into the leather binding and folded it carefully around. The leather healed itself while I watched, securing the secrets inside until I would have opportunity to open it again and read the history spelled out for me there.

The music and colors died, and a shiver overtook me. The Fallen Ones, if they came for the key, would never be satisfied with claiming it alone. I had discovered the terrible truth of the lock, that only my blood drawn by the pendant around my neck could restore the leather and open it. This, I would not tell the others. Already they worried.

With the first recovered writing placed squarely in my bookshelf, I opened the door to the room and walked out to join my companions. I absently wiped away a remaining trace of blood at my collar and positioned the key over the place.

There they stood, awaiting, gathering.

I looked around the Great Hall from Cibrien to Winger, from Ryuichi to Daen. My Ancients, my loves. Together again, yet so torn apart. The Whispering words came into my mind and I knew I would soon go back to my writing room with the mist rolling past its windows and the magic of all I had discovered captured in the pages there.

At the edge of the room I turned and pressed my hand to the necklace again.

"Someone else is coming. I can feel him."

•••